ADVENTURES To go
Your Home for Multi-Genre Reading Entertainment.

ADVENTURES *To go*

Your Home for Multi-Genre Reading Entertainment.

WWW.OFFBEATREADS.COM

ADVENTURES *To go*

FALL, 2022   ISSUE #5

WHAT

WHERE

EDITOR'S NOTE

Winter came quickly this year, and so did this issue of *Adventures To Go*. Even though this rag is a quarterly and we plan each issue in advance as much as possible, it's a bit like carrying a murdered body up a steep hill. The legs start burning right away, yet you must keep on climbing until every step is taken. I've mentioned before how this publication is a labor of love, so I'm not complaining. But surely you know how even the things you love can weigh heavily on one's shoulders.

I'm writing this just three days after Veteran's Day, and am glad to point you to the cover photograph, taken by Christian Kieffer for Warbird Pinup Girls. For the few potential readers choosing to peer through the wrong lens, our cover choice needs no defending. Don't think for one minute that we are celebrating war or anything of the kind. Who doesn't like photography superbly done? And Paige is stunningly beautiful. She gives a perfectly fitting nod to a truly glamorous time gone by. Unlike today, the beauty and glamour were organic and real. Of course, there is never a good time for war. But in that war against a real evil, I'm glad our boys had authentic, gorgeous, strong women to think about. Women have a way of stepping up when duty calls. That B-17 behind Paige—how many rivets were put in by women? I wonder. Perhaps all of them. (In *Adventures* Issue 4, we have a photo from 1943 of a woman drilling on a Vengeance dive bomber.) We officially pay tribute to our veterans and their families. If you'd like to support those who serve, we have a page on our website dedicated to veteran-owned and veteran-hiring businesses.

Letters to the editor:

Comments/Questions are accepted. Put *Letter to Editor* in Subject and send to: OffBeatReads@pm.me *Email content could be published in future *Adventures on the Go*.

"

Susan Glaspell was a multi-talented and underrated author. In this issue, we include a short from her titled,

The Man of Flesh and Blood. Also in the pages ahead: the still immensely popular Kurt Vonnegut's *2BRO2B*; originally from **Galaxy Science Fiction Magazine,** a Frederik Pohl story, *The Tunnel Under The World*; a new original by Darryle Purcell; in his own words Lieut. Pat O'Brien tells his real-life tale in *Outwitting the Hun*. Learn about upcoming author Miranda Maples in our interview with her (don't miss her new book at OffBeatReads.com). In a new addition, Elmedina Hota serves up poetry on an elegant silver platter in ***Dark Corners***. How's that for variety?

I have no idea why you would be carrying a dead body up a steep hill. Have you committed murder? Are you helping a friend hide her sin? That's it — you've already dug the grave… just a few more steps.

Robert Kimbrell

NEW BOOK! 265-PAGE HARDCOVER NOW AVAILABLE ON AMAZON WORLD-WIDE!
THE NEW WWII NOSE-ART PICTORIAL BY PHOTOGRAPHER AND AUTHOR CHRISTIAN KIEFFER
Warbird Pinup Girls
THE COLLECTION
Warbird Pinup Girls
CHRISTIAN MICHAEL KIEFFER
THE COLLECTION
2009-2022
WWW.AMAZON.COM/DP/B09XSZPPY1

JUST PASSING THROUGH

BY DARRYLE PURCELL

Twenty-one-year-old Pete Adams was feeling his oats that afternoon as he strutted down the sidewalk of Hollywood Boulevard like a bantam rooster. With his wavy blond hair rippling with the wind, the six-foot-tall UCLA senior knew he was unquestionably special and God's gift to humanity, even though he didn't believe in God. He smiled and winked toward his age-equals as he passed them, while sneering at the myriad of older tourists who, expecting weirdoes in Hollywood, ignored him as they looked down and discussed the various celebrities honored with sidewalk stars.

"Stupid boomers!" he muttered, knowing full well that no one would dare challenge his right to be lord of the sidewalk. After all, he thought, the clutter of dinosaurs milling along the boulevard were wastes of oxygen who had spent their lives defending dead cultural values that had nothing to do with his generation's indisputable tenets.

He stopped in front of one of Tinseltown's oldest landmarks, Rinty's Bar and Grill. The establishment opened in 1925 as a speakeasy, which, at that time, had paid off enough federal and local officials to exist without fear of being raided. And, it was named after the very popular Warner Bros. German shepherd star, Rin Tin Tin. That well-loved canine ham had surpassed Douglas Fairbanks and Rudolph Valentino as Hollywood's top dog by earning a fortune in box office receipts.

With the four-legged film hero's celebrity status, the bar became a hangout for stars and screen hopefuls well into the talking-picture age. By the late-1940s, Rinty's served less celebrities and more locals, thus staying economically viable in the community. In 2023, almost a century after it opened, the establishment offered an oasis to an equal balance of neighborhood regulars and out-of-town tourists seeking a taste of old Hollywood.

Adams, feeling a slight thirst for his favorite cocktail, decided Rinty's was as good a place as any to grace with a visit. He entered the somewhat dark facility, which sported a dozen ancient-wood tables with chairs and an ornate 30-foot bar. Two large oil paintings of the famous canine celebrity flanked a large, oak-framed mirror behind the bar. Several glass-covered movie posters from Rinty's films adorned the walls, the best of which were the classically illustrated *Rinty of the Desert*, *Tracked by the Police* and *On the Border*. If the ghosts of Charlie Chaplin, Mary Pickford, Buster Keaton and Tom Mix had walked into Rinty's Bar and Grill that day, they would have felt right at home in that, other than the prices, the place hadn't changed a bit in the last almost-100 years.

"What a dump!" Adams stated loud enough for the nine customers and lone bartender to hear and ignore.

Johnny Embers didn't lift his half-staff eyelids toward the rude man, as he handed an elderly gentleman at the bar a bottle of amber ale and a fresh, icy mug.

"Thanks, Johnny," the bald man with the small white beard said.

"Always a pleasure, Casey," the tall, black bartender, who was also in his 70s, responded.

"Is this a barroom or a hospice?" Adams snarled. "You all look like customers in the Grim Reaper's waiting room."

Some people snorted and looked away while the rest sat quietly, waiting for the other shoe to drop.

"We've got ourselves another millennial prince," the old man quietly told Johnny, as he lifted his baseball cap with the Screaming Eagles emblem off the bar and placed it squarely on his head. "Think he's here to enlighten us about the error of our ways?"

"I think he's here to get his ass kicked," the unsmiling bartender answered.

Adams held up one finger as he stepped up to the bar and said loud enough for all to hear, "My man! I'll take a Mai Tai."

"My boy!" Embers responded sharply. "Unless you have papers signed by Democrat President Jefferson Davis, I am definitely not your man!"

"I, uh, didn't mean…"

"Oh, I think everyone in the room knows what you meant with every inconsiderate word that slithered out of your mouth," Embers said. "We don't serve your kind here!"

Adams puffed up like a frog, if said frog had been a chorus boy. "My kind? You don't know what my kind is! And, it doesn't matter! You have to serve members of all designations!"

"All but one," the elderly man at the bar said, as he spun around on his stool to face the youthful turd. "Assholes! This establishment doesn't serve assholes, asshole!"

A few of the customers seated at the tables chuckled.

"Your words are offensive and triggering!" Adams shouted. "I'll have this place shut down!"

"Triggering? Damn! I'd love to trigger you, but I left my gun in the car."

"And I'll have you arrested for discrimination for referring to *my kind*!"

"Sonny boy, or whatever you think you are," the old man said, "you have offended everyone in this room. And we don't care what you identify as within the LSMFT group. Even if you're a polygamous raccoon fetishist, not that there's anything wrong with that, you are still an asshole!"

Adams' eyes opened wide, he reached back with is right arm and threw a punch toward the older man's jaw, which was stopped halfway there by an almost invisibly fast response. The youth squealed as the man in the cap gripped the boy's fist firmly in his left hand. Tears formed in Adams' eyes.

"When you came in, I thought you were a boy," the old man said. "But you hit like a girl! And now that you're this close, your penis-breath is disgusting!"

Adams dropped to his knees as his fist was slowly being crushed. "Who the fuck do you think you are, Bruce Lee?" he stammered.

The old man chuckled. "The only celebrity martial arts I know are what I learned on television," he formed a peace sign with his right hand, "from Moe Howard!" Then he poked Adams in the eyes and released the troublemaker. The obnoxious youth fell back onto his butt and covered his injured eyes with his unbroken left hand.

Most of the seated customers cheered as the old man took a big drink from his cold glass of amber ale.

"So now what're we gonna do with him, Casey?" Johnny asked.

"Perhaps, if you will help me, we can show this guy to the back door. We wouldn't want him to offend anyone else by letting him hobble out the front door and onto the boulevard."

Johnny and Casey each took an arm and dragged the sputtering fool into the backroom, but no farther.

Adams looked up at the two men and asked, "Where's the backdoor?"

"Right over there, asshole," Casey pointed at the door. "But, instead, we thought we'd send you on a nice trip to someplace where you could learn a few things about life, and your not-so-special existence in it."

"Yeah," Johnny added, as he yanked to boy to his feet. "Perhaps you might learn to appreciate older Americans and our values by seeing how others live."

"And, I'm going to let you wear my hat," Casey said, as he shoved his baseball cap onto the turd's head. "That eagle is my old military unit patch from when I served in Vietnam. I was there to, you know, stop Communism before it reached our shores."

The two older men chuckled as they stepped away from Adams and began to glow. What looked like colorful lightning bolts arced from their fingertips, creating a vibrating circle of light. Pete Adams opened his sore eyes wide as he saw dirt streets and strangely costumed people walking on them inside the lighted area.

"What the…?"

Johnny shoved the youth hard enough to send him through the lighted opening and onto his face in the dirt street. Then the circle closed and the glow dimmed.

Johnny and Casey returned to the bar.

"Think he'll learn anything?" Johnny asked.

"Maybe he'll figure out he's not so special after all."

"As I remember, the last one we sent off to learn something landed in a thick rainforest," Johnny said.

"Yep," Casey answered, as he motioned that his beer was empty. "I wonder if he figured out how to survive in the jungle."

"If he didn't," Johnny said, while handing Casey another amber ale and a fresh glass, "he was probably eaten by something, or someone. Life's a jungle wherever you go."

"Today's youthful traveler is going to get a harsh lesson in tact. The people he's currently meeting in Tehran may not be as polite as we were."

"Yeah, they might not take kindly to his new cap either," the bartender giggled.

"Thanks to assholes like him, I'm beginning to really enjoy my retirement," Casey said. "This has been the most fun I've had since back in the '50s when we were growing up in Roswell, New Mexico."

The End

ACTRESS RUTH ROMAN

Adventures: Hi Miranda, we're really glad to have this time with you. Who is Miranda Maples, and what does she do?

Miranda: First off, thank you for taking the time to interview me. This is my first interview, and I'm so happy it is with *Adventures To Go!* Besides being an author, I am also a part-time librarian. I love working in a library, because not only am I surrounded by books all day, but I am also able to connect my community with resources that are impactful, as well as fun. I love being able to help people explore the vast wealth of knowledge that is available through libraries.

I am an East Tennessee native, and I love exploring the woods, taking walks alone (I get a lot of ideas for stories when walking), baking, and spending time traveling when possible. I am currently reveling in the dazzling fall foliage of October. I grew up on a farm, and it's my dream to have a large piece of land with an old house that I can fill with beautiful objects.

Adventures: As of this moment, your book *The Dead Born*, has been released or will be released very soon. I had the opportunity to read it at the beginning of the publishing process, it is great! Will you explain to readers what it is about?

Miranda: Absolutely. I am so happy you liked my book! The Dead Born is about a traumatized novelist with supernatural abilities who tries to solve her childhood friend's murder. Jacey Forestar returns to her hometown of Poplar Hill to pay her respects. Jacey decides to use her psychic gifts to find out who murdered her friend. Moving back into the gloomy old house where she grew up, she is haunted by visions of her long-dead family members, and a demonic entity roaming the dark halls. Jacey must conquer her trauma and harness her dark gifts to defeat the demonic forces and save her own soul.

Adventures: Any teasers about the plot in book two?

Miranda: Yes indeed! In book two, which is titled "Reborn: Book Two of the Southern Saints and Witches Series", we find Jacey going on a quest to find a mysterious woman she saw in a vision at the end of book one. This woman is Jacey's relative, and she has the answers to why Jacey and her bloodline became cursed. This next installment will be even more intense, and a lot of questions will be answered. Yet, Jacey is in even more danger now because she discovers a deep plot that reaches further than she ever dreamt was possible.

Adventures: How did you get started writing?

Miranda: I wrote my first short story when I was in middle school. It was a horror piece about a psychotic neighborhood cannibal. I suppose the first time I realized that I wanted to write for more than just fun was when I read a short story titled The Pear-Shaped Man in one of my mother's issues of now defunct Omni magazine. It has stuck with me all these years, and I think it is because it seems so mundane at first, but it builds into this creepy story in a way that is so unsettling. It's just the way the author uses description to disturb the reader. I realized, hey I want to do that! (I only found out years later that George RR Martin wrote this!) So I finally completed my novel a couple of years ago, and decided it needed to be out in the world. In a way, I've been writing my first novel my whole life, and I also realized no one was beating down my door to read my work, so I got over my fear of rejection, and sent out queries, and it was picked up by OffBeat Publishing.

Adventures: Where do you see yourself being in say, five years? Will you always write?

Miranda: Yes, I am a writer, it's who I am at my core, and it's what I absolutely love doing more than anything else. I love creating worlds and characters and entertaining people with the written word. In five years, ideally, I will not only still be a novelist, but also a working screenwriter. I love cinema and TV, and aside from books, I love escaping into a good movie or TV show. I believe that movies and TV have the same power to inspire, scare, and move people, and I want to be a part of that as well.

Thank you so much for taking the time to interview me, it was such a pleasure!

For more about Miranda and to be notified when her forthcoming books launch, visit OffBeatReads.com and MirandaMaples.com

MOMENT IN HISTORY

December 1957: Five hundred students attended a tennis clinic to learn from Althea Gibson, the U.S. and Wimbledon tennis champion. Photo taken at   Midwood HS. (World Telegram & Sun photo by Ed. Ford.)

2 B R 0 2 B

BY KURT VONNEGUT

Everything was perfectly swell.

There were no prisons, no slums, no insane asylums, no cripples, no poverty, no wars.

All diseases were conquered. So was old age.

Death, barring accidents, was an adventure for volunteers.

The population of the United States was stabilized at forty-million souls.

One bright morning in the Chicago Lying-in Hospital, a man named Edward K. Wehling, Jr., waited for his wife to give birth. He was the only man waiting. Not many people were born a day any more.

Wehling was fifty-six, a mere stripling in a population whose average age was one hundred and twenty-nine.

X-rays had revealed that his wife was going to have triplets. The children would be his first.

Young Wehling was hunched in his chair, his head in his hand. He was so rumpled, so still and colorless as to be virtually invisible. His camouflage was perfect, since the waiting room had a disorderly and demoralized air, too. Chairs and ashtrays had been moved away from the walls. The floor was paved with spattered dropcloths.

The room was being redecorated. It was being redecorated as a memorial to a man who had volunteered to die.

A sardonic old man, about two hundred years old, sat on a stepladder, painting a mural he did not like. Back in the days when people aged visibly, his age would have been guessed at thirty-five or so. Aging had touched him that much before the cure for aging was found.

The mural he was working on depicted a very neat garden. Men and women in white, doctors and nurses, turned the soil, planted seedlings, sprayed bugs, spread fertilizer.

Men and women in purple uniforms pulled up weeds, cut down plants that were old and sickly, raked leaves, carried refuse to trash-burners.

Never, never, never—not even in medieval Holland nor old Japan— had a garden been more formal, been better tended. Every plant had all the loam, light, water, air and nourishment it could use.

A hospital orderly came down the corridor, singing under his breath a popular song:

> *If you don't like my kisses, honey,*
> *Here's what I will do:*
> *I'll go see a girl in purple,*
> *Kiss this sad world toodle-oo.*
> *If you don't want my lovin',*
> *Why should I take up all this space?*
> *I'll get off this old planet,*
> *Let some sweet baby have my place.*

The orderly looked in at the mural and the muralist. "Looks so real," he said, "I can practically imagine I'm standing in the middle of it."

"What makes you think you're not in it?" said the painter. He gave a satiric smile. "It's called 'The Happy Garden of Life,' you know."

"That's good of Dr. Hitz," said the orderly.

He was referring to one of the male figures in white, whose head was a portrait of Dr. Benjamin Hitz, the hospital's Chief Obstetrician. Hitz was a blindingly handsome man.

"Lot of faces still to fill in," said the orderly. He meant that the faces of many of the figures in the mural were still blank. All blanks were to be filled with portraits of important people on either the hospital staff or from the Chicago Office of the Federal Bureau of Termination.

"Must be nice to be able to make pictures that look like something," said the orderly.

The painter's face curdled with scorn. "You think I'm proud of this daub?" he said. "You think this is my idea of what life really looks like?"

"What's your idea of what life looks like?" said the orderly.

The painter gestured at a foul dropcloth. "There's a good picture of it," he said. "Frame that, and you'll have a picture a damn sight more honest than this one."

"You're a gloomy old duck, aren't you?" said the orderly.

"Is that a crime?" said the painter.

The orderly shrugged. "If you don't like it here, Grandpa—" he said, and he finished the thought with the trick telephone number that people who didn't want to live any more were supposed to call. The zero in the telephone number he pronounced "naught."

The number was: "2 B R 0 2 B."

It was the telephone number of an institution whose fanciful sobriquets included: "Automat," "Birdland," "Cannery," "Catbox," "De-louser," "Easy-go," "Good-by, Mother," "Happy Hooligan," "Kiss-me-quick," "Lucky Pierre," "Sheepdip," "Waring Blendor," "Weep-no-more" and "Why Worry?"

"To be or not to be" was the telephone number of the municipal gas chambers of the Federal Bureau of Termination.

The painter thumbed his nose at the orderly. "When I decide it's time to go," he said, "it won't be at the Sheepdip."

"A do-it-yourselfer, eh?" said the orderly. "Messy business, Grandpa. Why don't you have a little consideration for the people who have to clean up after you?"

The painter expressed with an obscenity his lack of concern for the tribulations of his survivors. "The world could do with a good deal more mess, if you ask me," he said.

The orderly laughed and moved on.

Wehling, the waiting father, mumbled something without raising his head. And then he fell silent again.

A coarse, formidable woman strode into the waiting room on spike heels. Her shoes, stockings, trench coat, bag and overseas cap were all purple, the purple the painter called "the color of grapes on Judgment Day."

The medallion on her purple musette bag was the seal of the Service Division of the Federal Bureau of Termination, an eagle perched on a turnstile.

The woman had a lot of facial hair—an unmistakable mustache, in fact. A curious thing about gas-chamber hostesses was that, no matter how lovely and feminine they were when recruited, they all sprouted mustaches within five years or so.

"Is this where I'm supposed to come?" she said to the painter.

"A lot would depend on what your business was," he said. "You aren't about to have a baby, are you?"

"They told me I was supposed to pose for some picture," she said. "My name's Leora Duncan." She waited.

"And you dunk people," he said.

"What?" she said.

"Skip it," he said.

"That sure is a beautiful picture," she said. "Looks just like heaven or something."

"Or something," said the painter. He took a list of names from his smock pocket. "Duncan, Duncan, Duncan," he said, scanning the list. "Yes—here you are. You're entitled to be immortalized. See any faceless body here you'd like me to stick your head on? We've got a few choice ones left."

She studied the mural bleakly. "Gee," she said, "they're all the same to me. I don't know anything about art."

"A body's a body, eh?" he said. "All righty. As a master of fine art, I recommend this body here." He indicated a faceless figure of a woman who was carrying dried stalks to a trash-burner.

"Well," said Leora Duncan, "that's more the disposal people, isn't it? I mean, I'm in service. I don't do any disposing."

The painter clapped his hands in mock delight. "You say you don't know anything about art, and then you prove in the next breath that you know more about it than I do! Of course the sheave-carrier is wrong for a hostess! A snipper, a pruner—that's more your line." He pointed to a figure in purple who was sawing a dead branch from an apple tree. "How about her?" he said. "You like her at all?"

"Gosh—" she said, and she blushed and became humble—"that—that puts me right next to Dr. Hitz."

"That upsets you?" he said.

"Good gravy, no!" she said. "It's—it's just such an honor."

"Ah, You... you admire him, eh?" he said.

"Who doesn't admire him?" she said, worshiping the portrait of Hitz. It was the portrait of a tanned, white-haired, omnipotent Zeus, two hundred and forty years old. "Who doesn't admire him?" she said again. "He was responsible for setting up the very first gas chamber in Chicago."

"Nothing would please me more," said the painter, "than to put you next to him for all time. Sawing off a limb—that strikes you as appropriate?"

"That is kind of like what I do," she said. She was demure about what she did. What she did was make people comfortable while she killed them.

And, while Leora Duncan was posing for her portrait, into the waiting room bounded Dr. Hitz himself. He was seven feet tall, and he boomed with importance, accomplishments, and the joy of living.

"Well, Miss Duncan! Miss Duncan!" he said, and he made a joke. "What are you doing here?" he said. "This isn't where the people leave. This is where they come in!"

"We're going to be in the same picture together," she said shyly.

"Good!" said Dr. Hitz heartily. "And, say, isn't that some picture?"

"I sure am honored to be in it with you," she said.

"Let me tell you," he said, "I'm honored to be in it with you. Without women like you, this wonderful world we've got wouldn't be possible."

He saluted her and moved toward the door that led to the delivery rooms. "Guess what was just born," he said.

"I can't," she said.

"Triplets!" he said.

"Triplets!" she said. She was exclaiming over the legal implications of triplets.

The law said that no newborn child could survive unless the parents of the child could find someone who would volunteer to die. Triplets, if they were all to live, called for three volunteers.

"Do the parents have three volunteers?" said Leora Duncan.

"Last I heard," said Dr. Hitz, "they had one, and were trying to scrape another two up."

"I don't think they made it," she said. "Nobody made three appointments with us. Nothing but singles going through today, unless somebody called in after I left. What's the name?"

"Wehling," said the waiting father, sitting up, red-eyed and frowzy. "Edward K. Wehling, Jr., is the name of the happy father-to-be."

He raised his right hand, looked at a spot on the wall, gave a hoarsely wretched chuckle. "Present," he said.

"Oh, Mr. Wehling," said Dr. Hitz, "I didn't see you."

"The invisible man," said Wehling.

"They just phoned me that your triplets have been born," said Dr. Hitz. "They're all fine, and so is the mother. I'm on my way in to see them now."

"Hooray," said Wehling emptily.

"You don't sound very happy," said Dr. Hitz.

"What man in my shoes wouldn't be happy?" said Wehling. He gestured with his hands to symbolize care-free simplicity. "All I have to do is pick out which one of the triplets is going to live, then deliver my maternal grandfather to the Happy Hooligan, and come back here with a receipt."

Dr. Hitz became rather severe with Wehling, towered over him. "You don't believe in population control, Mr. Wehling?" he said.

"I think it's perfectly keen," said Wehling tautly.

"Would you like to go back to the good old days, when the population of the Earth was twenty billion—about to become forty billion, then eighty billion, then one hundred and sixty billion? Do you know what a drupelet is, Mr. Wehling?" said Hitz.

"Nope," said Wehling sulkily.

"A drupelet, Mr. Wehling, is one of the little knobs, one of the little pulpy grains of a blackberry," said Dr. Hitz. "Without population control, human beings would now be packed on this surface of this old planet like drupelets on a blackberry! Think of it!"

Wehling continued to stare at the same spot on the wall.

"In the year 2000," said Dr. Hitz, "before scientists stepped in and laid down the law, there wasn't even enough drinking water to go around, and nothing to eat but sea-weed—and still people insisted on their right to reproduce like jackrabbits. And their right, if possible, to live forever."

"I want those kids," said Wehling quietly. "I want all three of them."

"Of course you do," said Dr. Hitz. "That's only human."

"I don't want my grandfather to die, either," said Wehling.

"Nobody's really happy about taking a close relative to the Catbox," said Dr. Hitz gently, sympathetically.

"I wish people wouldn't call it that," said Leora Duncan.

"What?" said Dr. Hitz.

"I wish people wouldn't call it 'the Catbox,' and things like that," she said. "It gives people the wrong impression."

"You're absolutely right," said Dr. Hitz. "Forgive me." He corrected himself, gave the municipal gas chambers their official title, a title no one ever used in conversation. "I should have said, 'Ethical Suicide Studios,'" he said.

"That sounds so much better," said Leora Duncan.

"This child of yours—whichever one you decide to keep, Mr. Wehling," said Dr. Hitz. "He or she is going to live on a happy, roomy, clean, rich planet, thanks to population control. In a garden like that mural there." He shook his head. "Two centuries ago, when I was a young man, it was a hell that nobody thought could last another twenty years. Now centuries of peace and plenty stretch before us as far as the imagination cares to travel."

He smiled luminously.

The smile faded as he saw that Wehling had just drawn a revolver.

Wehling shot Dr. Hitz dead. "There's room for one—a great big one," he said.

And then he shot Leora Duncan. "It's only death," he said to her as she fell. "There! Room for two."

And then he shot himself, making room for all three of his children.

Nobody came running. Nobody, seemingly, heard the shots.

The painter sat on the top of his stepladder, looking down reflectively on the sorry scene.

The painter pondered the mournful puzzle of life demanding to be born and, once born, demanding to be fruitful ... to multiply and to live as long as possible—to do all that on a very small planet that would have to last forever.

All the answers that the painter could think of were grim. Even grimmer, surely, than a Catbox, a Happy Hooligan, an Easy Go. He thought of war. He thought of plague. He thought of starvation.

He knew that he would never paint again. He let his paintbrush fall to the drop-cloths below. And then he decided he had had about enough of life in the Happy Garden of Life, too, and he came slowly down from the ladder.

He took Wehling's pistol, really intending to shoot himself.

But he didn't have the nerve.

And then he saw the telephone booth in the corner of the room. He went to it, dialed the well-remembered number: "2 B R 0 2 B."

"Federal Bureau of Termination," said the very warm voice of a hostess.

"How soon could I get an appointment?" he asked, speaking very carefully.

"We could probably fit you in late this afternoon, sir," she said. "It might even be earlier, if we get a cancellation."

"All right," said the painter, "fit me in, if you please." And he gave her his name, spelling it out.

"Thank you, sir," said the hostess. "Your city thanks you; your country thanks you; your planet thanks you. But the deepest thanks of all is from future generations."

THE END

Because humankind fails to learn from past lessons, we find that many circumstances from yesteryear are repeating themselves yet again. The commentaries that follow here and in future issues were originally published by *The Mohave Valley Daily News between 1993 & 2013*--and in many ways they apply to today.
We are grateful to republish these commentaries written by Darryle Purcell in full and unedited. His own brand of humor and style can deliver insight, provoke thought, and even boil blood.

Ferret aficionados put the bite on prairie dogs

June 21, 2001

THEY SAY IT'S A DOG-EAT-DOG WORLD OUT THERE.... THAT IS UNLESS YOU'RE A prairie dog. Then, according to an Associated Press story that appeared in Sunday's Daily News, it's a ferret-eat-dog world.

The story reports that Kaiser Permanente attempted to "relocate" 500 prairie dogs that just happened to live where the company is building an assisted-living facility in Colorado. Kaiser spokesman Steve Krizman is quoted as saying, "There is no one taking prairie dogs right now." Therefore, the company is shipping the prairie dogs to an Arizona black-footed ferret breeding program to become ferret chow.

The last paragraph of the story reads, "Prairie dogs are typically quarantined for a period to make sure they aren't carrying disease. They are usually killed before being given to the ferrets."

Now, I'm not your typical animal-rights kind of guy. Oh, I like dogs, except for those mincing little yappers with Richard Simmons haircuts. But I also like hamburgers and a snake can really tick me off by just looking at me.

However, in this case, I feel a bit sorry for the prairie dogs.

I'm sure Kaiser will build a very nice assisted-living facility. And, obviously the 500 prairie dogs should be moved. Otherwise they might mess up the miniature golf course with extra holes, trip a few walkerassisted residents, or foul the hot tubs. But do they really need someone to take them? Did Kaiser look in the classified section for "prairie dogs wanted," or "room to rent, prairie dogs preferred," only to find "There is no one taking prairie dogs right now"?

Does Kaiser have an employee who solves problems such as what to do with extra critters?

I can picture the board meeting where Third Vice President of Rodent Remedies Michelle Marmot pipes up, "Let's sell the little beasts for food. We can tell everyone we are relocating them, herd them onto miniature cattle cars and deliver them to our ferret camps in the Arizona desert. We'll medically check them out for a couple of weeks to make sure they are disease-free, then we just make sure most of them are dead before we feed them to the ferrets. We'll call it Code Name: Soylent Brown."

Now, I know there are some local politicos who might think I would tend to favor weasel-like creatures. But they also know I am against any form of affirmative action. Programs that discriminate for any reason are wrong. Therefore, what makes ferrets, black footed or not, more important than prairie dogs? Prairie dogs have a society. They live together in communities while the infamous untrustworthy ferrets are loners that raid those rodent civilizations, dragging helpless dog-children off in the night to devour them.

If they had been born animals, Franklin Roosevelt, Jonas Salk, Henry Kissinger and Whoopi Goldberg could have been prairie dogs. On the other hand, Bela Lugosi, Ho Chi Minh, Dr. Mengele and James Carville could have been ferrets. Which creatures would you rather deal with?

I would think there is a lot of uninhabited desert land out there, miles from everything, where a community of displaced prairie dogs could move in without even being noticed.

As for the ferret-breeding program, Arizona Game and Fish could come up with a less-insidious dining plan. Perhaps desert tortoise on a half shell or spotted owl under glass could be served. And there is always an abundance of the little yapping lap dogs with Richard Simmons haircuts running around.

quick

2 out of 3 with someone near.

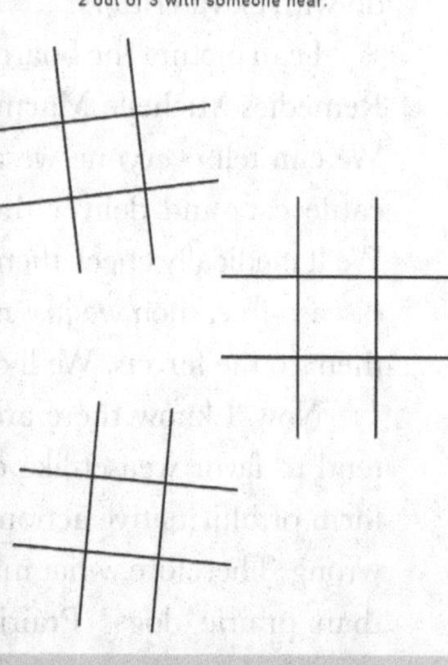

Literature written by Murasaki Shikibu in the 11th century titled, "The Tale of Genji" is considered by many to be the world's first novel.

SUDOKU

(MEDIUM DIFFICULTY; ANSWERS IN BACK OF BOOK)

9	1	6	2	4				
2	3							
			1		8			2
5	2	1						7
	8	9				5	1	
7	6			9				3
				8		7	2	1
	9				4	6		5
	7	3			5			

There is nothing noble in being superior to your fellow man; true nobility is being superior to your former self.
ERNEST HEMINGWAY

OUTWITTING THE HUN

BY LIEUT. PAT O'BRIEN

My Escape from a German Prison Camp
Royal Flying Corps
Originally Published March, 1918

TO
THE NORTH STAR
WHOSE GUIDING LIGHT MARKED THE
PATHWAY TO FREEDOM FOR A WEARY
FUGITIVE, THIS BOOK IS INSCRIBED
IN HUMBLE GRATITUDE
AND ABIDING FAITH

LIEUT. PAT O'BRIEN, R. F. C.

PREFACE

There is a common idea that the age of miracles is past. Perhaps it is, but if so, the change must have come about within the past few weeks—after I escaped into Holland. For if anything is certain in this life it is this: this book never would have been written but for the succession of miracles set forth in these pages.

Miracles, luck, coincidence, Providence—it doesn't matter much what you call it—certainly played an important part in the series of hairbreadth escapes in which I figured during my short but eventful appearance in the great drama now being enacted across the seas. Without it, all my efforts and sufferings would have been quite unavailing.

No one realizes this better than I do and I want to repeat it right here because elsewhere in these pages I may appear occasionally to overlook or minimize it: without the help of Providence I would not be here to-day.

But this same Providence which brought me home safely, despite all the dangers which beset me, may work similar miracles for others, and it is in the hope of encouraging other poor devils who may find themselves in situations as hopeless apparently as mine oftentimes were that this book is written.

When this cruel war is over—which I trust may be sooner than I expect it to be—I hope I shall have an opportunity to revisit the scenes of my adventures and to thank in person in an adequate manner every one who extended a helping hand to me when I was a wretched fugitive. All of them took great risks in befriending an escaped prisoner, and they did it without the slightest hope of reward. At the same time I hope I shall have a chance to pay my compliments to those who endeavored to take advantage of my distress.

In the meanwhile, however, I can only express my thanks in this ineffective manner, trusting that in some mysterious way a copy of this book may fall into the hands of every one who befriended me. I hope particularly that every good Hollander who played the part of the Good Samaritan to me so bountifully after my escape from Belgium will see these pages and feel that I am absolutely sincere when I say that words cannot begin to express my sense of gratitude to the Dutch people.

It is needless for me to add how deeply I feel for my fellow-prisoners in Germany who were less fortunate than I. Poor, poor fellows!—they are the real victims of the war. I hope that every one of them may soon be restored to that freedom whose value I never fully realized until after I had had to fight so hard to regain it.

PAT O'BRIEN.
MOMENCE, ILLINOIS, *JANUARY 14, 1918.*

CHAPTER I

THE FOLLY OF DESPAIR

Less than nine months ago eighteen officers of the Royal Flying Corps, which had been training in Canada, left for England on the *Megantic*.

If any of them was over twenty-five years of age, he had successfully concealed the fact, because they don't accept older men for the R. F. C.

Nine of the eighteen were British subjects; the other nine were Americans, who, tired of waiting for their own country to take her place with the Allies, had joined the British colors in Canada. I was one of the latter.

We were going to England to earn our "wings"—a qualification which must be won before a member of the R. F. C. is allowed to hunt the Huns on the western front.

That was in May, 1917.

By August 1st most of us were full-fledged pilots, actively engaged at various parts of the line in daily conflict with the enemy.

By December 15th every man Jack of us who had met the enemy in France, with one exception, had appeared on the casualty list. The exception was H. K. Boysen, an American, who at last report was fighting on the Italian front, still unscathed. Whether his good fortune has stood by him up to this time I don't know, but if it has I would be very much surprised.

Of the others five were killed in action—three Americans, one Canadian, and one Englishman. Three more were in all probability killed in action, although officially they are listed merely as "missing." One of these was an American, one a Canadian, and the third a Scotchman. Three more, two of them Americans, were seriously wounded. Another, a Canadian, is a prisoner in Germany. I know nothing of the others.

What happened to me is narrated in these pages. I wish, instead, I could tell the story of each of my brave comrades, for not one of them was downed, I am sure, without upholding the best traditions of the R. F. C. Unfortunately, however, of the eighteen who sailed on the *Megantic* last May, I happened to be the first to fall into the hands of the Huns, and what befell my comrades after that, with one exception, I know only second hand.

The exception was the case of poor, brave Paul Raney—my closest chum—whose last battle I witnessed from my German prison—but that is a story I shall tell in its proper place.

In one way, however, I think the story of my own "big adventure" and my miraculous escape may, perhaps, serve a purpose as useful as that of the heroic fate of my less fortunate comrades. Their story, it is true, might inspire others to deeds of heroism, but mine, I hope, will convey the equally valuable lesson of the folly of despair.

Many were the times in the course of my struggles when it seemed absolutely useless to continue. In a hostile country, where discovery meant death, wounded, sick, famished, friendless, hundreds of miles from the nearest neutral territory the frontier of which was so closely guarded that even if I got there it seemed too much to hope that I could ever get through, what was the use of enduring further agony?

And yet here I am, in the Land of Liberty—although in a somewhat obscure corner, the little town of Momence, Illinois, where I was born— not very much the worse for wear after all I've been through, and, as I write these words, not eight months have passed since my seventeen comrades and I sailed from Canada on the *Megantic*!

Can it be possible that I was spared to convey a message of hope to others who are destined for similar trials? I am afraid there will be many of them.

Years ago I heard of the epitaph which is said to have been found on a child's grave:

If I was so soon to be done for,

O Lord, what was I ever begun for?

The way it has come to me since I returned from Europe is:

If, O Lord, I was *not* to be done for,

What were my sufferings e'er begun for?

Perhaps the answer lies in the suggestion I have made.

At any rate, if this record of my adventures should prove instrumental in sustaining others who need encouragement, I shall not feel that my sufferings were in vain.

It is hardly likely that any one will quite duplicate my experiences, but I haven't the slightest doubt that many will have to go through trials equally nerve-racking and suffer disappointments just as disheartening.

It would be very far from the mark to imagine that the optimism which I am preaching now so glibly sustained me through all my troubles. On the contrary, I am free to confess that I frequently gave way to despair and often, for hours at a time, felt so dejected and discouraged that I really didn't care what happened to me. Indeed, I rather hoped that something *would* happen to put an end to my misery.

But, despite all my despondency and hopelessness, the worst never happened, and I can't help thinking that my salvation must have been designed to show the way to others.

CHAPTER II

I BECOME A FIGHTING-SCOUT

I started flying, in Chicago, in 1912. I was then eighteen years old, but I had had a hankering for the air ever since I can remember.

As a youngster I followed the exploits of the Wrights with the greatest interest, although I must confess I sometimes hoped that they wouldn't really conquer the air until I had had a whack at it myself. I got more whacks than I was looking for later on.

Needless to say, my parents were very much opposed to my risking my life at what was undoubtedly at that time one of the most hazardous "pastimes" a young fellow could select, and every time I had a smash-up or some other mishap I was ordered never to go near an aviation field again.

So I went out to California. There another fellow and I built our own machine, which we flew in various parts of the state.

In the early part of 1916, when trouble was brewing in Mexico, I joined the American Flying Corps. I was sent to San Diego, where the army flying school is located, and spent about eight months there, but as I was anxious to get into active service and there didn't seem much chance of America ever getting into the war, I resigned and, crossing over to Canada, joined the Royal Flying Corps at Victoria, B. C.

I was sent to Camp Borden, Toronto, first to receive instruction and later to instruct. While a cadet I made the first loop ever made by a cadet in Canada, and after I had performed the stunt I half expected to be kicked out of the service for it. Apparently, however, they considered the source and let it go at that. Later on I had the satisfaction of introducing the loop as part of the regular course of instruction for cadets in the R. F. C., and I want to say right here that Camp Borden has turned out some of the best fliers that have ever gone to France.

In May, 1917, I and seventeen other Canadian fliers left for England on the *Megantic*, where we were to qualify for service in France.

Our squadron consisted of nine Americans, C. C. Robinson, H. A. Miller, F. S. McClurg, A. A. Allen, E. B. Garnett, H. K. Boysen, H. A. Smeeton, A. Taylor, and myself; and nine Britishers, Paul H. Raney, J. R. Park, C. Nelmes, C. R. Moore, T. L. Atkinson, F. C. Conry, A. Muir, E. A. L. F. Smith, and A. C. Jones.

Within a few weeks after our arrival in England all of us had won our "wings"—the insignia worn on the left breast by every pilot on the western front.

We were all sent to a place in France known as the Pool Pilots' Mess. Here men gather from all the training squadrons in Canada and England and await assignments to the particular squadron of which they are to become members.

The Pool Pilots' Mess is situated a few miles back of the lines. Whenever a pilot is shot down or killed the Pool Pilots' Mess is notified to send another to take his place.

There are so many casualties every day in the R. F. C. at one point of the front or another that the demand for new pilots is quite active, but when a fellow is itching to get into the fight as badly as I and my friends were I must confess that we got a little impatient, although we realized that every time a new man was called it meant that some one else had, in all probability, been killed, wounded, or captured.

One morning an order came in for a scout pilot, and one of my friends was assigned. I can tell you the rest of us were as envious of him as if it were the last chance any of us were ever going to have to get to the front. As it was, however, hardly more than three hours had elapsed before another wire was received at the Mess and I was ordered to follow my friend. I afterward learned that as soon as he arrived at the squadron he had prevailed upon the commanding officer of the squadron to wire for me.

At the Pool Pilots' Mess it was the custom of the officers to wear "shorts"—breeches that are about eight inches long, like the Boy Scouts wear, leaving a space of about eight inches of open country between the top of the puttees and the end of the "shorts." The Australians wore them in Salonica and at the Dardanelles.

When the order came in for me, I had these "shorts" on, and I didn't have time to change into other clothes. Indeed, I was in such a sweat to get to the front that if I had been in my pajamas I think I would have gone that way. As it was, it was raining and I threw an overcoat over me, jumped into the machine, and we made record time to the aerodrome to which I had been ordered to report.

As I alighted from the automobile my overcoat blew open and displayed my manly form attired in "shorts" instead of in the regulation flying breeches, and the sight aroused considerable commotion in camp.

"Must be a Yankee!" I overheard one officer say to another as I approached. "No one but a Yank would have the cheek to show up that way, you know!"

But they laughed good-naturedly as I came up to them and welcomed me to the squadron, and I was soon very much at home.

My squadron was one of four stationed at an aerodrome about eighteen miles back of the Ypres line. There were eighteen pilots in our squadron, which was a scout-squadron, scout-machines carrying but one man.

A scout, sometimes called a fighting-scout, has no bomb-dropping or reconnoitering to do. His duty is just to fight, or, as the order was given to me, "You are expected to pick fights and not wait until they come to you!"

When bomb-droppers go out over the lines in the daytime, a scout-squadron usually convoys them. The bomb-droppers fly at about twelve thousand feet, the scouts a thousand feet or so above them to protect them.

If at any time they should be attacked, it is the duty of the scouts to dive down and carry on the fight, the orders of the bomb-droppers being to go on dropping bombs and not to fight unless they have to. There is seldom a time that machines go out over the lines on this work in the daytime that they are not attacked at some time or other, and so the scouts usually have plenty of work to do. In addition to these attacks, however, the squadron is invariably under constant bombardment from the ground, but that doesn't worry us very much, as we know pretty well how to avoid being hit from that quarter.

On my first flight, after joining the squadron, I was taken out over the lines to get a look at things, map out my location in case I was ever lost, locate the forests, lakes, and other landmarks, and get the general lay of the land.

One thing that was impressed upon me very emphatically was the location of the hospitals, so that in case I was ever wounded and had the strength to pick my landing I could land as near as possible to a hospital. All these things a new pilot goes through during the first two or three days after joining a squadron.

Our regular routine was two flights a day, each of two hours' duration. After doing our regular patrol, it was our privilege to go off on our own hook, if we wished, before going back to the squadron.

I soon found out that my squadron was some hot squadron, our fliers being almost always assigned to special-duty work, such as shooting up trenches at a height of fifty feet from the ground!

I received my baptism into this kind of work the third time I went out over the lines, and I would recommend it to any one who is hankering for excitement. You are not only apt to be attacked by hostile aircraft from above, but you are swept by machine-gun fire from below. I have seen some of our machines come back from this work sometimes so riddled with bullets that I wondered how they ever held together. Before we started out on one of these jobs we were mighty careful to see that our motors were in perfect condition, because they told us the "war-bread was bad in Germany."

One morning, shortly after I joined the squadron, three of us started over the line on our own accord. We soon observed four enemy machines, two-seaters, coming toward us. This type of machine is used by the Huns for artillery work and bomb-dropping, and we knew they were on mischief bent. Each machine had a machine-gun in front, worked by the pilot, and the observer also had a gun with which he could spray all around.

When we first noticed the Huns our machines were about six miles back of the German lines and we were lying high up in the sky, keeping the sun behind us, so that the enemy could not see us.

We picked out three of the machines and dove down on them. I went right by the man I picked for myself and his observer in the rear seat kept pumping at me to beat the band. Not one of my shots took effect as I went right under him, but I turned and gave him another burst of bullets and down he went in a spinning nose dive, one of his wings going one way and one another. As I saw him crash to the ground I knew that I had got my first hostile aircraft. One of my comrades was equally successful, but the other two German machines got away. We chased them back until things got too hot for us by reason of the appearance of other German machines, and then we called it a day.

This experience whetted my appetite for more of the same kind, and I did not have long to wait.

It may be well to explain here just what a spinning nose dive is. A few years ago the spinning nose dive was considered one of the most dangerous things a pilot could attempt, and many men were killed getting into this spin and not knowing how to come out of it. In fact, lots of pilots thought that when once you got into a spinning nose dive there was no way of coming out of it. It is now used, however, in actual flying.

The machines that are used in France are controlled in two ways, both by hands and by feet, the feet working the yoke or rudder bar which controls the rudder that steers the machine. The lateral controls and fore and aft, which cause the machine to rise or lower, are controlled by a contrivance called a "joy-stick." If, when flying in the air, a pilot should release his hold on this stick, it will gradually come back toward the pilot.

In that position the machine will begin to climb. So if a pilot is shot and loses control of this "joy-stick" his machine begins to ascend, and climbs until the angle formed becomes too great for it to continue or the motor to pull the plane; for a fraction of a second it stops, and the motor then being the heaviest, it causes the nose of the machine to fall forward, pitching down at a terrific rate of speed and spinning at the same time. If the motor is still running, it naturally increases the speed much more than it would if the motor were shut off, and there is great danger that the wings will double up, causing the machine to break apart. Although spins are made with the motor on, you are dropping like a ball being dropped out of the sky and the velocity increases with the power of the motor.

This spinning nose dive has been frequently used in "stunt" flying in recent years, but is now put to practical use by pilots in getting away from hostile machines, for when a man is spinning, it is almost impossible to hit him, and the man making the attack invariably thinks his enemy is going down to certain death in the spin.

This is all right when a man is over his own territory, because he can right his machine and come out of it; but if it happens over German territory, the Huns would only follow him down, and when he came out of the spin they would be above him, having all the advantage, and would shoot him down with ease.

It is a good way of getting down into a cloud, and is used very often by both sides, but it requires skill and courage by the pilot making it if he ever expects to come out alive.

A spin being made by a pilot intentionally looks exactly like a spin that is made by a machine actually being shot down, so one never knows whether it is forced or intentional until the pilot either rights his machine and comes out of it or crashes to the ground.

Another dive similar to this one is known as just the plain "dive." Assume, for instance, that a pilot flying at a height of several thousand feet is shot, loses control of his machine, and the nose of the plane starts down with the motor full on. He is going at a tremendous speed and in many instances is going so straight and swiftly that the speed is too great for the machine, because it was never constructed to withstand the enormous pressure forced against the wings, and they consequently crumple up.

If, too, in an effort to straighten the machine, the elevators should become affected, as often happens in trying to bring a machine out of a dive, the strain is again too great on the wings, and there is the same disastrous result. Oftentimes, when the petrol-tank is punctured by a tracer-bullet from another machine in the air, the plane that is hit catches on fire and either gets into a spin or a straight dive and heads for the earth, hundreds of miles an hour, a mass of flame, looking like a brilliant comet in the sky.

The spinning nose dive is used to greater advantage by the Germans than by our own pilots, for the reason that when a fight gets too hot for the

German he will put his machine in a spin, and as the chances are nine out of ten that we are fighting over German territory, he simply spins down out of our range, straightens out before he reaches the ground, and goes on home to his aerodrome. It is useless to follow him down inside the German lines, for you would in all probability be shot down before you could attain sufficient altitude to cross the line again.

It often happens that a pilot will be chasing another machine when suddenly he sees it start to spin. Perhaps they are fifteen or eighteen thousand feet in the air, and the hostile machine spins down for thousands of feet. He thinks he has hit the other machine and goes home happy that he has brought down another Hun. He reports the occurrence to the squadron, telling how he shot down his enemy; but when the rest of the squadron come in with their report, or some artillery observation balloon sends in a report, it develops that when a few hundred feet from the ground the supposed dead man in the spin has come out of the spin and gone merrily on his way for his own aerodrome.

CHAPTER III

CAPTURED BY THE HUNS

I shall not easily forget the 17th of August, 1917. I killed two Huns in a double-seated machine in the morning, another in the evening, and then I was captured myself. I may have spent more eventful days in my life, but I can't recall any just now.

That morning, in crossing the line on early morning patrol, I noticed two German balloons. I decided that as soon as my patrol was over I would go off on my own hook and see what a German balloon looked like at close quarters.

These observation balloons are used by both sides in conjunction with the artillery. A man sits up in the balloon with a wireless apparatus and directs the firing of the guns. From his point of vantage he can follow the work of his own artillery with a remarkable degree of accuracy and at the same time he can observe the enemy's movements and report them.

The Germans are very good at this work and they use a great number of these balloons. It was considered a very important part of our work to keep them out of the sky.

There are two ways of going after a balloon in a machine. One of them is to cross the lines at a low altitude, flying so near the ground that the man with the anti-aircraft gun can't bother you. You fly along until you get to the level of the balloon, and if, in the mean time, they have not drawn the balloon down, you open fire on it and the bullets you use will set it on fire if they land.

The other way is to fly over where you know the balloons to be, put your machine in a spin so that they can't hit you, get above them, spin over the balloon, and then open fire. In going back over the line you cross at a few hundred feet.

This is one of the hardest jobs in the service. There is less danger in attacking an enemy's aircraft.

Nevertheless, I had made up my mind either to get those balloons or make them descend, and I only hoped that they would stay on the job until I had a chance at them.

When our two hours' duty was up, therefore, I dropped out of the formation as we crossed the lines and turned back again.

I was at a height of fifteen thousand feet, considerably higher than the balloons. Shutting my motor off, I dropped down through the clouds, thinking to find the balloons at about five or six miles behind the German lines.

Just as I came out of the cloud-banks I saw below me, about a thousand feet, a two-seater hostile machine doing artillery observation and directing the German guns. This was at a point about four miles behind the German lines.

Evidently the German artillery saw me and put out ground signals to attract the Hun machine's attention, for I saw the observer quit his work and grab his gun, while the pilot stuck the nose of his machine straight down.

But they were too late to escape me. I was diving toward them at a speed of probably two hundred miles an hour, shooting all the time as fast as possible. Their only chance lay in the possibility that the force of my dive might break my wings. I knew my danger in that direction, but as soon as I came out of my dive the Huns would have their chance to get me, and I knew I had to get them first and take a chance on my wings holding out.

Fortunately, some of my first bullets found their mark and I was able to come out of my dive at about four thousand feet. They never came out of theirs!

But right then came the hottest situation in the air I had experienced up to that time. The depth of my dive had brought me within reach of the machine-guns from the ground and they also put a "barrage" around me of shrapnel from anti-aircraft guns, and I had an opportunity to "ride the barrage," as they call it in the R. F. C. To make the situation more interesting, they began shooting "flaming onions" at me.

"Flaming onions" are rockets shot from a rocket-gun. They are used to hit a machine when it is flying low and they are effective up to about five thousand feet. Sometimes they are shot up one after another in strings of about eight, and they are one of the hardest things to go through. If they hit the machine it is bound to catch fire and then the jig is up.

All the time, too, I was being attacked by "Archie"—the anti-aircraft fire. I escaped the machine-guns and the "flaming onions," but "Archie" got me four or five times. Every time a bullet plugged me, or rather my machine, it made a loud bang, on account of the tension on the material covering the wings.

None of their shots hurt me until I was about a mile from our lines, and then they hit my motor. Fortunately I still had altitude enough to drift on to our own side of the lines, for my motor was completely out of commission. They just raised the dickens with me all the time I was descending, and I began to think I would strike the ground before crossing the line, but there was a slight wind in my favor and it carried me two miles behind our lines. There the balloons I had gone out to get had the satisfaction of "pin-pointing" me. Through the directions which they were able to give to their artillery, they commenced shelling my machine where it lay.

Their particular work is to direct the fire of their artillery, and they are used just as the artillery observation airplanes are. Usually two men are stationed in each balloon. They ascend to a height of several thousand feet about five miles behind their own lines and are equipped with wireless and signaling apparatus. They watch the burst of their own artillery, check up the position, get the range, and direct the next shot.

When conditions are favorable they are able to direct the shots so accurately that it is a simple matter to destroy the object of their attack. It was such a balloon as this that got my position, marked me out, called for an artillery shot, and they commenced shelling my machine where it lay. If I had got the two balloons instead of the airplane, I probably would not have lost my machine, for he would in all probability have gone on home and not bothered about getting my range and causing the destruction of my machine.

I landed in a part of the country that was literally covered with shell-holes. Fortunately my machine was not badly damaged by the forced landing. I leisurely got out, walked around it to see what the damage was, and concluded that it could be easily repaired. In fact, I thought, if I could find a space long enough between shell-holes to get a start before leaving the ground, that I would be able to fly on from there.

I was still examining my plane and considering the matter of a few slight repairs, without any particular thought for my own safety in that unprotected spot, when a shell came whizzing through the air, knocked me to the ground, and landed a few feet away. It had no sooner struck than I made a run for cover and crawled into a shell-hole. I would have liked to have got farther away, but I didn't know where the next shell would burst, and I thought I was fairly safe there, so I squatted down and let them blaze away.

The only damage I suffered was from the mud which splattered up in my face and over my clothes. That was my introduction to a shell-hole, and I resolved right there that the infantry could have all the shell-hole fighting they wanted, but it did not appeal to me, though they live in them through many a long night and I had only sought shelter there for a few minutes.

After the Germans had completely demolished my machine and ceased firing I waited there a short time, fearing perhaps they might send over a lucky shot, hoping to get me, after all. But evidently they concluded enough shells had been wasted on one man. I crawled out cautiously, shook the mud off, and looked over in the direction where my machine had once been. There wasn't enough left for a decent souvenir, but nevertheless I got a few, such as they were, and, readily observing that nothing could be done with what was left, I made my way back to infantry headquarters, where I was able to telephone in a report.

A little later one of our automobiles came out after me and took me back to our aerodrome. Most of my squadron thought I was lost beyond a doubt and never expected to see me again; but my friend, Paul Raney, had held out that I was all right, and, as I was afterward told, "Don't send for another pilot; that Irishman will be back if he has to walk." And he knew that the only thing that kept me from walking was the fact that our own automobile had been sent out to bring me home.

I had lots to think about that day, and I had learned many things; one was not to have too much confidence in my own ability. One of the men in the squadron told me that I had better not take those chances; that it was going to be a long war and I would have plenty of opportunities to be killed without deliberately "wishing them on" myself. Later I was to learn the truth of his statement.

That night my "flight"—each squadron is divided into three flights consisting of six men each—got ready to go out again. As I started to put on my tunic I noticed that I was not marked up for duty as usual.

I asked the commanding officer, a major, what the reason for that was, and he replied that he thought I had done enough for one day. However, I knew that if I did not go, some one else from another "flight" would have to take my place, and I insisted upon going up with my patrol as usual, and the major reluctantly consented. Had he known what was in store for me I am sure he wouldn't have changed his mind so readily.

As it was, we had only five machines for this patrol, anyway, because as we crossed the lines one of them had to drop out on account of motor trouble. Our patrol was up at 8 p.m., and up to within ten minutes of that hour it had been entirely uneventful.

At 7.50 p.m., however, while we were flying at a height of sixteen thousand feet, we observed three other English machines which were about three thousand feet below us pick a fight with nine Hun machines.

I knew right then that we were in for it, because I could see over toward the ocean a whole flock of Hun machines which evidently had escaped the attention of our scrappy comrades below us.

So we dove down on those nine Huns.

At first the fight was fairly even. There were eight of us to nine of them. But soon the other machines which I had seen in the distance, and which were flying even higher than we were, arrived on the scene, and when they, in turn, dove down on us, there was just twenty of them to our eight!

THE AEROPLANE WHICH LIEUTENANT O'BRIEN USED IN HIS LAST
BATTLE WITH THE HUNS WHEN HE WAS BROUGHT DOWN AND
MADE PRISONER

FOUR OF THEM SINGLED ME OUT. I WAS DIVING AND THEY DOVE RIGHT DOWN
after me, shooting as they came. Their tracer-bullets were coming closer to
me every moment. These tracer-bullets are balls of fire which enable the
shooter to follow the course his bullets are taking and to correct his aim
accordingly. They do no more harm to a pilot if he is hit than an ordinary
bullet, but if they hit the petrol-tank, good night! When a machine catches
fire in flight there is no way of putting it out. It takes less than a minute for
the fabric to burn off the wings, and then the machine drops like an arrow,
leaving a trail of smoke like a comet.

As their tracer-bullets came closer and closer to me I realized that my
chances of escape were nil. Their very next shot, I felt, must hit me.

Once, some days before, when I was flying over the line I had watched
a fight above me. A German machine was set on fire and dove down
through our formation in flame on its way to the ground. The Hun was
diving at such a sharp angle that both his wings came off, and as he passed
within a few hundred feet of me I saw the look of horror upon his face.

Now, when I expected any moment to suffer a similar fate, I could not
help thinking of that poor Hun's last look of agony.

I realized that my only chance lay in making an Immermann turn. This maneuver was invented by a German—one of the greatest who ever flew and who was killed in action some time ago. This turn, which I made successfully, brought one of their machines right in front of me, and as he sailed along barely ten yards away I had "the drop" on him, and he knew it.

His white face and startled eyes I can still see. He knew beyond question that his last moment had come, because his position prevented his taking aim at me, while my gun pointed straight at him. My first tracer-bullet passed within a yard of his head, the second looked as if it hit his shoulder, the third struck him in the neck, and then I let him have the whole works and he went down in a spinning nose dive.

All this time the three other Hun machines were shooting away at me. I could hear the bullets striking my machine one after another. I hadn't the slightest idea that I could ever beat off those three Huns, but there was nothing for me to do but fight, and my hands were full.

In fighting, your machine is dropping, dropping all the time. I glanced at my instruments and my altitude was between eight and nine thousand feet. While I was still looking at the instruments the whole blamed works disappeared. A burst of bullets went into the instrument board and blew it to smithereens, another bullet went through my upper lip, came out of the roof of my mouth and lodged in my throat, and the next thing I knew was when I came to in a German hospital the following morning at five o'clock, German time.

I was a prisoner of war!

CHAPTER IV

CLIPPED WINGS

The hospital in which I found myself on the morning after my capture was a private house made of brick, very low and dirty, and not at all adapted for use as a hospital. It had evidently been used but a few days, on account of the big push that was taking place at that time of the year, and in all probability would be abandoned as soon as they had found a better place.

In all, the house contained four rooms and a stable, which was by far the largest of all. Although I never looked into this "wing" of the hospital, I was told that it, too, was filled with patients, lying on beds of straw around on the ground. I do not know whether they, too, were officers or privates.

The room in which I found myself contained eight beds, three of which were occupied by wounded German officers. The other rooms, I imagined, had about the same number of beds as mine. There were no Red Cross nurses in attendance, just orderlies, for this was only an emergency hospital and too near the firing-line for nurses. The orderlies were not old men nor very young boys, as I expected to find, but young men in the prime of life, who evidently had been medical students. One or two of them, I discovered, were able to speak English, but for some reason they would not talk. Perhaps they were forbidden by the officer in charge to do so.

In addition to the bullet wound in my mouth, I had a swelling from my forehead to the back of my head almost as big as my shoe—and that is saying considerable. I couldn't move an inch without suffering intense pain, and when the doctor told me that I had no bones broken I wondered how a fellow would feel who had.

German officers visited me that morning and told me that my machine went down in a spinning nose dive from a height of between eight and nine thousand feet, and they had the surprise of their lives when they discovered that I had not been dashed to pieces. They had to cut me out of my machine, which was riddled with shots and shattered to bits.

A German doctor removed the bullet from my throat, and the first thing he said to me when I came to was, "You are an American!"

There was no use denying it, because the metal identification disk on my wrist bore the inscription, "Pat O'Brien, U. S. A. Royal Flying Corps."

Although I was suffering intense agony, the doctor, who spoke perfect English, insisted upon conversing with me.

"You may be all right as a sportsman," he declared, "but you are a damned murderer just the same for being here. You Americans who got into this thing before America came into the war are no better than common murderers and you ought to be treated the same way!"

The wound in my mouth made it impossible for me to answer him, and I was suffering too much pain to be hurt very much by anything he could say.

THE IDENTIFICATION DISK WORN BY LIEUTENANT O'BRIEN WHEN
HE WAS CAPTURED BY THE HUNS. IT REVEALED TO THEM THAT
HE WAS AN AMERICAN

HE ASKED ME IF I WOULD LIKE AN APPLE! I COULD JUST AS EASILY HAVE EATEN
a brick.

When he got no answers out of me he walked away disgustedly.

"You don't have to worry any more," he declared, as a parting shot; "for you the war is over!"

I was given a little broth later in the day, and as I began to collect my thoughts I wondered what had happened to my comrades in the battle which had resulted so disastrously to me. As I began to realize my plight I worried less about my physical condition than the fact that, as the doctor had pointed out, for me the war was practically over. I had been in it but a short time, and now I would be a prisoner for the duration of the war!

The next day some German flying officers visited me, and I must say they treated me with great consideration. They told me of the man I had brought down. They said he was a Bavarian and a fairly good pilot. They gave me his hat as a souvenir and complimented me on the fight I had put up.

My helmet, which was of soft leather, was split from front to back by a bullet from a machine-gun and they examined it with great interest. When they brought me my uniform I found that the star of my rank which had been on my right shoulder-strap had been shot off clean. The one on my left shoulder-strap they asked me for as a souvenir, as also my R. F. C. badges, which I gave them. They allowed me to keep my "wings," which I wore on my left breast, because they were aware that that is the proudest possession of a British flying officer.

I think I am right in saying that the only chivalry in this war on the German side of the trenches has been displayed by the officers of the German Flying Corps, which comprises the pick of Germany. They pointed out to me that I and my comrades were fighting purely for the love of it, whereas they were fighting in defense of their country, but still, they said, they admired us for our sportsmanship. I had a notion to ask them if dropping bombs on London and killing so many innocent people was in defense of their country, but I was in no position or condition to pick a quarrel at that time.

That same day a German officer was brought into the hospital and put in the bunk next to mine. Of course, I casually looked at him, but did not pay any particular attention to him at that time. He lay there for three or four hours before I did take a real good look at him. I was positive that he could not speak English, and naturally I did not say anything to him.

Once when I looked over in his direction his eyes were on me and to my surprise he said, very sarcastically, "What the hell are you looking at?" and then smiled. At this time I was just beginning to say a few words, my wound having made talking difficult, but I said enough to let him know what I was doing there and how I happened to be there. Evidently he had heard my story from some of the others, though, because he said it was too bad I had not broken my neck; that he did not have much sympathy with the Flying Corps, anyway. He asked me what part of America I came from, and I told him "California."

After a few more questions he learned that I hailed from San Francisco, and then added to my distress by saying, "How would you like to have a good juicy steak right out of the Hofbräu?" Naturally, I told him it would "hit the spot," but I hardly thought my mouth was in shape just then to eat it. I immediately asked, of course, what he knew about the Hofbräu, and he replied, "I was connected with the place a good many years, and I ought to know all about it."

After that this German officer and I became rather chummy—that is, as far as I could be chummy with an enemy, and we whiled away a good many long hours talking about the days we had spent in San Francisco, and frequently in the conversation one of us would mention some prominent Californian, or some little incident occurring there, with which we were both familiar.

He told me when war was declared he was, of course, intensely patriotic and thought the only thing for him to do was to go back and aid in the defense of his country. He found that he could not go directly from San Francisco because the water was too well guarded by the English, so he boarded a boat for South America. There he obtained a forged passport and in the guise of a Montevidean took passage for New York and from there to England.

He passed through England without any difficulty on his forged passport, but concluded not to risk going to Holland, for fear of exciting too much suspicion, so went down through the Strait of Gibraltar to Italy, which was neutral at that time, up to Austria, and thence to Germany. He said when they put in at Gibraltar, after leaving England, there were two suspects taken off the ship, men that he was sure were neutral subjects, but much to his relief his own passport and credentials were examined and passed O. K.

The Hun spoke of his voyage from America to England as being exceptionally pleasant, and said he had had a fine time because he associated with the English passengers on board, his fluent English readily admitting him to several spirited arguments on the subject of the war which he keenly enjoyed.

One little incident he related revealed the remarkable tact which our enemy displayed in his associations at sea, which no doubt resulted advantageously for him. As he expressed it, he "made a hit" one evening when the crowd had assembled for a little music by suggesting that they sing "God Save the King." Thereafter his popularity was assured and the desired effect accomplished, for very soon a French officer came up to him and said, "It's too bad that England and ourselves haven't men in our army like you." It was too bad, he agreed, in telling me about it, because he was confident he could have done a whole lot more for Germany if he had been in the English army.

In spite of his apparent loyalty, however, the man didn't seem very enthusiastic over the war and frankly admitted one day that the old political battles waged in California were much more to his liking than the battles he had gone through over here. On second thought he laughed as though it were a good joke, but he evidently intended me to infer that he had taken a keen interest in politics in San Francisco.

When my "chummy enemy" first started his conversation with me the German doctor in charge reprimanded him for talking to me, but he paid no attention to the doctor, showing that some real Americanism had soaked into his system while he had been in the U. S. A.

I asked him one day what he thought the German people would do after the war; if he thought they would make Germany a republic, and, much to my surprise, he said, very bitterly, "If I had my way about it, I would make her a republic to-day and hang the damned Kaiser in the bargain." And yet he was considered an excellent soldier. I concluded, however, that he must have been a German Socialist, though he never told me so.

On one occasion I asked him for his name, but he said that I would probably never see him again and it didn't matter what his name was. I did not know whether he meant that the Germans would starve me out or just what was on his mind, for at that time I am sure he did not figure on dying. The first two or three days I was in the hospital I thought surely he would be up and gone long before I was, but blood poisoning set in about that time and just a few hours before I left for Courtrai he died.

One of those days, while my wound was still very troublesome, I was given an apple; whether it was just to torment me, knowing that I could not eat it, or whether for some other reason, I do not know. But, anyway, a German flying officer there had several in his pockets and gave me a nice one. Of course, there was no chance of my eating it, so when the officer had gone and I discovered this San Francisco fellow looking at it rather longingly I picked it up, intending to toss it over to him. But he shook his head and said, "If this was San Francisco, I would take it, but I cannot take it from you here." I was never able to understand just why he refused the apple, for he was usually sociable and a good fellow to talk to, but apparently he could not forget that I was his enemy. However, that did not stop one of the orderlies from eating the apple.

One practice about the hospital which impressed me particularly was that if a German soldier did not stand much chance of recovering sufficiently to take his place again in the war, the doctors did not exert themselves to see that he got well. But if a man had a fairly good chance of recovering and they thought he might be of some further use, everything that medical skill could possibly do was done for him. I don't know whether this was done under orders or whether the doctors just followed their own inclinations in such cases.

My teeth had been badly jarred up from the shot, and I hoped that I might have a chance to have them fixed when I reached Courtrai, the prison where I was to be taken. So I asked the doctor if it would be possible for me to have this work done there, but he very curtly told me that though there were several dentists at Courtrai, they were busy enough fixing the teeth of their own men without bothering about mine. He also added that I would not have to worry about my teeth; that I wouldn't be getting so much food that they would be put out of commission by working overtime. I wanted to tell him that from the way things looked he would not be wearing his out very soon, either.

My condition improved during the next two days and on the fourth day of my captivity I was well enough to write a brief message to my squadron reporting that I was a prisoner of war and "feeling fine," although, as a matter of fact, I was never so depressed in my life. I realized, however, that if the message reached my comrades, it would be relayed to my mother in Momence, Illinois, and I did not want to worry her more than was absolutely necessary. It was enough for her to know that I was a prisoner. She did not have to know that I was wounded.

I had hopes that my message would be carried over the lines and dropped by one of the German flying officers. That is a courtesy which is usually practised on both sides. I recalled how patiently we had waited in our aerodrome for news of our men who had failed to return, and I could picture my squadron speculating on my fate.

That is one of the saddest things connected with service in the R. F. C. You don't care much what happens to you, but the constant casualties among your friends is very depressing.

You go out with your "flight" and get into a muss. You get scattered and when your formation is broken up you finally wing your way home alone.

Perhaps you are the first to land. Soon another machine shows in the sky, then another, and you patiently wait for the rest to appear. Within an hour, perhaps, all have shown up save one, and you begin to speculate and wonder what has happened to him.

Has he lost his way? Has he landed at some other aerodrome? Did the Huns get him?

When darkness comes you realize that, at any rate, he won't be back that night, and you hope for a telephone-call from him telling of his whereabouts.

If the night passes without sign or word from him he is reported as missing, and then you watch for his casualty to appear in the war-office lists.

One day, perhaps a month later, a message is dropped over the line by the German Flying Corps with a list of pilots captured or killed by the Huns, and then, for the first time, you know definitely why it was your comrade failed to return the day he last went over the line with his squadron.

I was still musing over this melancholy phase of the scout's life when an orderly told me there was a beautiful battle going on in the air, and he volunteered to help me outside the hospital that I might witness it, and I readily accepted his assistance.

That afternoon I saw one of the gamest fights I ever expect to witness.

There were six of our machines against perhaps sixteen Huns. From the type of the British machines I knew that they might possibly be from my own aerodrome. Two of our machines had been apparently picked out by six of the Huns and were bearing the brunt of the fight. The contest seemed to me to be so unequal that victory for our men was hardly to be thought of, and yet at one time they so completely outmaneuvered the Huns that I thought their superior skill might save the day for them, despite the fact that they were so hopelessly outnumbered. One thing I was sure of: they would never give in.

Of course it would have been a comparatively simple matter for our men, when they saw how things were going against them, to have turned their noses down, landed behind the German lines, and given themselves up as prisoners, but that is not the way of the R. F. C.

A battle of this kind seldom lasts many minutes, although every second seems like an hour to those who participate in it and even onlookers suffer more thrills in the course of the struggle than they would ordinarily experience in a lifetime. It is apparent even to a novice that the loser's fate is death.

Of course the Germans around the hospital were all watching and rooting for their comrades, but the English, too, had one sympathizer in that group who made no effort to stifle his admiration for the bravery his comrades were displaying.

The end came suddenly. Four machines crashed to earth almost simultaneously. It was an even break—two of theirs and two of ours. The others apparently returned to their respective lines.

The wound in my mouth was bothering me considerably, but by means of a pencil and paper I requested one of the German officers to find out for me who the English officers were who had been shot down.

A little later he returned and handed me a photograph taken from the body of one of the victims. It was a picture of Paul Raney, of Toronto, and myself, taken together! Poor Raney! He was the best friend I had and one of the best and gamest men who ever fought in France!

It was he, I learned long after, who, when I was reported missing, had checked over all my belongings and sent them back to England with a signed memorandum—which is now in my possession. Poor fellow, he little realized then that but a day or two later he would be engaged in his last heroic battle, with me a helpless onlooker!

The same German officer who brought me the photograph also drew a map for me of the exact spot where Raney was buried in Flanders. I guarded it carefully all through my subsequent adventures and finally turned it over to his father and mother when I visited them in Toronto to perform the hardest and saddest duty I have ever been called upon to execute—to confirm to them in person the tidings of poor Paul's death.

The other British pilot who fell was also from my squadron and a man I knew well—Lieutenant Keith, of Australia. I had given him a picture of myself only a few hours before I started on my own disastrous flight. He was one of the star pilots of our squadron and had been in many a desperate battle before, but this time the odds were too great for him. He put up a wonderful fight and he gave as much as he took.

LIEUT. PAUL H. RANEY OF TORONTO AND LIEUT. PAT O'BRIEN

(Raney was killed in action before the eyes of O'Brien, who was a prisoner of war. This picture, found on the body of Raney when he fell behind the German lines, was handed to O'Brien to identify the victim.)

THE NEXT TWO DAYS PASSED WITHOUT INCIDENT AND I WAS THEN TAKEN TO the Intelligence Department of the German Flying Corps, which was located about an hour from the hospital. There I was kept two days, during which time they put a thousand and one questions to me. While I was there I turned over to them the message I had written in the hospital and asked them to have one of their fliers drop it on our side of the line.

They asked me where I would like it dropped, thinking perhaps I would give my aerodrome away, but when I smiled and shook my head they did not insist upon an answer.

"I'll drop it over ——," declared one of them, naming my aerodrome, which revealed to me that their flying corps is as efficient as other branches of the service in the matter of obtaining valuable information.

And right here I want to say that the more I came to know of the enemy the more keenly I realized what a difficult task we're going to have to lick him. In all my subsequent experience the fact that there is a heap of fight left in the Huns still was thoroughly brought home to me. We shall win the war eventually, if we don't slow up too soon in the mistaken idea that the Huns are ready to lie down.

The flying officers who questioned me were extremely anxious to find out all they could about the part America is going to play in the war, but they evidently came to the conclusion that America hadn't taken me very deeply into her confidence, judging from the information they got, or failed to get, from me.

At any rate, they gave me up as a bad job and I was ordered to the officers' prison at Courtrai, Belgium.

CHAPTER V

THE PRISON-CAMP AT COURTRAI

From the Intelligence Department I was conveyed to the officers' prison-camp at Courtrai in an automobile. It was about an hour's ride. My escort was one of the most famous flyers in the world, barring none. He was later killed in action, but I was told by an English airman who witnessed his last combat that he fought a game battle and died a hero's death.

The prison, which had evidently been a civil prison of some kind before the war, was located right in the heart of Courtrai. The first building we approached was large, and in front of the archway, which formed the main entrance, was a sentry box. Here we were challenged by the sentry, who knocked on the door; the guard turned the key in the lock and I was admitted. We passed through the archway and directly into a courtyard, on which faced all of the prison buildings, the windows, of course, being heavily barred.

After I had given my pedigree—my name, age, address, etc.—I was shown to a cell with bars on the windows overlooking this courtyard. I was promptly told that at night we were to occupy these rooms, but I had already surveyed the surroundings, taken account of the number of guards and the locked door outside, and concluded that my chances of getting away from some other place could be no worse than in that particular cell.

As I had no hat, my helmet being the only thing I wore over the lines, I was compelled either to go bareheaded or wear the red cap of the Bavarian whom I had shot down on that memorable day. It can be imagined how I looked attired in a British uniform and a bright red cap. Wherever I was taken, my outfit aroused considerable curiosity among the Belgians and German soldiers.

When I arrived at prison that day I still wore this cap, and as I was taken into the courtyard, my overcoat covering my uniform, all that the British officers who happened to be sunning themselves in the courtyard could see was the red cap. They afterward told me they wondered who the "big Hun" was with the bandage on his mouth. This cap I managed to keep with me, but was never allowed to wear it on the walks we took. I either went bareheaded or borrowed a cap from some other prisoner.

At certain hours each day the prisoners were allowed to mingle in the courtyard, and on the first occasion of this kind I found that there were eleven officers imprisoned there besides myself.

They had here interpreters who could speak all languages. One of them was a mere boy who had been born in Jersey City, New Jersey, and had spent all his life in America until the beginning of 1914. Then he moved with his folks to Germany, and when he became of military age the Huns forced him into the army. I think if the truth were known he would much rather have been fighting for America than against her.

I found that most of the prisoners remained at Courtrai only two or three days. From there they were invariably taken to prisons in the interior of Germany.

Whether it was because I was an American or because I was a flier, I don't know, but this rule was not followed in my case. I remained there two weeks.

During that period, Courtrai was constantly bombed by our airmen. Not a single day or night passed without one or more air raids. In the two weeks I was there I counted twenty-one of them. The town suffered a great deal of damage. Evidently our people were aware that the Germans had a lot of troops concentrated in this town, and, besides, the headquarters staff was stationed there. The Kaiser himself visited Courtrai while I was in the prison, I was told by one of the interpreters, but he didn't call on me and, for obvious reasons, I couldn't call on him.

The courtyard was not a very popular place during air raids. Several times when our airmen raided that section in the daytime I went out and watched the machines and the shrapnel bursting all around; but the Germans did not crowd out there, for their own anti-aircraft guns were hammering away to keep our planes as high in the sky as possible, and shells were likely to fall in the prison yard any moment. Of course, I watched these battles at my own risk.

Many nights from my prison window I watched with peculiar interest the air raids carried on, and it was a wonderful sight with the German searchlights playing on the sky, the "flaming onions" fired high and the burst of the anti-aircraft guns, but rather an uncomfortable sensation when I realized that perhaps the very next minute a bomb might be dropped on the building in which I was a prisoner. But perhaps all of this was better than no excitement at all, for prison life soon became very monotonous.

One of the hardest things I had to endure throughout the two weeks I spent there was the sight of the Hun machines flying over Courtrai, knowing that perhaps I never would have another chance to fly, and I used to sit by the hour watching the German machines maneuvering over the prison, as they had an aerodrome not far away, and every afternoon the students—I took them for students because their flying was very poor—appeared over the town.

One certain Hun seemed to find particular satisfaction in flying right down over the prison nightly, for my special discomfort and benefit it seemed, as if he knew an airman imprisoned there was vainly longing to try his wings again over their lines. But I used to console myself by saying, "Never mind, old boy; there was never a bird whose wings could not be clipped if they got him just right, and your turn will come some day."

One night there was an exceptionally heavy air raid going on. A number of German officers came into my room, and they all seemed very much frightened. I jokingly remarked that it would be fine if our airmen hit the old prison—the percentage would be very satisfactory—one English officer and about ten German ones. They didn't seem to appreciate the joke, however, and, indeed, they were apparently too much alarmed at what was going on overhead to laugh even at their own jokes. Although these night raids seemed to take all the starch out of the Germans while they were going on, the officers were usually as brave as lions the next day and spoke contemptuously of the raid of the night before.

I saw thousands of soldiers in Courtrai, and although they did not impress me as having very good or abundant food, they were fairly well clothed. I do not mean to imply that conditions pointed to an early end of the war. On the contrary, from what I was able to observe on that point, unless the Huns have an absolute crop failure, they can, in my opinion, go on for years! The idea of our being able to win the war by starving them out strikes me as ridiculous. This is a war that must be won by *fighting*, and the sooner we realize that fact the sooner it will be over.

Rising-hour in the prison was seven o'clock. Breakfast came at eight. This consisted of a cup of coffee and nothing else. If the prisoner had the foresight to save some bread from the previous day, he had bread for breakfast also, but that never happened in my case. Sometimes we had two cups of coffee—that is, near-coffee. It was really chicory or some cereal preparation. We had no milk or sugar.

For lunch they gave us boiled sugar-beets or some other vegetable, and once in a while some kind of pickled meat, but that happened very seldom. We also received a third of a loaf of bread—war-bread. This war-bread was as heavy as a brick, black, and sour. It was supposed to last us from noon one day to noon the next. Except for some soup, this was the whole lunch menu.

Dinner came at 5.30 p.m., when we sometimes had a little jam made out of sugar-beets, and a preparation called tea which you had to shake vigorously or it settled in the bottom of the cup and then about all you had was hot water. This "tea" was a sad blow to the Englishmen. If it hadn't been called tea, they wouldn't have felt so badly about it, perhaps, but it was adding insult to injury to call that stuff "tea" which, with them, is almost a national institution.

Sometimes with this meal they gave us butter instead of jam, and once in a while we had some kind of canned meat.

This comprised the usual run of eatables for the day—I can eat more than that for breakfast! In the days that were to come, however, I was to fare considerably worse.

MAILING–CARD SENT BY GERMAN GOVERNMENT TO PAT O'BRIEN'S
SISTER, MRS. CLARA CLEGG OF MOMENCE, ILLINOIS

OBVERSE SIDE OF CARD SHOWN ABOVE

WWE WERE ALLOWED TO SEND OUT AND BUY A FEW THINGS, BUT AS MOST OF THE prisoners were without funds, this was but an empty privilege. Once I took advantage of the privilege to send my shoes to a Belgian shoemaker to be half-soled. They charged me twenty marks—five dollars!

Once in a while a Belgian Ladies' Relief Society visited the prison and brought us handkerchiefs, American soap—which sells at about one dollar and fifty cents a bar in Belgium—tooth-brushes, and other little articles, all of which were American-made, but whether they were supplied by the American Relief Committee or not I don't know. At any rate, these gifts were mighty useful and were very much appreciated.

One day I offered a button off my uniform to one of these Belgian ladies as a souvenir, but a German guard saw me and I was never allowed to go near the visitors afterward.

The sanitary conditions in this prison-camp were excellent as a general proposition. One night, however, I discovered that I had been captured by "cooties."

This was a novel experience to me and one that I would have been very willing to have missed, because in the Flying Corps our aerodromes are a number of miles back of the lines and we have good billets, and our acquaintance with such things as "cooties" and other unwelcome visitors is very limited.

When I discovered my condition I made a holler and roused the guard, and right then I got another example of German efficiency.

This guard seemed to be even more perturbed about my complaint than I was myself, evidently fearing that he would be blamed for my condition.

The commandant was summoned, and I could see that he was very angry. Some one undoubtedly got a severe reprimand for it.

I was taken out of my cell by a guard with a rifle and conducted about a quarter of a mile from the prison to an old factory building which had been converted into an elaborate fumigating plant. There I was given a pickle bath in some kind of solution, and while I was absorbing it my clothes, bedclothes, and whatever else had been in my cell were being put through another fumigating process.

While I was waiting for my things to dry—it took, perhaps, half an hour—I had a chance to observe about one hundred other victims of "cooties"—German soldiers who had become infested in the trenches. We were all nude, of course, but apparently it was not difficult for them to recognize me as a foreigner even without my uniform on, for none of them made any attempt to talk to me, although they all were very busy talking *about* me. I could not understand what they were saying, but I know I was the butt of most of their jokes, and they made no effort to conceal the fact that I was the subject of their conversation.

When I got back to my cell I found that it had been thoroughly fumigated, and from that time on I had no further trouble with "cooties" or other visitors of the same kind.

As we were not allowed to write anything but prison cards, writing was out of the question; and as we had no reading-matter to speak of, reading was nil. We had nothing to do to pass away the time, so consequently cards became our only diversion, for we did, fortunately, have some of those.

There wasn't very much money, as a rule, in circulation, and I think for once in my life I held most of that, not due to any particular ability on my part in the game, but I happened to have several hundred francs in my pockets when shot down. But we held a lottery there once a day, and I don't believe there was ever another lottery held that was watched with quite such intense interest as that. The drawing was always held the day before the prize was to be awarded, so we always knew the day before who was the lucky man. There was as much speculation as to who would win the prize as if it had been the finest treasure in the world. The great prize was one-third of a loaf of bread.

Through some arrangement which I never quite figured out, it happened that among the eight or ten officers who were there with me there was always one-third of a loaf of bread over. There was just one way of getting that bread, and that was to draw lots. Consequently that was what started the lottery. I believe if a man had ever been inclined to cheat he would have been sorely tempted in this instance, but the game was played absolutely square, and if a man had been caught cheating, the chances are that he would have been shunned by the rest of the officers as long as he was in prison. I was fortunate enough to win the prize twice.

One man—I think he was the smallest eater in the camp—won it on three successive days, but it was well for him that his luck deserted him on the fourth day, for he probably would have been handled rather roughly by the rest of the crowd, who were growing suspicious. But we handled the drawing ourselves and knew there was nothing crooked about it, so he was spared.

We were allowed to buy pears, and, being small and very hard, they were used as the stakes in many a game. But the interest in these little games was as keen as if the stakes had been piles of money instead of two or three half-starved pears. No man was ever so reckless, however, in all the betting, as to wager his own rations.

By the most scheming and sacrificing I ever did in my life I managed to hoard two pieces of bread (grudgingly spared at the time from my daily rations), but I was preparing for the day when I should escape—if I ever should. It was not a sacrifice easily made, either, but instead of eating bread I ate pears until I finally got one piece of bread ahead; and when I could force myself to stick to the pear diet again I saved the other piece from that day's allowance, and in days to come I had cause to credit myself fully for the foresight.

Whenever a new prisoner came in and his German hosts had satisfied themselves as to his life history and taken down all the details—that is, all he would give them—he was immediately surrounded by his fellow-prisoners, who were eager for any bit of news or information he could possibly give them, and as a rule he was glad to tell us because, if he had been in the hands of the Huns for any length of time, he had seen very few English officers.

The conditions of this prison were bad enough when a man was in normally good health, but it was barbarous to subject a wounded soldier to the hardships and discomforts of the place. However, this was the fate of a poor private we discovered there one day in terrific pain, suffering from shrapnel in his stomach and back. All of us officers asked to have him sent to a hospital, but the doctors curtly refused, saying it was against orders. So the poor creature went on suffering from day to day and was still there when I left, another victim of German cruelty.

At one time in this prison-camp there were a French marine, a French flying officer, and two Belgian soldiers, and of the United Kingdom one from Canada, two from England, three from Ireland, a couple from Scotland, one from Wales, a man from South Africa, one from Algeria, and a New-Zealander, the last being from my own squadron, a man whom

I thought had been killed, and he was equally surprised, when brought into the prison, to find me there. In addition there were a Chinaman and myself from the U. S. A.

It was quite a cosmopolitan group, and as one typical Irishman said, "Sure, and we have every nation that's worth mentioning, including the darn Germans, with us whites." Of course, this was not translated to the Germans, nor was it even spoken in their hearing, or we probably would not have had quite so cosmopolitan a bunch. Each man in the prison was ready to uphold his native country in any argument that could possibly be started, and it goes without saying that I never took a back seat in any of them with my praise for America, with the Canadian and Chinaman chiming in on my side. But they were friendly arguments; we were all in the same boat and that was no place for quarreling.

Every other morning, the weather allowing, we were taken to a large swimming-pool and were allowed to have a bath. There were two pools, one for the German officers and one for the men. Although we were officers, we had to use the pool occupied by the men. While we were in swimming a German guard with a rifle across his knees sat at each corner of the pool and watched us closely as we dressed and undressed. English interpreters accompanied us on all of these trips, so at no time could we talk without their knowing what was going on.

Whenever we were taken out of the prison for any purpose they always paraded us through the most crowded streets—evidently to give the populace an idea that they were getting lots of prisoners. The German soldiers we passed on these occasions made no effort to hide their smiles and sneers.

The Belgian people were apparently very curious to see us, and they used to turn out in large numbers whenever the word was passed that we were out. At times the German guards would strike the women and children who crowded too close to us. One day I smiled and spoke to a pretty Belgian girl, and when she replied a German made a run for her. Luckily she stepped into the house before he reached her or I am afraid my salutation would have resulted seriously for her and I would have been powerless to have assisted her.

Whenever we passed a Belgian home or other building which had been wrecked by bombs dropped by our airmen our guards made us stop a moment or two while they passed sneering remarks among themselves.

One of the most interesting souvenirs I have of my imprisonment at Courtrai is a photograph of a group of us taken in the prison courtyard. The picture was made by one of the guards, who sold copies of it to those of us who were able to pay his price—one mark apiece.

As we faced the camera, I suppose we all tried to look our happiest, but the majority of us, I am afraid, were too sick at heart to raise a smile even for this occasion. One of our Hun guards is shown in the picture seated at the table. I am standing directly behind him, attired in my flying tunic, which they allowed me to wear all the time I was in prison, as is the usual custom with prisoners of war. Three of the British officers shown in the picture, in the foreground, are clad in "shorts."

Through all my subsequent adventures I was able to retain a print of this interesting picture, and although when I gaze at it now it only serves to increase my gratification at my ultimate escape, it fills me with regret to think that my fellow-prisoners were not so fortunate. All of them, by this time, are undoubtedly eating their hearts up in the prison-camps of interior Germany. Poor fellows!

A GROUP OF PRISONERS OF WAR IN THE PRISON–CAMP AT
COURTRAI, BELGIUM

(Lieutenant O'Brien, in his R. F. C. flying-tunic, is standing in the center behind the German guard seated at the table. This picture was taken by one of the German guards and sold to Lieutenant O'Brien for one mark.)

DESPITE THE SCANTY FARE AND THE RESTRICTIONS WE WERE UNDER IN THIS prison, we did manage on one occasion to arrange a regular banquet. The planning which was necessary helped to pass the time.

At this time there were eight of us. We decided that the principal thing we needed to make the affair a success was potatoes, and I conceived a plan to get them. Every other afternoon they took us for a walk in the country, and it occurred to me that it would be a comparatively simple matter for us to pretend to be tired and sit down when we came to the first potato-patch.

It worked out nicely. When we came to the first potato-patch that afternoon we told our guards that we wanted to rest a bit and we were allowed to sit down. In the course of the next five minutes each of us managed to get a potato or two. Being Irish, I got six.

When we got back to the prison I managed to steal a handkerchief full of sugar which, with some apples that we were allowed to purchase, we easily converted into a sort of jam.

We now had potatoes and jam, but no bread. It happened that the Hun who had charge of the potatoes was a great musician. It was not very difficult to prevail upon him to play us some music, and while he went out to get his zither I went into the bread pantry and stole a loaf of bread.

Most of us had saved some butter from the day before and we used it to fry our potatoes. By bribing one of the guards he bought some eggs for us. They cost twenty-five cents apiece, but we were determined to make this banquet a success, no matter what it cost.

The cooking was done by the prison cook, whom, of course, we had to bribe.

When the meal was ready to serve it consisted of scrambled eggs, fried potatoes, bread and jam, and a pitcher of beer which we were allowed to buy.

That was the 29th of August. Had I known that it was to be the last real meal that I was to eat for many weeks I might have enjoyed it even more than I did, but it was certainly very good.

We had cooked enough for eight, but while we were still eating another joined us. He was an English officer who had just been brought in on a stretcher. For seven days, he told us, he had lain in a shell-hole, wounded, and he was almost famished, and we were mighty glad to share our banquet with him.

We called on each man for a speech, and one might have thought that we were at a first-class club meeting. A few days after that our party was broken up and some of the men I suppose I shall never see again.

One of the souvenirs of my adventure is a check given me during this "banquet" by Lieut. James Henry Dickson, of the Tenth Royal Irish Fusileers, a fellow-prisoner. It was for twenty francs and was made payable to the order of "Mr. Pat O'Brien, 2nd Lieut." Poor Jim forgot to scratch out the "London" and substitute "Courtrai" on the date line, but its value as a souvenir is just as great. When he gave it to me he had no idea that I would have an opportunity so soon afterward to cash it in person, although I am quite sure that whatever financial reverses I may be destined to meet my want will never be great enough to induce me to realize on that check.

There was one subject that was talked about in this prison whenever conversation lagged, and I suppose it is the same in the other prisons, too. What were the chances of escape?

Every man seemed to have a different idea and one way I suppose was about as impracticable as another. None of us ever expected to get a chance to put our ideas into execution, but it was interesting speculation, and, anyway, one could never tell what opportunities might present themselves.

One suggestion was that we disguise ourselves as women. "O'Brien would stand a better chance disguised as a horse!" declared another, referring to the fact that my height (I am six feet two inches) would make me more conspicuous as a woman than as a man.

Another suggested that we steal a German Gotha—a type of aeroplane used for long-distance bombing. It is these machines which are used for bombing London. They are manned by three men, one sitting in front with a machine-gun, the pilot sitting behind him, and an observer sitting in the rear with another machine-gun. We figured that at a pinch perhaps seven or eight of us could make our escape in a single machine. They have two motors of very high horse-power, fly very high and make wonderful speed. But we had no chance to put this idea to the test.

I worked out another plan by which I thought I might have a chance if I could ever get into one of the German aerodromes. I would conceal myself in one of the hangars, wait until one of the German machines started out, and as he taxied along the ground I would rush out, shout at the top of my voice, and point excitedly at his wheels. This, I figured, would cause the pilot to stop and get out to see what was wrong. By that time I would be up to him and as he stooped over to inspect the machine I could knock him senseless, jump into the machine, and be over the lines before the Huns could make up their minds just what had happened.

It was a fine dream, but my chance was not to come that way.

There were dozens of other ways which we considered. One man would be for endeavoring to make his way right through the lines. Another thought the safest plan would be to swim some river that crossed the lines.

The idea of making one's way to Holland, a neutral country, occurred to every one, but the one great obstacle in that direction, we all realized, was the great barrier of barbed and electrically charged wire which guards every foot of the frontier between Belgium and Holland and which is closely watched by the German sentries.

This barrier was a threefold affair. It consisted first of a barbed-wire wall six feet high. Six feet beyond that was a nine-foot wall of wire powerfully charged with electricity. To touch it meant electrocution. Beyond that, at a distance of six feet was another wall of barbed wire six feet high.

Beyond the barrier lay Holland and liberty, but how to get there was a problem which none of us could solve and few of us ever expected to have a chance to try.

Mine came sooner than I expected.

CHAPTER VI

A LEAP FOR LIBERTY

I had been in prison at Courtrai nearly three weeks when, on the morning of September 9th, I and six other officers were told that we were to be transferred to a prison-camp in Germany.

One of the guards told me during the day that we were destined for a reprisal camp in Strassburg. They were sending us there to keep our airmen from bombing the place.

He explained that the English carried German officers on hospital-ships for a similar purpose, and he excused the German practice of torpedoing these vessels on the score that they also carried munitions! When I pointed out to him that France would hardly be sending munitions to England, he lost interest in the argument.

Some days before I had made up my mind that it would be a very good thing to get hold of a map of Germany which I knew was in the possession of one of the German interpreters, because I realized that if ever the opportunity came to make my escape such a map might be of the greatest assistance to me.

With the idea of stealing this map, accordingly, a lieutenant and I got in front of this interpreter's window one day and engaged in a very hot argument as to whether Heidelberg was on the Rhine or not, and we argued back and forth so vigorously that the German came out of his room, map in hand, to settle it. After the matter was entirely settled to our satisfaction he went back into his room and I watched where he put the map.

When, therefore, I learned that I was on my way to Germany I realized that it was more important than ever for me to get that map, and, with the help of my friend, we got the interpreter out of his room on some pretext or another, and while he was gone I confiscated the map from the book in which he kept it and concealed it in my sock underneath my legging. As I had anticipated, it later proved of the utmost value to me.

I got it none too soon, for half an hour later we were on our way to Ghent. Our party consisted of five British officers and one French officer. At Ghent, where we had to wait for several hours for another train to take us direct to the prison in Germany, two other prisoners were added to our party.

In the interval we were locked in a room at a hotel, a guard sitting at the door with a rifle on his knee. It would have done my heart good for the rest of my life if I could have got away then and fooled that Hun, he was so cocksure.

Later we were marched to the train that was to convey us to Germany. It consisted of some twelve coaches, eleven of them containing troops going home on leave, and the twelfth reserved for us. We were placed in a fourth-class compartment, with old, hard, wooden seats, a filthy floor, and no lights save a candle placed there by a guard. There were eight of us prisoners and four guards.

As we sat in the coach we were an object of curiosity to the crowd who gathered at the station.

"Hope you have a nice trip!" one of them shouted, sarcastically.

"Drop me a line when you get to Berlin, will you?" shouted another in broken English.

"When shall we see you again?" asked a third.

"Remember me to your friends, will you? You'll find plenty where you're going!" shouted another.

The German officers made no effort to repress the crowd; in fact, they joined in the general laughter which followed every sally.

I called to a German officer who was passing our window.

"You're an officer, aren't you?" I asked, respectfully enough.

"Yes. What of it?" he rejoined.

"Well, in England," I said, "we let your officers who are prisoners ride first-class. Can't you fix it so that we can be similarly treated, or be transferred at least to a second-class compartment?"

"If I had my way," he replied, "you'd ride with the hogs!"

Then he turned to the crowd and told them of my request and how he had answered me, and they all laughed hilariously.

This got me pretty hot.

"That would be a damned sight better than riding with the Germans!" I yelled after him, but if he considered that a good joke, too, he didn't pass it on to the crowd.

Some months later when I had the honor of telling my story to King George he thought this incident was one of the best jokes he had ever heard. I don't believe he ever laughed harder in his life.

Before our train pulled out our guards had to present their arms for inspection, and their rifles were loaded in our presence to let us know that they meant business.

From the moment the train started on its way to Germany the thought kept coming to my head that unless I could make my escape before we reached that reprisal camp I might as well make up my mind that, as far as I was concerned, the war was over.

It occurred to me that if the eight of us in that car could jump up at a given signal and seize those four Hun guards by surprise, we'd have a splendid chance of besting them and jumping off the train when it first slowed down, but when I passed the idea on to my comrades they turned it down. Even if the plan had worked out as gloriously as I had pictured, they pointed out, the fact that so many of us had escaped would almost inevitably result in our recapture. The Huns would have scoured Belgium till they had got us and then we would all be shot. Perhaps they were right.

Nevertheless, I was determined that, no matter what the others decided to do, I was going to make one bid for freedom, come what might.

As we passed through village after village in Belgium and I realized that we were getting nearer and nearer to that dreaded reprisal camp, I concluded that my one and only chance of getting free before we reached it was through the window! I would have to go through that window while the train was going full speed, because if I waited until it had slowed up or stopped entirely, it would be a simple matter for the guards to overtake or shoot me.

I opened the window. The guard who sat opposite me—so close that his feet touched mine and the stock of his gun which he held between his knees occasionally struck my foot—made no objection, imagining, no doubt, that I found the car too warm or that the smoke, with which the compartment was filled, annoyed me.

As I opened the window the noise the train was making as it thundered along grew louder. It seemed to say: "You're a fool if you do; you're a fool if you don't! You're a fool if you do; you're a fool if you don't!" And I said to myself, "The 'no's' have it," and closed down the window again.

As soon as the window was closed the noise of the train naturally subsided and its speed seemed to diminish, and my plan appealed to me stronger than ever.

I knew the guard in front of me didn't understand a word of English, and so, in a quiet tone of voice, I confided to the English officer who sat next me what I planned to do.

"For God's sake, Pat, chuck it!" he urged. "Don't be a lunatic! This railroad is double-tracked and rock-ballasted and the other track is on your side. You stand every chance in the world of knocking your brains out against the rails, or hitting a bridge or a whistling post, and, if you escape those, you will probably be hit by another train on the other track. You haven't one chance in a thousand to make it!"

There was a good deal of logic in what he said, but I figured that, once I was in that reprisal camp, I might never have even one chance in a thousand to escape, and the idea of remaining a prisoner of war indefinitely went against my grain. I resolved to take my chance now even at the ride of breaking my neck.

The car was full of smoke. I looked across at the guard. He was rather an old man, going home on leave, and he seemed to be dreaming of what was in store for him rather than paying any particular attention to me. Once in a while I had smiled at him and I figured that he hadn't the slightest idea of what was going through my mind all the time we had been traveling.

I began to cough as though my throat were badly irritated by the smoke, and then I opened the window again. This time the guard looked up and showed his disapproval, but did not say anything.

It was then four o'clock in the morning and would soon be light. I knew I had to do it right then or never, as there would be no chance to escape in the daytime.

I had on a trench coat that I had used as a flying-coat and wore a knapsack which I had constructed out of a gas-bag brought into Courtrai by a British prisoner. In this I had two pieces of bread, a piece of sausage, and a pair of flying-mittens. All of them had to go with me through the window.

The train was now going at a rate of between thirty and thirty-five miles an hour, and again it seemed to admonish me, as it rattled along over the ties: "You're a fool if you do; you're a fool if you don't! You're a fool if you don't; you're a fool if you do! You're a fool if you don't—"

I waited no longer. Standing up on the bench as if to put the bag on the rack, and taking hold of the rack with my left hand and a strap that hung from the top of the car with my right, I pulled myself up, shoved my feet and legs out of the window, and let go!

There was a prayer on my lips as I went out and I expected a bullet between my shoulders, but it was all over in an instant.

I landed on my left side and face, burying my face in the rock ballast, cutting it open and closing my left eye, skinning my hands and shins and straining my ankle. For a few moments I was completely knocked out, and if they shot at me through the window, in the first moments after my escape, I had no way of knowing.

Of course, if they could have stopped the train right then, they could easily have recaptured me, but at the speed it was going and in the confusion which must have followed my escape, they probably didn't stop within half a mile from the spot where I lay.

I came to within a few minutes, and when I examined myself and found no bones broken I didn't stop to worry about my cuts and bruises, but jumped up with the idea of putting as great a distance between me and that track as possible before daylight came. Still being dazed, I forgot all about the barbed-wire fence along the right-of-way and ran full tilt into it.

Right there I lost one of my two precious pieces of bread, which fell out of my knapsack, but I could not stop to look for it then.

The one thing that was uppermost in my mind was that for the moment I was free and it was up to me now to make the most of my liberty.

CHAPTER VII

CRAWLING THROUGH GERMANY

The exact spot at which I made my desperate leap I don't know. Perhaps, after the war is over, some one on that train will be good enough to tell me, and then I may go back and look for the dent I must have made in the rock ballast.

As I have said, I didn't stop very long that morning after I once regained my senses.

I was bleeding profusely from the wounds caused by the fall, but I checked it somewhat with handkerchiefs I held to my face and I also held the tail of my coat so as to catch the blood as it fell and not leave telltale traces on the ground.

Before I stopped I had gone about a mile. Then I took my course from the stars and found that I had been going just opposite to the direction I should be making, but I could not go back across the track there.

Heading west, therefore, I kept this course for about two and a half hours, but as I was very weak from loss of blood I didn't cover very much ground in that time. Just before daylight I came to a canal which I knew I had to cross, and I swam it with everything I had on.

This swim, which proved to be the first of a series that I was destined to make, taught me several things.

In the first place, I had forgotten to remove my wrist-watch. This watch had been broken in my fall from the air, but I had had it repaired at Courtrai. In the leap from the train the crystal had been broken again, but it was still going and would probably have been of great service to me in my subsequent adventures, but the swim across the canal ruined it.

Then, too, I had not thought to take my map out of my sock, and the water damaged that, too.

Thereafter, whenever I had any swimming to do, I was careful to take such matters into consideration, and my usual practice was to make a bundle of all the things that would be damaged by water and tie it to my head. In this way I was able to keep them dry.

It was now daylight and I knew that it would be suicidal for me to attempt to travel in the daytime. My British uniform would have been fatal to me. I decided to hide in the daytime and travel only at night.

Not far from the canal I could see a heavily wooded piece of ground, and I made my way there. By this time I had discovered that my left ankle had been strained in my leap from the train, and when I got to the woods I was glad to lie down and rest. The wound in my mouth had been opened, too, when I jumped, and it would have been difficult for me to have swallowed had not the piece of bread, which was to serve for my breakfast, got wet when I swam the canal. I found a safe hiding-place in which to spend the day and I tried to dry some of my clothes, but a slight drizzling rainfall made that out of the question. I knew that I ought to sleep, as I planned to travel at night, but, sore as I was, caked with mud and blood, my clothing soaked through, and my hunger not nearly appeased, sleep was out of the question. This seemed to me about the longest day I had ever spent, but I was still to learn how long a day can really be and how much longer a night!

When night came I dragged myself together and headed northeast.

My clothing consisted of my Flying Corps uniform, two shirts, no underwear, leather leggings, heavy shoes, a good pair of wool socks, and a German cap. I had a wallet containing several hundred francs in paper money and various other papers. I also had a jack-knife which I had stolen one day from the property-room at Courtrai where all the personal effects taken from prisoners were kept. For a day or two I carried the knapsack, but as I had nothing to carry in it I discarded it.

I traveled rapidly, considering my difficulties, and swam a couple of canals that night, covering in all perhaps ten miles before daylight. Then I located in some low bushes, lying there all day in my wet clothes and finishing my sausage for food. That was the last of my rations.

That night I made perhaps the same distance, but became very hungry and thirsty before the night was over.

For the next six days I still figured that I was in Germany, and I was living on nothing but cabbage, sugar-beets, and an occasional carrot, always in the raw state, just as I got them out of the fields. The water I drank was often very rank, as I had to get it from canals and pools. One night I lay in a cabbage-patch for an hour lapping the dew from the leaves with my tongue!

During this period I realized that I must avoid meeting any one at all hazards. I was in the enemy's country and my uniform would have been a dead give-away. Any one who captured me or who gave information from which my capture resulted might have been sure of a handsome reward. I knew that it was necessary for me to make progress as fast as possible, but the main consideration was to keep out of sight, even if it took me a year to get to Holland, which was my objective. From my map, I estimated that I was about thirty-five miles from Strassburg when I made my leap from the train, and if I could travel in a straight line I had perhaps one hundred and fifty miles to travel. As it was, however, I was compelled to make many detours, and I figured that two hundred and fifty miles was nearer the extent of the journey ahead of me.

In several parts of this country I had to travel through forests of young pine-trees about twelve feet high. They were very close together and looked almost as if they had been set out. They proved to be a serious obstacle to me, because I could not see the stars through them, and I was relying upon the heavens to guide me to freedom. I am not much of an astronomer, but I know the Pole Star when I see it. But for it I wouldn't be here to-day!

I believe it rained every night and day while I was making my way through Germany to Luxembourg.

My invariable program at this stage of my journey was to travel steadily all night until about six in the morning, when I would commence looking around for a place wherein to hide during the day. Low bushes or woods back from the road, as far as possible from the traveled pathway, usually served me for this purpose. Having found such a spot, I would drop down and try to sleep. My overcoat was my only covering, and that was usually soaked through either from the rain or from swimming.

The only sleep I got during those days was from exhaustion, and it usually came to me toward dusk when it was time for me to start again.

It was a mighty fortunate thing for me that I was not a smoker. Somehow I have never used tobacco in any form and I was now fully repaid for whatever pleasure I had foregone in the past as a result of my habits in that particular, because my sufferings would certainly have been intensified now if in addition to lack of food and rest I had had to endure a craving for tobacco.

About the sixth night I was so drowsy and exhausted when the time came for me to be on the move that I was very much tempted to sleep through the night. I knew, however, that that would be a bad precedent to establish and I wouldn't give in.

I plugged wearily along and about eleven o'clock, after I had covered perhaps four miles, I sat down to rest for a moment on a shock of brush which was sheltered from the drizzle somewhat by other shocks which were stacked there. It was daylight when I awoke, and I found myself right in a German's backyard. You can imagine that I lost no time getting out of that neighborhood, and I made up my mind right then that I would never give way to that "tired feeling" again.

In the daytime, in my hiding-place, wherever it happened to be, I had plenty of opportunity to study my map, and before very long I knew it almost by heart. Unfortunately, however, it did not show all the rivers and canals which I encountered, and sometimes it fooled me completely.

It must have been about the ninth night that I crossed into Luxembourg, but while this principality is officially neutral, it offered me no safer a haven than Belgium would. The Huns have violated the neutrality of both and discovery would have been followed by the same consequences as capture in Germany proper.

In the nine days I had covered perhaps seventy-five miles and I was that much nearer liberty, but the lack of proper food, the constant wearing of wet clothes, and the loss of sleep and rest had reduced me to a very much weakened condition. I doubted very much whether I would be able to continue, but I plugged along.

CHAPTER VIII

NINE DAYS IN LUXEMBOURG

I was now heading northwest and I thought that by keeping that course I would get out of Luxembourg and into Belgium, where I expected to be a little better off, because the people in Luxembourg were practically the same as Germans.

One of the experiences I had in Luxembourg which I shall never forget occurred the first day that I spent there. I had traveled all night and I was feeling very weak. I came to a small wood with plenty of low underbrush, and I picked out a thick clump of bushes which was not in line with any paths, crawled in, and lay down to spend the day.

The sun could just reach me through an opening in the trees above, and I took off all my clothes except my shirt and hung them on the bushes to dry in the sun. As the sun moved I moved the clothes around correspondingly, because, tired as I was, I could take only cat-naps.

That afternoon I awoke from one of these naps with a start. There were voices not a dozen feet from me! My first impulse was to jump to my feet and sell my life as dearly as I could, but on second thoughts I decided to look before I leaped. Peeping through the underbrush, I could just discern two men calmly chopping down a tree and conversing as they worked. I thanked my lucky stars that I had not jumped up on my first impulse, for I was apparently quite safe as long as I lay where I was.

It then occurred to me that if the tree upon which they were working should happen to fall in my direction it would crush me to death! It was tall enough to reach me and big enough to kill me if it landed in my direction, and as I could see only the heads of the men who were chopping it down, I was unable to tell which way they planned to have it fall.

There was this much in my favor: the chances of the tree falling in just my direction were not very great and there was more than an even chance that the men would be wise enough to fell it so that it would not, because if it landed in the bushes the task of trimming the branches off the trunk would be so much harder.

But, even without this feeling of security, there was really nothing else I could do but wait and see what fate had in store for me. I lay there watching the top of the tree for more than an hour. Time and again I saw it sway and fancied it was coming in my direction, and it was all I could do to keep my place, but a moment later I would hear the crash of the men's axes and I knew that my imagination had played me a trick.

I was musing on the sorry plight I was in—weak, nearly starving to death, a refugee in a hostile country and waiting patiently to see which way a tree was going to fall—when there came a loud crack and I saw the top of the tree sway and fall almost opposite to the place where I lay! I had guessed right.

Later I heard some children's voices, and again peering through the underbrush, I saw that they had brought the men their lunch. You can't realize how I felt to see them eating their lunch so near at hand and to know that, hungry as I was, I could have none of it. I was greatly tempted to go boldly up to them and take a chance of getting a share, but I did not know whether they were Germans or not, and I had gone through too much to risk my liberty even for food. I swallowed my hunger instead.

Shortly afterward it began to rain, and about four o'clock the men left. I crawled out as fast as I could, and scurried around looking for crumbs, but found none, and when darkness came I went on my way once more.

That night I came to a river, and as it was the first time my clothes had been dry for a long time, I thought I would try to keep them that way as long as possible. I accordingly took off all my things and made them into two bundles, planning to carry one load across and then swim back for the other.

The river was quite wide, but I am a fairly good swimmer, and I figured I could rest awhile after the first trip before going back for the second bundle.

The first swim was uneventful. When I landed on the other side I drank till my thirst was quenched, and then swam back. After resting awhile I started across a third time, with my shoes and several other things firmly tied to my head. Just about ten feet from the opposite bank one of the shoes worked its way loose and sank in about eight feet of water. There was nothing to do but finish the trip and then go back and dive for the missing shoe, as I could not go on with a single shoe.

Diving in my weakened condition was considerable strain, but I had to have that shoe, and I kept at it for nearly an hour before I eventually found it, and I was pretty nearly all in by that time.

That was the last time I ever took my shoes off, for my feet were becoming so swollen that I figured if I took my shoes off I might be unable to get them on again.

This stunt of crossing the river and diving for the lost shoe had consumed about three hours, and after resting some fifteen minutes I went on my way again. I had hardly gone a mile when I came to another river, about the same size as the one I had just crossed. I walked along the bank awhile, thinking that I might be lucky enough to find a boat or a bridge, but after walking about half an hour I received one of those disappointments which "come once in a lifetime." I found that this river was the one I had just swum! I had swum it on the bend and was still on the wrong side! Had I made only a short detour in the first place, I would have avoided all the annoyance of the past three hours and saved my strength and time. I was never so mad in my life at myself as I was to think that I had not paid more attention to the course of the stream before I undertook to cross it, but, as a matter of fact, there was really no way of telling. The river was not shown on my map at all.

Now I *had* to cross it, whereas before I could have turned it. I walked boldly into the water, not bothering to take my clothes off this time, nor did I ever bother to take them off afterward when swimming canals or rivers.

I found it was impossible to keep them dry, anyway, and so I might just as well swim in them and save time.

All the next day I spent in a forest, to which my night's travel had brought me about five o'clock in the morning. I kept on my way through the woods until daylight came, and then, thinking the place would afford fairly good concealment, I concluded to rest until night.

The prospects of even a good sleep were dismal, however, for about the time the sun's face should have appeared a drizzling rain began and I gave up my search for a dry spot which would serve as a bed. Some of the leaves were beginning to fall, but of course there were not enough of them to have formed a covering for the ground, and the dampness seemed to have penetrated everywhere.

I wandered around through the woods for two or three hours, looking for shelter, but without any success, for, though the trees were large, the forest was not dense and there was practically no brush or shrubbery. Consequently, one could get a fairly clear view for some distance, and I knew it would be unwise to drop off to sleep just any place, or some one would surely happen onto me.

Once I came very near the edge of the woods and heard voices of men driving by in a wagon, but I couldn't make out just what they were, and instinct told me I had better not come out of the woods, so I turned back. Here and there small artificial ditches had been dug, which at a dry season might have cradled a weary fugitive, but now they, too, were filled with water. Once I singled out a good big tree with large branches and thought I might climb into it and go to sleep, but the longer I looked at it the more I realized that it would require more energy than I had in my present weak and exhausted condition, so I didn't attempt that.

Finally I chose a spot that looked a bit drier than the rest, concluded to take a chance on being discovered, and threw myself down for a nap. I was extremely nervous, though, throughout that whole day and would scarcely get settled into a comfortable position and doze off for a few minutes when, startled by some sound in the woods, I would suddenly waken.

After what seemed like a year or more, night finally came, and with it a "dud" sky, low-hanging clouds, and still more rain. There was not a star in the sky, of course, and that made it very bad, because without the aid of the stars I had absolutely no way of knowing in which direction I was going. It was just a case of taking a chance. I probably would have been better off if I had simply picked out a place and stayed there until the weather improved, but naturally I was impatient to be on my way when each day without food only lessened my strength and my ultimate chances of reaching the frontier.

So I left the woods and struck off in the direction which I thought was north. I hadn't been at all sure of my bearings the day before, and as it had rained the sun failed entirely to help me out; but I was almost sure I had the right direction, and trusted to luck. That night I found more rivers, canals, and swamps than I ever found in my life before, but I had the good fortune to stumble on to some celery, and after my diet of beets it surely was a treat. Perhaps it's unnecessary to add that I took on a good supply of celery, and for days I went along chewing celery like a cow would a cud.

Along toward morning, when I supposed I had got in a fairly good lap of my journey—perhaps seven or eight miles—I began to recognize certain objects as familiar landmarks. At least, I thought I had seen them before, and as I traveled along I knew positively I had seen certain objects very recently. Off at my right—not over a quarter of a mile—I noticed some fairly good-sized woods, and thought I would go over there to hide that day, because it looked as though the sun was going to shine, and I hoped to get my clothes dry and perhaps get a decent sleep. I had this celery and a large beet, so I knew I would be able to live the day through.

Finally, I made my way over to the woods. It was still too dark in among the trees to do much in the way of selecting my quarters for the day, and I could not go a step farther. So I waited on the edge of the forest until dawn and then set out to explore the place with a view to finding some nook where I might sleep. Imagine my disgust and discouragement, too, when, an hour or so later, I came upon the exact place where I had spent the day before, and I realized that all night long I had been circling the very woods I was trying to get away from. I think perhaps I had gone all of a quarter of a mile in the right direction, but then had lost my bearings entirely and daylight found me with nothing accomplished.

The sun, however, did come out that day, and I welcomed its warm rays as they perhaps have never been welcomed before. I was very tired—just about all in—but I spent a better day in the woods than the previous one.

That night the stars came out; I located my friend, the North Star, and tried to make up for lost time. But when one is making only seven or eight miles a day, or rather a night, one night lost means a whole lot, especially when each day keeps him from freedom. Such ill fortune and discouragements as this were harder to endure, I believe, than the actual hunger, and the accompanying worry naturally reduced my weight. At times I was furiously angry with myself for the mistakes I made and the foolish things I did, but I always tried to see something funny about the situation, whatever it might be, that relieved the strain a bit and helped to pass the time. I think if a man is overburdened with a sense of humor and wants to get rid of it, this trip I took would be an excellent remedy for it. Right at this time I would have welcomed anything for a companion; I believe even a snake would have been a godsend to me.

With a name as Irish as mine, it is only natural that I looked for goats along the way, thinking that I might be able to milk them. There are very few cows in this country, and the opportunities for milking them fewer than the cows themselves, because they are housed in barns adjoining the homes and always alertly watched by their fortunate owners. I did hope that I might find a goat staked out some place in the fields, but in all my travels I never saw a goat or a pig, and only a few cows. Several times I searched nests for eggs, but somebody always had beaten me to it, as I never even found so much as a nest egg.

There was no chance of getting away with any "bullying" stuff in Luxembourg, I knew, because the young men have not been forced into the army and are still at home, and as they are decidedly pro-German, it would have been pretty hard for me to demand anything in that part of the country. It was not like taking things away from old men and women or robbing people that could not stop me if they chose to do so. I thought at this time that I was suffering about the worst hardships any human being could ever be called upon to endure, but I was later to find out that the best of my journey was made along about this time. There were plenty of vegetables, even though they were raw, and these were much better than the things I was afterward compelled to eat or go without.

We frequently hear of men who have lived for a certain number of days on their own resources in the woods just on a bet or to prove that the "back to nature" theory still has its merits and will still work. My advice to some of those nature-seekers is to, if in the future they wish to make a real good record, try the little countries of Luxembourg and Belgium, with a slice of Germany thrown in.

I suppose that during this experience of mine I made many mistakes and traveled many unnecessary miles which one with a knowledge of woodsmanship might have avoided, and I failed to take advantage of many things which would have been quite apparent to one who knew. It must not be forgotten, however, that I did not undertake this adventure voluntarily. It was "wished on me." I simply had to make the most of the knowledge I had.

At about this time blisters began to appear on my legs and my knees swelled. In addition I was pretty well convinced that I had lost the sight of my left eye. I hadn't seen a thing out of it since my leap from the train.

When I imagine the villainous appearance I must have presented at this time—my unhealed wounds, eighteen days' growth of beard, and general haggard and unkempt visage—I think the fear I felt about meeting strangers was perhaps unwarranted. The chances are they would have been infinitely more scared than I!

As it was, I was nearly out of Luxembourg before I really came face to face with any one. It was about six o'clock in the morning and I was traveling along a regular path. Just as I approached a cross-path I heard footsteps coming down it. I stopped short, stooped over, and pretended to be adjusting my shoe-lace, figuring that if the stranger turned into my path he would probably pass right by me. As luck would have it, he continued on his way and never noticed me at all.

After that I frequently noticed groups of Luxembourg peasants in the distance, but I usually saw them first and managed to avoid them.

About the eighteenth day after my leap from the train I crossed into Belgium. It had taken me just nine days to get through Luxembourg—a distance which a man could ordinarily cover in two, but, considering the handicaps under which I labored, I was very well satisfied with my progress.

CHAPTER IX

I ENTER BELGIUM

I have said it was about the eighteenth day after my escape that I entered Belgium, but that is more or less guesswork. I was possibly well into that country before I realized that I had crossed the line.

About the third day after I figured I was in Belgium I started to swim a canal just before daylight. I was then heading due north in the direction of the German lines. I was just about to wade into the canal when I heard a German yelling violently, and for the first time I knew I was being followed!

I ran up the bank of the canal quite a distance and then swam to the opposite side, as I reasoned they would not be looking for me there. I found a sheltered clump of bushes in a swamp near the canal, and in the driest part that I could find I crawled in and made myself as comfortable as possible. The sun came up soon and kept me warm, and I planned to camp right there, food or no food, until the Huns got tired of searching for me. I think I heard them once or twice that day, and my heart nearly stopped on each occasion, but evidently they decided to look in some other direction and I was not further molested.

At the same time I figured that it was absolutely necessary for me to change my course even at the expense of going somewhat out of my way.

Certainly if I went north they would get me. I decided to go due west, and I kept in that direction for four days.

As I was in a very weak condition, I did not cover more than five miles a night. I kept away from the roads and did all my journeying through fields, beet-patches, woods, swamps—anywhere, provided I was not likely to be seen and captured. Food was an important consideration to me, but it was secondary to concealment.

At last I brought up at the Meuse River at a place between Namur and Huy, and it was here that I came nearest of all to giving up the struggle.

The Meuse at this point is about half a mile wide—as wide as the Hudson River at West Point. Had I been in normal condition I wouldn't have hesitated a moment to swim across. San Diego Bay, California, is a mile and a half wide, and I had often swum across and back, and the San Joaquin, which is also a mile and a half wide, had never proved an obstacle to me.

In the wretched shape in which I then was, however, the Meuse looked like the Atlantic Ocean to me. I looked for a boat, but could find none. I tried to get a piece of wood upon which I hoped to ferry across, but I was equally unsuccessful.

Get across I must, and I decided there was nothing to do but swim it.

It was then about three o'clock in the morning. I waded in and was soon in beyond my depth and had to swim. After about an hour of it I was very much exhausted and I doubted whether I could make the opposite bank, although it was not more than thirty or forty feet away. I choked and gasped and my arms and legs were completely fagged out. I sank a little and tried to touch bottom with my feet, but the water was still beyond my depth.

There are times when every one will pray, and I was no exception. I prayed for strength to make those few wicked yards, and then, with all the will power I could summon, struck out for dear life. It seemed a lifetime before I finally felt the welcome mud of bottom and was able to drag myself up to the bank, but I got there. The bank was rather high, and I was shaking so violently that when I took hold of the grass to pull myself up, the grass shook out of my hands. I could not retain my grip. I was afraid I would faint then and there, but I kept pulling and crawling frantically up that infernal bank, and finally made it.

Then, for the first time in my life, I fainted—fainted from utter exhaustion.

It was now about four o'clock in the morning and I was entirely unprotected from observation. If any one had come along I would have been found lying there dead to the world.

Possibly two hours passed before I regained consciousness, and then, no doubt, only because the rain was beating in my face.

I knew that I had to get away, as it was broad daylight. Moreover, there was a towpath right there and any minute a boat might come along and find me. But it was equally dangerous for me to attempt to travel very far. Fortunately, I found some shrubbery near by, and I hid there all day, without food or drink.

That night I made a little headway, but when day broke I had a dreadful fever and was delirious. I talked to myself and thereby increased my chances of capture. In my lucid intervals, when I realized that I had been talking, the thought sent a chill through me, because in the silent night even the slightest sound carries far across the Belgian country. I began to fear that another day of this would about finish me.

I have a distinct recollection of a ridiculous conversation I carried on with an imaginary Pat O'Brien—a sort of duplicate of myself. I argued with him as I marched drearily along, and he answered me back in kind, and when we disagreed I called upon my one constant friend, the North Star, to stand by me.

"There you are, you old North Star!" I cried, aloud. "You want me to get to Holland, don't you? But this Pat O'Brien—this Pat O'Brien who calls himself a soldier—he's got a yellow streak—North Star—and he says it can't be done! He wants me to quit—to lie down here for the Huns to find me and take me back to Courtrai—after all you've done, North Star, to lead me to liberty. Won't you make this coward leave me, North Star? I don't want to follow him—I just want to follow you—because you—you are taking me away from the Huns and this Pat O'Brien—this fellow who keeps after me all the time and leans on my neck and wants me to lie down—this yellow Pat O'Brien wants me to go back to the Huns!"

After a spell of foolish chatter like that my senses would come back to me for a while and I would trudge along without a word until the fever came on me again.

I knew that I had to have food because I was about on my last legs. I was very much tempted to lie down then and there and call it a heat. Things seemed to be getting worse for me the farther I went, and all the time I had before me the specter of that electric barrier between Belgium and Holland, even if I ever reached there alive. What was the use of further suffering when I would probably be captured in the end, anyway?

Before giving up, however, I decided upon one bold move. I would approach one of the houses in the vicinity and get food there or die in the effort!

I picked out a small house, because I figured there would be less likelihood of soldiers being billeted there.

Then I wrapped a stone in my khaki handkerchief as a sort of camouflaged weapon, determined to kill the occupant of the house, German or Belgian, if that step were necessary in order to get food. I tried the well in the yard, but it would not work, and then I went up to the door and knocked.

It was one o'clock in the morning. An old lady came to the window and looked out. She could not imagine what I was, probably, because I was still attired in that old overcoat. She gave a cry, and her husband and a boy came to the door.

They could not speak English and I could not speak Flemish, but I pointed to my flying-coat and then to the sky and said "*fleger*" ("flier"), which I thought would tell them what I was.

Whether they understood or were intimidated by my hard-looking appearance, I don't know, but certainly it would have to be a brave old man and boy who would start an argument with such a villainous-looking character as stood before them that night! I had not shaved for a month, my clothes were wet, torn, and dirty, my leggings were gone—they had got so heavy I had discarded them—my hair was matted, and my cheeks were flushed with fever. In my hand I carried the rock in my handkerchief, and I made no effort to conceal its presence or its mission.

Anyway, they motioned me indoors and gave me my first hot meal in more than a month. True, it consisted only of warm potatoes. They had been previously cooked, but the old woman warmed them up in milk in one of the dirtiest kettles I had ever seen. I asked for bread, but she shook her head, although I think it must have been for lack of it rather than because she begrudged it to me. For if ever a man showed he was famished, I did that night. I swallowed those warm potatoes ravenously and I drank four glasses of water one after another. It was the best meal I had had since the "banquet" in the prison at Courtrai.

The woman of the house was probably seventy-five years old and had evidently worn wooden shoes all her life, for she had a callous spot on the side of her foot the size of half a dollar, and it looked so hard that I doubt whether you could have driven a nail into it with a hammer.

As I sat there drying myself—for I was in no hurry to leave the first human habitation I had entered in four weeks—I reflected on my unhappy lot and the unknown troubles and dangers that lay ahead of me. Here, for more than a month, I had been leading the life of a hunted animal—yes, worse than a hunted animal, for Nature clothes her less favored creatures more appropriately for the life they lead than I was clothed for mine— and there was not the slightest reason to hope that conditions would grow better.

Perhaps the first warm food I had eaten for over a month had released unused springs of philosophy in me, as food sometimes does for a man.

I pointed to my torn and water-soaked clothes and conveyed to them as best I could that I would be grateful for an old suit, but apparently they were too poor to have more than they actually needed themselves, and I rose to go. I had roused them out of bed, and I knew I ought not to keep them up longer than was absolutely necessary.

As I approached the door I got a glance at myself in a mirror. I was the awfulest sight I had ever laid eyes on! The glimpse I got of myself startled me almost as much as if I had seen a dreaded German helmet! My left eye was fairly well healed by this time, and I was beginning to regain the sight of it, but my face was so haggard and my beard so long and unkempt that I looked like Santa Claus on a "bat."

As they let me out of the door I pointed to the opposite direction to the one I intended taking and started off in the direction I had indicated. Later I changed my course completely to throw off any possible pursuit.

The next day I was so worn out from exposure and exhaustion that I threw away my coat, thinking that the less weight I had to carry the better it would be for me, but when night came I regretted my mistake, because the nights were now getting colder. I thought at first it would be best for me to retrace my steps and look for the coat I had so thoughtlessly discarded, but I decided to go on without it.

I then began to discard everything that I had in my pocket, finally throwing my wrist-watch into a canal. A wrist-watch does not add much weight, but when you plod along and have not eaten for a month it finally becomes rather heavy. The next thing I discarded was a pair of flying-mittens.

These mittens I had got at Camp Borden, in Canada, and had become quite famous, as my friends termed them "snow-shoes." In fact, they were a ridiculous pair of mittens, but the best pair I ever had, and I really felt worse when I lost those mittens than anything else. I could not think of anybody else ever using them, so I dug a hole in the mud and buried them, and could not help but laugh at the thought of what my friends would say had they seen me burying my mittens, because they were a standing joke in Canada, England, and France.

I had on two shirts, and as they were always both wet and didn't keep me warm, it was useless to wear both. One of these was a shirt that I had bought in France, the other an American army shirt. They were both khaki and one as apt to give me away as the other, so I discarded the French shirt. The American army shirt I brought back with me to England, and it is still in my possession.

When I escaped from the train I still had that Bavarian cap of bright red in my pocket and wore it for many nights, but I took great care that no one saw it. It also had proved very useful when swimming rivers, for I carried my map and a few other belongings in it, and I had fully made up my mind to bring it home as a souvenir. But the farther I went the heavier my extra clothing became, so I was compelled to discard even the cap. I knew that it would be a telltale mark if I simply threw it away, so one night after swimming a river I dug a hole in the soft mud on the bank and buried it, too, with considerably less ceremony than my flying-mittens had received, perhaps; and that was the end of my Bavarian hat.

My experience at the Belgian's house whetted my appetite for warm food, and I figured that what had been done once could be done again. Sooner or later I realized I would probably approach a Belgian and find a German instead, but in such a contingency I was determined to measure my strength against the Hun's if necessary to effect my escape.

As it was, however, most of the Belgians to whom I applied for food gave it to me readily enough, and if some of them refused me it was only because they feared I might be a spy or that the Germans would shoot them if their action were subsequently found out.

About the fifth day after I had entered Belgium I was spending the day as usual in a clump of bushes when I discerned in the distance what appeared to be something hanging on a line. All day long I strained my eyes trying to decide what it could be and arguing with myself that it might be something that I could add to my inadequate wardrobe, but the distance was so great that I could not identify it. I had a great fear that before night came it would probably be removed.

As soon as darkness fell, however, I crawled out of my hiding-place and worked up to the line and got a pair of overalls for my industry. It was a mighty joyful night for me. That pair of overalls was the first bit of civilian clothes I had thus far picked up, with the exception of a civilian cap which I had found at the prison and concealed on my person and which I still had. The overalls were rather small and very short, but when I put them on I found that they hung down far enough to cover my breeches.

It was perhaps three days later that I planned to search another house for further clothes. Entering Belgian houses at night is anything but a safe proposition, because their families are large and sometimes as many as seven or eight sleep in a single room. The barn is usually connected with the house proper, and there was always the danger of disturbing some dumb animal, even if the inmates of the house were not aroused.

Frequently I took a chance of searching a backyard at night in the hope of finding food scraps, but my success in that direction was so slight that I soon decided it wasn't worth the risk, and I continued to live on the raw vegetables that I could pick with safety in the fields and the occasional meal that I was able to get from the Belgian peasants in the daytime.

Nevertheless, I was determined to get more in the way of clothing, and when night came I picked out a house that looked as though it might furnish me with what I wanted. It was a moonlight night, and if I could get in the barn I would have a fair chance of finding my way around by the moonlight which would enter the windows.

The barn adjoined the main part of the house, but I groped around very carefully and soon I touched something hanging on a peg. I didn't know what it was, but I confiscated it and carried it out into the fields. There in the moonlight I examined my booty and found it was an old coat. It was too short as an overcoat and too long for an ordinary coat, but nevertheless I made use of it. It had probably been an overcoat for the Belgian who had worn it.

Some days later I got a scarf from a Belgian peasant, and with this equipment I was able to conceal my uniform entirely.

Later on, however, I decided that it was too dangerous to keep the uniform on anyway, and when night came I dug a hole and buried it.

I never realized until I had to part with it just how much I thought of that uniform. It had been with me through many hard trials, and I felt as if I were abandoning a friend when I parted with it. I was tempted to keep the wings off the tunic, but thought that that would be a dangerous concession to sentiment in the event that I was ever captured. It was the only distinction I had left, as I had given the Royal Flying Corps badges and the stars of my rank to the German Flying Officers as souvenirs, but I felt that it was safer to discard it. As it finally turned out, through all my subsequent experiences my escape would never have been jeopardized had I kept my uniform, but, of course, I had no idea what was in store for me.

There was one thing which surprised me very much as I journeyed through Belgium, and that was the scarcity of dogs. Apparently most of them have been taken by the Germans, and what are left are beasts of burden who are too tired at night to bark or bother intruders. This was a mighty good thing for me, for I would certainly have stirred them up in passing through backyards, as I sometimes did when I was making a short cut.

One night as I came out of a yard it was so pitch dark I could not see ten feet ahead of me, and I was right in the back of a little village, although I did not know it. I crawled along, fearing I might come to a crossroads at which there would in all probability be a German sentry.

My precaution served me in good stead, for I had come out in the main street of a village and within twenty feet of me, sitting on some bricks where they were building a little store, I could see the dim outline of a German spiked helmet!

I could not cross the street and the only thing to do was to back-track. It meant making a long detour and losing two hours of precious time and effort, but there was no help for it, and I plodded wearily back, cursing the Huns at every step.

The next night while crossing some fields I came to a road. It was one of the main roads of Belgium and was paved with cobblestones. On these roads you can hear a wagon or horse about a mile or two away. I listened intently before I moved ahead, and, hearing nothing, concluded that the way was clear.

As I emerged from the field and got my first glimpse of the road I got the shock of my life! In either direction, as far as I could see, the road was lined with German soldiers!

What they were doing in that part of Belgium I did not know, but you can be mighty sure I didn't spend any time trying to find out.

Again it was necessary to change my course and lose a certain amount of ground, but by this time I had become fairly well reconciled to these reverses and they did not depress me as much as they had at first.

At this period of my adventure if a day or a night passed without its thrill I began to feel almost disappointed, but such disappointments were rather rare.

One evening as I was about to swim a canal about two hundred feet wide I suddenly noticed, about one hundred yards away, a canal-boat moored to the side.

It was a sort of out-of-the-way place, and I wondered what the canal-boat had stopped for. I crawled up to see. As I neared the boat five men were leaving it, and I noticed them cross over into the fields. At a safe distance I followed them, and they had not gone very far before I saw what they were after. They were committing the common but heinous crime of stealing potatoes!

Without the means to cook them, potatoes didn't interest me a bit, and I thought that the boat itself would probably yield me more than the potato-patch. Knowing that the canal hands would probably take their time in the fields, I climbed up the stern of the boat leisurely and without any particular pains to conceal myself. Just as my head appeared above the stern of the boat I saw, silhouetted against the sky, the dreaded outline of a German soldier—spiked helmet and all! A chill ran down my spine as I dropped to the bank of the canal and slunk away. Evidently the sentry had not seen me or, if he had, he had probably figured that I was one of the foraging party, but I realized that it wouldn't pay in future to take anything for granted.

CHAPTER X

EXPERIENCES IN BELGIUM

I think that one of the worst things I had to contend with in my journey through Belgium was the number of small ditches. They intercepted me at every half-mile or so, sometimes more frequently. The canals and the big rivers I could swim. Of course, I got soaked to the skin every time I did it, but I was becoming hardened to that.

These little ditches, however, were too narrow to swim and too wide to jump. They had perhaps two feet of water in them and three feet of mud, and it was almost invariably a case of wading through. Some of them, no doubt, I could have jumped if I had been in decent shape, but with a bad ankle and in the weakened condition in which I was, it was almost out of the question.

One night I came to a ditch about eight or nine feet wide. I thought I was strong enough to jump it, and it was worth trying, as the discomfort I suffered after wading these ditches was considerable. Taking a long run, I jumped as hard as I could, but I missed it by four or five inches and landed in about two feet of water and three feet more of mud. Getting out of that mess was quite a job. The water was too dirty and too scanty to enable me to wash off the mud with which I was covered and it was too wet to scrape off. I just had to wait until it dried and scrape it off then.

In many sections of Belgium through which I had to pass I encountered large areas of swamp and marshy ground, and, rather than waste the time involved in looking for better underfooting—which I might not have found, anyway—I used to plod right through the mud. Apart from the discomfort of this method of traveling and the slow time I made, there was an added danger to me in the fact that the "squash-squash" noise which I made might easily be overheard by Belgians and Germans and give my position away. Nobody would cross a swamp or marsh in that part of the country unless he was trying to get away from somebody, and I realized my danger, but could not get around it.

It was a common sight in Belgium to see a small donkey and a common, ordinary milch cow hitched together, pulling a wagon. When I first observed the unusual combination I thought it was a donkey and ox or bull, but closer inspection revealed to me that cows were being used for the purpose.

From what I was able to observe, there must be very few horses left in Belgium except those owned by the Germans. Cows and donkeys are now doing the work formerly done by horses and mules. Altogether I spent nearly eight weeks wandering through Belgium and in all that time I don't believe I saw more than half a dozen horses in the possession of the native population.

One of the scarcest things in Germany, apparently, is rubber, for I noticed that their motor trucks, or lorries, unlike our own, had no rubber tires. Instead, heavy iron bands were employed. I could hear them come rumbling along the stone roads for miles before they reached the spot where I happened to be in hiding. When I saw these military roads in Belgium for the first time, with their heavy cobblestones that looked as if they would last for centuries, I realized at once why it was that the Germans had been able to make such a rapid advance into Belgium at the start of the war.

I noticed that the Belgians used dogs to a considerable extent to pull their carts, and I thought many times that if I could have stolen one of those dogs it would have made a very good companion for me, and might, if the occasion arose, help me out in a fight. But I had no way of feeding it and the animal would probably have starved to death. I could live on vegetables which I could always depend upon finding in the fields, but a dog couldn't, and so I gave up the idea.

The knack of making fire with two pieces of dry wood I had often read about, but I had never put it to a test, and for various reasons I concluded that it would be unsafe for me to build a fire even if I had matches. In the first place, there was no absolute need for it. I didn't have anything to cook, nor utensils to cook it in even if I had. While the air was getting to be rather cool at night, I was usually on the go at the time and didn't notice it. In the daytime, when I was resting or sleeping, the sun was usually out.

To have borrowed matches from a Belgian peasant would have been feasible, but when I was willing to take the chance of approaching any one it was just as easy to ask for food as matches.

In the second place, it would have been extremely dangerous to have built a fire even if I had needed it. You can't build a fire in Belgium, which is the most thickly populated country in Europe, without every one knowing it, and I was far from anxious to advertise my whereabouts.

The villages in the part of Belgium through which I was making my course were so close together that there was hardly ever an hour passed without my hearing some clock strike. Every village has its clock. Many times I could hear the clocks striking in two villages at the same time.

But the hour had very little interest to me. My program was to travel as fast as I could from sunset to sunrise and pay no attention to the hours in between, and in the daytime I had only two things to worry about: keep concealed and get as much sleep as possible.

The cabbage that I got in Belgium consisted of the small heads that the peasants had not cut. All the strength had concentrated in these little heads and they would be as bitter as gall. I would have to be pretty hungry to-day before I could ever eat cabbage again, and the same observation applies to carrots, turnips, and sugar-beets—especially sugar-beets.

It is rather a remarkable thing that to-day even the smell of turnips, raw or cooked, makes me sick, and yet a few short months ago my life depended upon them.

Night after night, as I searched for food, I was always in hopes that I might come upon some tomatoes or celery—vegetables which I really liked, but with the exception of once, when I found some celery, I was never so fortunate. I ate so much of the celery the night I came upon it that I was sick for two days thereafter, but I carried several bunches away with me and used to chew on it as I walked along.

Of course, I kept my eyes open all the time for fruit trees, but apparently it was too late in the year for fruit, as all that I ever was able to find were two pears which I got out of a tree. That was one of my red-letter days, but I was never able to repeat it.

In the brooks and ponds that I passed I often noticed fish of different kinds. That was either in the early morning, just before I turned in for the day, or on moonlight nights when the water seemed as clear in spots as in the daytime. It occurred to me that it would be a simple matter to rig a hook and line and catch some of the fish, but I had no means of cooking them and it was useless to fish for the sake of it.

One night in Belgium my course took me through a desolate stretch of country which seemed to be absolutely uncultivated. I must have covered twelve miles during the night without passing a single farm or cultivated field. My stock of turnips which I had plucked the night before was gone and I planned, of course, to get enough to carry me through the following day.

The North Star was shining brightly that night and there was absolutely nothing to prevent my steering an absolutely direct course for Holland and liberty, but my path seemed to lie through arid pastures. Far to the east or to the west I could hear faintly the striking of village bells, and I knew that if I changed my course I would undoubtedly strike farms and vegetables, but the North Star seemed to plead with me to follow it, and I would not turn aside.

When daylight came the consequence was I was empty-handed, and I had to find a hiding-place for the day. I thought I would approach the first peasant I came to and ask for food, but that day I had misgivings—a hunch—that I would get into trouble if I did, and I decided to go without food altogether for that day.

It was a foolish thing to do, I found, because I not only suffered greatly from hunger all that day, but it interfered with my sleep. I would drop off to sleep for half an hour, perhaps, and during that time I would dream that I was free, back home, living a life of comparative ease, and then I would wake up with a start and catch a glimpse of the bushes surrounding me, feel the hard ground beneath me and the hunger pangs gnawing at my insides, and then I would realize how far from home I really was, and I would lie there and wonder whether I would ever really see my home again. Then I would fall asleep again and dream this time, perhaps, of the days I spent in Courtrai, of my leap from the train window, of the Bavarian pilot whom I sent to eternity in my last air-fight, of my tracer-bullets getting closer and closer to his head, and then I would wake up again with a start and thank the Lord that I was only dreaming it all again instead of living through it!

That night I got an early start because I knew I had to have food, and I decided that, rather than look for vegetables, I would take a chance and apply to the first Belgian peasant I came to.

It was about eight o'clock when I came to a small house. I had picked up a heavy stone and had bound it in my handkerchief, and I was resolved to use it as a weapon if it became necessary. After all I had gone through I was resolved to win my liberty eventually at whatever cost.

As it happened, I found that night the first real friend I had encountered in all my traveling. When I knocked timidly on the door it was opened by a Belgian peasant, about fifty years of age. He asked me in Flemish what I wanted, but I shook my head and, pointing to my ears and mouth, intimated that I was deaf and dumb, and then I opened and closed my teeth several times to show him that I wanted food.

He showed me inside and sat me at the table. He apparently lived alone, for his ill-furnished room had but one chair, and the plate and knife and fork he put before me seemed to be all he had. He brought me some cold potatoes and several slices of stale bread, and he warmed me some milk on a small oil-stove.

I ate ravenously, and all the time I was engaged I knew that he was eying me closely.

Before I was half through he came over to me, touched me on the shoulder, and, stooping over so that his lips almost touched my ear, he said, in broken English, "You are an Englishman—I know it—and you can hear and talk if you wish. Am I not right?"

There was a smile on his face and a friendly attitude about him that told me instinctively that he could be trusted, and I replied, "You have guessed right—only I am an American, not an Englishman."

He looked at me pityingly and filled my cup again with warm milk.

His kindness and apparent willingness to help me almost overcame me, and I felt like warning him of the consequences he would suffer if the Huns discovered he had befriended me. I had heard that twenty Belgians had been shot for helping Belgians to escape into Holland, and I hated to think what might happen to this Good Samaritan if the Huns ever knew that he had helped an escaped American prisoner.

After my meal was finished I told him in as simple language as I could command of some of the experiences I had gone through, and I outlined my future plans.

"You will never be able to get to Holland," he declared, "without a passport. The nearer you get to the frontier the more German soldiers you will encounter, and without a passport you will be a marked man."

I asked him to suggest a way by which I could overcome this difficulty.

He thought for several moments and studied me closely all the time—perhaps endeavoring to make absolutely sure that I was not a German spy—and then, apparently deciding in my favor, told me what he thought it was best for me to do.

"If you will call on this man," mentioning the name of a Belgian in ----, a city through which I had to pass, he advised, "you will be able to make arrangements with him to secure a passport, and he will do everything he can to get you out of Belgium."

He told me where the man in question could be found and gave me some useful directions to continue my journey, and then he led me to the door. I thanked him a thousand times and wanted to pay him for his kindness and help, but he would accept nothing. He did give me his name, and you may be sure I shall never forget it, but to mention it here might, of course, result in serious consequences for him. When the war is over, however, or the Germans are thrown out of Belgium, I shall make it my duty to find that kind Belgian, if to do it I have to go through again all that I have suffered already.

CHAPTER XI

What the Belgian had told me about the need of a passport gave me fresh cause for worry. Suppose I should run into a German sentry before I succeeded in getting one?

I decided that until I reached the big city which the Belgian had mentioned—and which I cannot name for fear of identifying some of the people there who befriended me—I would proceed with the utmost precaution. Since I had discarded my uniform and had obtained civilian clothes I had not been quite as careful as I was at first. While I had done my traveling at night, I had not gone into hiding so early in the morning as before, and I had sometimes started again before it was quite dark, relying upon the fact that I would probably be mistaken for a Belgian on his way to or from work, as the case might be. From now on, I resolved, however, I would take no more chances.

That evening I came to a river perhaps seventy-five yards wide, and I was getting ready to swim it when I thought I would walk a little way to find, if possible, a better place to get to the river from the bank. I had not walked more than a few hundred feet when I saw a boat. It was the first time I had seen a boat in all my experiences.

It was firmly chained, but as the stakes were sunk in the soft bank it was not much of a job to pull them out. I got in, drank to my heart's content, shoved over to the other side, got out, drove a stake into the ground, and moored the boat. It would have been a simple matter to have drifted down the river, but the river was not shown on my map and I had no idea where it might lead me. Very reluctantly, therefore, I had to abandon the boat and proceed on foot.

I made several miles that night and before daylight found a safe place in which to hide for the day. From my hiding-place I could see through the bushes a heavy thick wood only a short distance away. I decided that I would start earlier than usual, hurry over to the wood, and perhaps in that way I could cover two or three miles in the daytime and gain just so much time. Traveling through the wood would be comparatively safe. There was a railroad going through the wood, but I did not figure that that would make it any the less safe.

About three o'clock that afternoon, therefore, I emerged from my hiding-place and hurried into the wood. After proceeding for half a mile or so I came to the railroad. I took a sharp look in both directions and, seeing no signs of trains or soldiers, I walked boldly over the tracks and continued on my way.

I soon came upon a clearing and knew that some one must be living in the vicinity. As I turned a group of trees I saw a small house and in the distance an old man working in a garden. I decided to enter the house and ask for food, figuring the woman would probably be old and would be no match for me even if she proved hostile. The old woman who came to the door in response to my knock was older even than I had expected. If she wasn't close to a hundred years, I miss my guess very much.

She could not speak English and I could not speak Flemish, of course, but, nevertheless, I made her understand that I wanted something to eat. She came out of the door and hollered for her husband in a shrill voice that would have done credit to a girl of eighteen. The old man came in from his garden and between the two of them they managed to get the idea that I was hungry, and they gave me a piece of bread—a very small piece—which was quite a treat.

The house they lived in consisted of just two rooms—the kitchen and a bedroom. The kitchen was perhaps fourteen feet square, eight feet of one side of it being taken up by an enormous fireplace. What was in the bedroom I had no way of telling, as I did not dare to be too inquisitive.

I made the old couple understand that I would like to stay in their house all night, but the old man shook his head. I bade them good-by and disappeared into the woods, leaving them to speculate as to the strange foreigner they had entertained.

From the greater density of the population in the section through which I was now passing I realized that I must be in the outskirts of the big city which the Belgian had mentioned and where I was to procure a passport.

Village after village intercepted me, and, although I tried to skirt them wherever possible, I realized that I would never make much progress if I continued that course. To gain a mile I would sometimes have to make a detour of two or three. I decided that I would try my luck in going straight through the next village I came to.

As I approached it I passed numbers of peasants who were ambling along the road. I was afraid to mingle with them because it was impossible for me to talk to them and it was dangerous to arouse suspicion even among the Belgians. For all I knew, one of them might be treacherous enough to deliver me to the Germans in return for the reward he might be sure of receiving.

About nine o'clock that evening I came to a point where ahead of me on the right was a Belgian police station—I knew it from its red lights—and on the other side of the street were two German soldiers in uniform leaning against a bicycle.

Here was a problem which called for instant decision. If I turned back, the suspicion of the soldiers would be instantly aroused, and if I crossed the road so as not to pass so closely to them, they might be equally suspicious. I decided to march bravely by the Huns, bluff my way through, and trust to Providence. If anybody imagines, however, that I was at all comfortable as I approached those soldiers, he must think that I am a much braver man than I claim to be. My heart beat so loud I was afraid they would hear it. Every step I took brought me so much nearer to what might prove to be the end of all my hopes. It was a nerve-racking ordeal.

I was now within a few feet of them. Another step and—

They didn't turn a hair! I passed right by them—heard what they were saying, although, of course, I didn't understand it, and went right on. I can't say I didn't walk a little faster as I left them behind, but I tried to maintain an even gait so as not to give them any idea of the inward exultation I was experiencing. No words can explain, however, how relieved I really felt—to know that I had successfully passed through the first of a series of similar tests which I realized were in store for me—although I did not know then how soon I was to be confronted with the second.

As it was, however, the incident gave me a world of confidence. It demonstrated to me that there was nothing in my appearance, at any rate, to attract the attention of the German soldiers. Apparently I looked like a Belgian peasant, and if I could only work things so that I would never have to answer questions and thus give away my nationality, I figured I would be tolerably safe.

As I marched along I felt so happy I couldn't help humming the air of one of the new patriotic songs that we used to sing at the aerodrome back of Ypres.

In this happy fame of mind I covered the next three miles in about an hour, and then I came to another little village. My usual course would have been to go around it—through fields, backyards, woods, or whatever else lay in my way—but I had gained so much time by going through the last village instead of detouring around it, and my appearance seemed to be so unsuspicious, that I decided to try the same stunt again.

I stopped humming and kept very much on the alert, but, apart from that, I walked boldly through the main street without any feeling of alarm.

I had proceeded perhaps a mile along the main street when I noticed ahead of me three German soldiers standing at the curb.

Again my heart started to beat fast, I must confess, but I was not nearly so scared as I had been an hour or so before. I walked ahead, determined to follow my previous procedure in every particular.

I had got to about fifteen feet away from the soldiers when one of them stepped onto the sidewalk and shouted:

"Halt!"

My heart stopped beating fast—for a moment, I believe, it stopped beating altogether! I can't attempt to describe my feelings. The thought that the jig was up, that all I had gone through and all I had escaped would now avail me nothing, mingled with a feeling of disgust with myself because of the foolish risk I had taken in going through the village, combined to take all the starch out of me, and I could feel myself wilting as the soldier advanced to the spot where I stood rooted in my tracks.

I had a bottle of water in one pocket and a piece of bread in the other, and as the Hun advanced to search me I held the bottle up in one hand and the piece of bread in the other so that he could see that was all I had.

It occurred to me that he would "frisk" me—that is, feel me over for arms or other weapons, then place me under arrest and march me off to the guard-house. I had not the slightest idea but that I was captured, and there didn't seem to be much use in resisting, unarmed as I was and with two other German soldiers within a few feet of us.

Like a flash it suddenly dawned on me, however, that for all this soldier could have known I was only a Belgian peasant and that his object in searching me, which he proceeded to do, was to ascertain whether I had committed the common "crime" of smuggling potatoes!

The Belgians are allowed only a certain amount of potatoes, and it is against the laws laid down by the Huns to deal in vegetables of any kind except under the rigid supervision of the authorities. Nevertheless, it was one of the principal vocations of the average poor Belgian to buy potatoes out in the country from the peasants and then smuggle them into the large cities and sell them clandestinely at a high price.

To stop this traffic in potatoes the German soldiers were in the habit of subjecting the Belgians to frequent search, and I was being held up by this soldier for no other reason than that he thought I might be a potato-smuggler!

He felt of my outside clothes and pockets, and, finding no potatoes, seemed to be quite satisfied. Had he but known who I was he could have earned an iron cross! Or perhaps, in view of the fact that I had a heavy water-bottle in my uplifted hand, it might have turned out to be a *wooden* cross!

He said something in German, which, of course, I did not understand, and then some Belgian peasants came along and seemed to distract his attention. Perhaps he had said, "It's all right, you may go on," or he may have been talking to the others in Flemish, but, at any rate, observing that he was more interested in the others than he was in me at the moment, I put the bottle in my pocket and walked on.

After I walked a few steps I took a furtive glance backward and noticed the soldier who had searched me rejoin his comrades at the curb and then stop another fellow who had come along, and then I disappeared in the darkness.

I cannot say that the outcome of this adventure left me in the same confident frame of mind that followed the earlier one. It was true I had come out of it all right, but I could not help thinking what a terribly close shave I had.

Suppose the soldier had questioned me? The ruse I had been following in my dealings with the Belgian peasants—pretending I was deaf and dumb—might possibly have worked here, too, but a soldier—a German soldier—might not so easily have been fooled. It was more than an even chance that it would at least have aroused his suspicions and resulted in further investigation. A search of my clothing would have revealed a dozen things which would have established my identity, and all my shamming of deafness would have availed me nothing.

As I wandered along I knew that I was now approaching the big city which my Belgian friend had spoken of and which I would have to enter if I was to get the passport, and I realized now how essential it was to have something to enable me to get through the frequent examinations to which I expected to be subjected.

While I was still debating in my mind whether it was going to be possible for me to enter the city that night, I saw in the distance what appeared to be an arc-light, and as I neared it that was what it turned out to be. Beneath the light I could make out the forms of three guards, and the thought of having to go through the same kind of ordeal that I had just experienced filled me with misgivings. Was it possible that I could be fortunate enough to get by again?

As I slowed up a little, trying to make up my mind what was best to do, I was overtaken by a group of Belgian women who were shuffling along the road, and I decided to mingle with them and see if I couldn't convey the impression that I was one of their party.

As we approached the arc-light the figures of those three soldiers with their spiked helmets loomed up before me like a regiment. I felt as if I were walking right into the jaws of death. Rather than go through what was in store for me I felt that I would infinitely prefer to be fighting again in the air with those four desperate Huns who had been the cause of my present plight; then, at least, I would have a chance to fight back, but now I had to risk my life and take what was coming to me without a chance to strike a blow in my own defense.

I shall never forget my feelings as we came within the shaft of light projected by that great arc-light, nor the faces of those three guards as we passed by them. I didn't look directly at them, but out of the corner of my eye I didn't miss a detail. I held a handkerchief up to my face as we passed them, and endeavored to imitate the slouching gait of the Belgians as well as I could; and apparently it worked. We walked right by those guards and they paid absolutely no attention to us.

If ever a fellow felt like going down on his knees and praying, I did at that moment, but it wouldn't have done to show my elation or gratitude in that conspicuous way.

It was then well after eleven o'clock, and I knew it would be unsafe for me to attempt to find a lodging-place in the city, and the only thing for me to do was to locate the man whose name the Belgian had given me. He had given me a good description of the street and had directed me how to get there, and I followed his instructions closely.

After walking the streets for about half an hour I came upon one of the landmarks my friend had described to me, and ten minutes afterward I was knocking at the door of the man who was to make it possible for me to reach Holland—and liberty. At least that was what I hoped.

CHAPTER XII

THE FORGED PASSPORT

For obvious reasons I cannot describe the man to whom I applied for the passport, nor the house in which he lived. While, in view of what subsequently happened, I would not be very much concerned if he got into trouble for having dealt with me, I realize that the hardships he had endured in common with all the other inhabitants of that conquered city may possibly have distorted his ideas of right and justice, and I shall not deliberately bring further disaster on him by revealing his identity.

This man—we will call him Huyliger, because that is as unlike his name as it is mine—was very kind to me on that memorable night when I aroused him from his sleep and in a few words of explanation told him of my plight.

He invited me inside, prepared some food for me, and, putting on a dressing-gown, came and sat by me while I ate, listening with the greatest interest to the short account I gave him of my adventures.

He could speak English fluently, and he interrupted me several times to express his sympathy for the sufferings I had endured.

"O'Brien," he said, after I had concluded my story, "I am going to help you. It may take several days—perhaps as long as two weeks, but eventually we will provide the means to enable you to get into Holland!"

I thanked him a thousand times and told him that I didn't know how I could possibly repay him.

"Don't think of that," he replied; "the satisfaction of knowing that I have aided in placing one more victim of the Huns beyond their power to harm him will more than repay me for all the risk I shall run in helping you. You'd better turn in now, O'Brien, and in the morning I'll tell you what I plan to do."

He showed me to a small room on the second floor, shook hands with me, and left me to prepare for the first real night's rest I had been able to take in nearly two months.

As I removed my clothes and noticed that my knees were still swollen to twice their normal size, that my left ankle was black and blue from the wrench I had given it when I jumped from the train, and that my ribs showed through my skin, I realized what a lot I had been through. As a matter of fact, I could not have weighed more than one hundred and fifty pounds at that time, whereas I had tipped the scales at one hundred and ninety when I was with my squadron in France.

I lost no time in getting into bed and still less in getting to sleep. I don't know what I dreamed of that night, but I had plenty of time to go through the experiences of my whole life, for when I was aroused by a knock on the door, and Huyliger came in, in response to my invitation to enter, he told me that it was nearly noon. I had slept for nearly twelve hours.

I cannot say that the thought did not run through my head that perhaps, after all, I was living in a fool's paradise, and that when Huyliger reappeared it would be with a couple of German soldiers behind him, but I dismissed such misgivings summarily, realizing that I was doing Huyliger an injustice to let such things enter my head even for an instant. I had no right to doubt his sincerity, and it would do me no good to entertain such suspicions. If he was going to prove treacherous to me, I was powerless, anyway, to cope with him.

In a few moments my host appeared with a tray containing my breakfast. I don't suppose I shall ever forget that meal. It consisted of a cup of coffee—real coffee, not the kind I had had at Courtrai—several slices of bread, some hot potatoes, and a dish of scrambled eggs.

Every mouthful of that meal tasted like angel-food to me, and Huyliger sat on the edge of the bed and watched me enjoying the meal, at the same time outlining the plans he had made for my escape.

In brief, the scheme was to conceal me in a convent until conditions were ripe for me to make my way to the border. In the mean while I was to be dressed in the garb of a priest, and when the time came for me to leave the city I was to pretend that I was a Spanish sailor, because I could speak a little Spanish, which I had picked up on the coast. To attempt to play the part of a Belgian would become increasingly difficult, he pointed out, and would bring inevitable disaster in the event that I was called upon to speak.

Huyliger said I would be given sufficient money to bribe the German guards at the Dutch frontier, and he assured me that everything would work out according to schedule.

"Yours is not the first case, O'Brien, we have handled successfully," he declared. "Only three weeks ago I heard from an English merchant who had escaped from a German detention camp and come to me for assistance, and whom I had been able to get through the lines. His message telling me of his safe arrival in Rotterdam came to me in an indirect way, of course, but the fact that the plans we had made carried through without mishap makes me feel that we ought to be able to do as much for you."

I told Huyliger I was ready to follow his instructions and would do anything he suggested.

"I want to rejoin my squadron as soon as I possibly can, of course," I told him, "but I realize that it will take a certain length of time for you to make the necessary arrangements, and I will be as patient as I can."

The first thing to do, Huyliger told me, was to prepare a passport. He had a blank one and it was a comparatively simple matter to fill in the spaces, using a genuine passport which Huyliger possessed as a sample of the handwriting of the passport clerk. My occupation was entered as that of a sailor. My birthplace we gave as Spain, and we put my age at thirty. As a matter of fact, at that time I could easily have passed for thirty-five, but we figured that with proper food and a decent place to sleep in at night I would soon regain my normal appearance and the passport would have to serve me, perhaps, for several weeks to come.

Filling in the blank spaces on the passport was, as I have said, a comparatively easy matter, but that did not begin to fill the bill. Every genuine passport bore an official rubber stamp, something like an elaborate postmark, and I was at a loss to know how to get over that difficulty.

THE FORGED PASSPORT PREPARED IN A BELGIAN CITY TO AID LIEUTENANT O'BRIEN'S ESCAPE INTO HOLLAND, BUT WHICH WAS NEVER USED

FORTUNATELY, HOWEVER, HUYLIGER HAD HALF OF A RUBBER STAMP WHICH had evidently been thrown away by the Germans, and he planned to construct the other half out of the cork from a wine bottle. He was very skilful with a penknife, and although he spoiled a score or more of corks before he succeeded in getting anything like the result he was after, the finished article was far better than our most sanguine expectations. Indeed, after we had pared it over here and there and removed whatever imperfections our repeated tests disclosed, we had a stamp which made an impression so closely resembling the original that, without a magnifying-glass, we were sure it would have been impossible to tell that it was a counterfeit.

Huyliger procured a camera and took a photograph of me to paste on the passport in the place provided for that purpose, and we then had a passport which was entirely satisfactory to both of us and would, we hoped, prove equally so to our friends the Huns.

It had taken two days to fix up the passport. In the mean while, Huyliger informed me that he had changed his plans about the convent, and that instead he would take me to an empty house where I could remain in safety until he told me it was advisable for me to proceed to the frontier.

This was quite agreeable to me, as I had had some misgivings as to the kind of a priest I would make, and it seemed to me to be safer to remain aloof from every one in a deserted house than to have to mingle with people or come in contact with them even with the best of disguises.

That night I accompanied Huyliger to a fashionable section of the city where the house in which I was to be concealed was located.

This house turned out to be a four-story structure of brick. Huyliger told me that it had been occupied by a wealthy Belgian before the war, but since 1914 it had been uninhabited save for the occasional habitation of some refugee whom Huyliger was befriending.

Huyliger had a key and let me in, but he did not enter the house with me, stating that he would visit me in the morning.

I explored the place from top to bottom as well as I could without lights. The house was elaborately furnished, but, of course, the dust lay a quarter of an inch thick almost everywhere. It was a large house, containing some twenty rooms. There were two rooms in the basement, four on the first floor, four on the second, five on the third, and five on the top. In the days that were to come I was to have plenty of opportunity to familiarize myself with the contents of that house, but at the time I did not know it, and I was curious enough to want to know just what the house contained.

Down in the basement there was a huge pantry, but it was absolutely bare, except of dust and dirt. A door which evidently led to a sub-basement attracted my attention, and I thought it might be a good idea to know just where it led in case it became necessary for me to elude searchers.

In that cellar I found case after case of choice wine—Huyliger subsequently told me that there were eighteen hundred bottles of it. I was so happy at the turn my affairs had taken and in the rosy prospects which I now entertained that I was half inclined to indulge in a little celebration then and there. On second thoughts, however, I remembered the old warning of the folly of shouting before you are well out of the woods, and I decided that it would be just as well to postpone the festivities for a while and go to bed instead.

In such an elaborately furnished house I had naturally conjured up ideas of a wonderfully large bed, with thick hair mattresses, downy quilts, and big soft pillows. Indeed, I debated for a while which particular bedroom I should honor with my presence that night. Judge of my disappointment, therefore, when, after visiting bedroom after bedroom, I discovered that there wasn't a bed in any one of them that was in a condition to sleep in. All the mattresses had been removed and the rooms were absolutely bare of everything in the way of wool, silk, or cotton fabrics. The Germans had apparently swept the house clean.

There was nothing to do, therefore, but to make myself as comfortable as I could on the floor, but as I had grown accustomed by this time to sleeping under far less comfortable conditions I swallowed my disappointment as cheerfully as I could and lay down for the night.

In the morning Huyliger appeared and brought me some breakfast, and after I had eaten it he asked me what connections I had in France or England from whom I could obtain money.

I told him that I banked at Cox & Co., London, and that if he needed any money I would do anything I could to get it for him, although I did not know just how such things could be arranged.

"Don't worry about that, O'Brien," he replied. "We'll find a way of getting at it, all right. What I want to know is how far you are prepared to go to compensate me for the risks I am taking and for the service I am rendering you."

The change in the man's attitude stunned me. I could hardly believe my ears.

"Of course, I shall pay you as well as I can for what you have done, Huyliger," I replied, trying to conceal as far as possible the disappointment his demand had occasioned me. "But don't you think that this is hardly the proper time or occasion to talk of compensation? All I have on me, as you know, is a few hundred francs, and that, of course, you are welcome to, and when I get back, if I ever do, I shall not easily forget the kindness you have shown me. I am sure you need have no concern about my showing my gratitude in a substantial way."

"That's all right, O'Brien," he insisted, looking at me in a knowing sort of way. "You may take care of me afterward, and then again you may not. I'm not satisfied to wait. I want to be taken care of *now*!"

"Well, what do you want me to do? How much do you expect in the way of compensation? How can I arrange to get it to you? I am willing to do anything that is reasonable."

"I want —— pounds!" he replied, and he named a figure that staggered me. If I had been Lord Kitchener instead of just an ordinary lieutenant in the R. F. C., he would hardly have asked a larger sum. Perhaps he thought I was.

"Why, my dear man," I said, smilingly, thinking that perhaps he was joking, "you don't really mean that, do you?"

"I certainly do, O'Brien, and what is more," he threatened, "I intend to get every cent I have asked, and you are going to help me get it!"

He pulled out an order calling for the payment to him of the amount he had mentioned, and demanded that I sign it.

I waved it aside.

"Huyliger," I said, "you have helped me out so far, and perhaps you have the power to help me further. I appreciate what you have done for me, although now, I think, I see what your motive was, but I certainly don't intend to be blackmailed, and I tell you right now that I won't stand for it!"

"Very well," he said. "It is just as you say. But before you make up your mind so obstinately I would advise you to think it over. I'll be back this evening."

My first impulse, after the man had left, was to get out of that house just as soon as I could. I had the passport he had prepared for me, and I figured that even without further help from him I could now get to the border without very much difficulty, and when I got there I would have to use my own ingenuity to get through.

It was evident, however, that Huyliger still had an idea that I might change my mind with regard to the payment he had demanded, and I decided that it would be foolish to do anything until he paid me a second visit.

At the beginning of my dealings with Huyliger I had turned over to him some pictures, papers, and other things that I had on me when I entered his house, including my identification disk, and I was rather afraid that he might refuse to return them to me.

All day long I remained in the house without a particle of food other than the breakfast Huyliger had brought to me. From the windows I could see plenty to interest me and help pass the time away, but of my experiences while in that house I shall tell in detail later on, confining my attention now to a narration of my dealings with Huyliger.

That night he appeared, as he had promised.

"Well, O'Brien," he asked, as he entered the room where I was awaiting him, "what do you say? Will you sign the order or not?"

It had occurred to me during the day that the amount demanded was so fabulous that I might have signed the order without any danger of its ever being paid, but the idea of this man, who had claimed to be befriending me, endeavoring to make capital out of my plight galled me so that I was determined not to give in to him, whether I could do so in safety or not.

"No, Huyliger," I replied. "I have decided to get along as best I can without any further assistance from you. I shall see that you are reasonably paid for what you have done, but I will not accept any further assistance from you at any price, and, what is more, I want you to return to me at once all the photographs and other papers and belongings of mine which I turned over to you a day or two ago!"

"I'm sorry about that, O'Brien," he retorted, with a show of apparent sincerity, "but that is something I cannot do."

"If you don't give me back those papers at once," I replied, hotly, "I will take steps to get them and damned quick, too!"

"I don't know just what you could do, O'Brien," he declared, coolly, "but as a matter of fact the papers and pictures you refer to are out of the country. I could not give them back to you if I wanted to."

Something told me the man was lying.

"See here, Huyliger!" I threatened, advancing toward him, putting my hand on his shoulder and looking him straight in the eye, "I want those papers and I want them here before midnight to-night. If I don't get them, I shall sleep in this place just once more, and then, at eight o'clock to-morrow morning, I shall go to the German authorities, give myself up, show them the passport that you fixed up for me, tell them how I got it, and explain everything!"

Huyliger paled. We had no lights in the house, but we were standing near a landing at the time and the moonlight was streaming through a stained-glass window.

The Belgian turned on his heel and started to go down the stairs.

"Mind you," I called after him, "I shall wait for you till the city clock strikes twelve, and if you don't show up with those papers by that time, the next time you will see me is when you confront me before the German authorities! I am a desperate man, Huyliger, and I mean every word I say!"

He let himself out of the door and I sat on the top stair and wondered just what he would do. Would he try to steal a march on me and get in a first word to the authorities, so that my story would be discredited when I put it to them?

Of course my threat to give myself up to the Huns was a pure bluff. While I had no desire to lose the papers which Huyliger had, and which included the map of the last resting-place of my poor chum Raney, I certainly had no intention of cutting off my nose to spite my chin by surrendering to the Germans. I would have been shot, as sure as fate, for, after all I had been able to observe behind the German lines, I would be regarded as a spy and treated as such.

At the same time I thought I had detected a yellow streak in Huyliger, and I figured that he would not want to take the risk of my carrying out my threat, even though he believed there was but a small chance of my doing so. If I did, he would undoubtedly share my fate, and the pictures and papers he had of mine were really of no use to him, and I have never been able to ascertain why it was he wished to retain them unless they contained something—some information about me—which accounted for his complete change of attitude toward me in the first place, and he wanted the papers as evidence to account to his superiors or associates for his conduct toward me.

When he first told me that the plan of placing me in a convent disguised as a priest had been abandoned he explained it by saying that the Cardinal had issued orders to the priests to help no more fugitives, and I have since wondered whether there was anything in my papers which had turned him against me and led him to forsake me after all he had promised to do for me.

For perhaps two hours I sat on that staircase musing about the peculiar turn in my affairs, when the front door opened and Huyliger ascended the stairs.

"I have brought you such of your belongings as I still had, O'Brien," he said, softly. "The rest, as I told you, I cannot give you. They are no longer in my possession."

I looked through the little bunch he handed me. It included my identification disk, most of the papers I valued, and perhaps half of the photographs.

"I don't know what your object is in retaining the rest of my pictures, Huyliger," I replied, "but, as a matter of fact, the ones that are missing were only of sentimental value to me, and you are welcome to them if you want them. We'll call it a heat."

I don't know whether he understood the idiom, but he sat down on the stairs just below me and cogitated for a few moments.

"O'Brien," he started, finally, "I'm sorry things have gone the way they have. I feel sorry for you and I would really like to help you. I don't suppose you will believe me, but the matter of the order which I asked you to sign was not of my doing. However, we won't go into that. The proposition was made to you and you turned it down, and that's an end of it. At the same time, I hate to leave you to your own resources and I'm going to make one more suggestion to you for your own good. I have another plan to get you into Holland, and if you will go with me to another house I will introduce you to a man who I think will be in a position to help you."

"How many millions of pounds will he want for his trouble?" I asked, sarcastically.

"You can arrange that when you see him. Will you go?"

I suspected there was something fishy about the proposition, but I felt that I could take care of myself and decided to see the thing through. I knew Huyliger would not dare to deliver me to the authorities because of the fact that I had the telltale passport, which would be his death-knell as well as my own.

Accordingly I said I would be quite willing to go with him whenever he was ready, and he suggested that we go the next evening.

I pointed out to him that I was entirely without food and asked him whether he could not arrange to bring or send me something to eat while I remained in the house.

"I'm sorry, O'Brien," he replied, "but I'm afraid you'll have to get along as best you can. When I brought you your breakfast this morning I took a desperate chance. If I had been discovered by one of the German soldiers entering this house with food in my possession, I would not only have paid the penalty myself, but you would have been discovered, too. It is too dangerous a proposition. Why don't you go out by yourself and buy your food at the stores? That would give you confidence, and you'll need plenty of it when you continue your journey to the border."

There was a good deal of truth in what he said, and I really could not blame him for not wanting to take any chances to help me, in view of the relations between us.

"Very well," I said; "I've gone without food for many hours at a time before and I suppose I shall be able to do so again. I shall look for you to-morrow evening."

The next evening he came and I accompanied him to another house not very far from the one in which I had been staying and not unlike it in appearance. It, too, was a substantial dwelling-house which had been untenanted since the beginning, save perhaps for such occasional visits as Huyliger and his associates made to it.

Huyliger let himself in and conducted me to a room on the second floor, where he introduced me to two men. One, I could readily see by the resemblance, was his own brother. The other was a stranger.

Very briefly they explained to me that they had procured another passport for me—a genuine one—which would prove far more effective in helping to get me to the frontier than the counterfeit one they had manufactured for me.

I think I saw through their game right at the start, but I listened patiently to what they had to say.

"Of course, you will have to return to us the passport we gave you before we can give you the real one," said Huyliger's brother.

"I haven't the slightest objection," I replied, "if the new passport is all you claim for it. Will you let me see it?"

There was considerable hesitation on the part of Huyliger's brother and the other chap at this.

"Why, I don't think that's necessary at all, Mr. O'Brien," said the former. "You give us the old passport and we will be very glad to give you the new one for it. Isn't that fair enough?"

"It may be fair enough, my friends," I retorted, seeing that it was useless to conceal further the fact that I was fully aware of their whole plan and why I had been brought to this house. "It may be fair enough, my friends," I said, "but you will get the passport that I have here," patting my side and indicating my inside breast pockct, "only off my dead body!"

I suppose the three of them could have made short work of me then and there if they had wanted to go the limit, and no one would ever have been the wiser, but I had gone through so much and I was feeling so mean toward the whole world just at that moment that I was determined to sell my life as dearly as possible.

"I have that passport here," I repeated, "and I'm going to keep it. If you gentlemen think you can take it from me, you are welcome to try!"

To tell the truth, I was spoiling for a fight and I half wished they would start something. The man who had lived in the house had evidently been a collector of ancient pottery, for the walls were lined with great pieces of earthenware which had every earmark of possessing great value. They certainly possessed great weight. I figured that if the worst came to the worst that pottery would come in mighty handy. A single blow with one of those big vases would put a man out as neatly as possible, and as there was lots of pottery and only three men I believed I had an excellent chance of holding my own in the combat which I had invited.

I had already picked out in my mind what I was going to use, and I got up, stood with my back to the wall, and told them that if they ever figured on getting the passport, then would be their best chance.

Apparently they realized that I meant business and they immediately began to expostulate at the attitude I was taking.

One of the men spoke excellent English. In fact, he told me that he could speak five languages, and if he could lie in the others as well I know he did in my own tongue, he was not only an accomplished linguist, but a most versatile liar into the bargain.

They argued and expostulated with me for some time.

"My dear fellow," said the linguist, "it is not that we want to deprive you of the passport. Good Heavens! if it will aid you in getting out of the country, I wish you could have six just like it. But for our own protection you owe it to us to proceed on your journey as best you can without it, because as long as you have it in your possession you jeopardize our lives, too. Don't you think it is fairer that you should risk your own safety rather than place the lives of three innocent men in danger?"

"That may be as it is, my friends," I retorted, as I made my way to the door, "and I am glad you realize your danger. Keep it in mind, for in case any of you should happen to feel inclined to notify the German authorities that I am in this part of the country, think it over before you do so. Remember always that if the Germans get me, they get the passport, too, and if they get the passport, your lives won't be worth a damn! When I tell the history of that clever little piece of pasteboard I will implicate all three of you, and whomever else is working with you, and as I am an officer I rather think my word will be taken before yours. Good night!"

The bluff evidently worked, because I was able to get out of the city without molestation from the Germans.

I have never seen these men since. I hope I never shall, because I am afraid I might be tempted to do something for which I might afterward be sorry.

I do not mean to imply that all Belgians are like this. I had evidently fallen into the hands of a gang who were endeavoring to make capital out of the misfortunes of those who were referred to them for help. In all countries there are bad as well as good, and in a country which has suffered so much as poor Belgium it is no wonder if some of the survivors have lost their sense of moral perspective.

I know the average poor peasant in Belgium would divide his scanty rations with a needy fugitive sooner than a wealthy Belgian would dole out a morsel from his comparatively well-stocked larder. Perhaps the poor have less to lose than the rich if their generosity or charity is discovered by the Huns.

There have been many Belgians shot for helping escaped prisoners and other fugitives, and it is not to be wondered at that they are willing to take as few chances as possible. A man with a family, especially, does not feel justified in helping a stranger when he knows that he and his whole family may be shot or sent to prison for their pains.

Although I suffered much from the attitude of Huyliger and his associates, I suppose I ought to hold no grudge against them in view of the unenviable predicament which they are in themselves.

CHAPTER XIII

FIVE DAYS IN AN EMPTY HOUSE

The five days I spent in that house seemed to me like five years. During all that time I had very little to eat—less, in fact, than I had been getting in the fields. I did not feel it so much, perhaps, because of the fact that I was no longer exposed to the other privations which had helped to make my condition so wretched. I now had a good place to sleep, at any rate, and I did not awake every half-hour or so as I had been accustomed to do in the fields and woods, and, of course, my hunger was not aggravated by the physical exertions which had been necessary before.

Nevertheless, perhaps because I had more time now to think of the hunger pains which were gnawing at me all the time, I don't believe I was ever so miserable as I was at that period of my adventure. I felt so mean toward the world I would have committed murder, I think, with very little provocation.

German soldiers were passing the house at all hours of the day. I watched them hour after hour from the keyhole of the door—to have shown myself at the window was out of the question because the house in which I was concealed was supposed to be untenanted.

Because of the fact that I was unable to speak either Flemish or German I could not go out and buy food, although I still had the money with which to do it. That was one of the things that galled me—the thought that I had the wherewithal in my jeans to buy all the food I needed, and yet no way of getting it without endangering my liberty and life.

At night, however, after it was dark, I would steal quietly out of the house to see what I could pick up in the way of food. By that time, of course, the stores were closed, but I scoured the streets, the alleys, and the byways for scraps of food, and occasionally got up courage enough to appeal to Belgian peasants whom I met on the streets, and in that way I managed to keep body and soul together.

It was quite apparent to me, however, that I was worse off in the city than I had been in the fields, and I decided to get out of that house just as soon as I knew definitely that Huyliger had made up his mind to do nothing further for me.

When I was not at the keyhole of the door I spent most of my day on the top floor in a room which looked out on the street. By keeping well away from the window I could see much of what was going on without being seen myself. In my restlessness I used to walk back and forth in that room, and I kept it up so constantly that I believe I must have worn a path on the floor. It was nine steps from one wall to the other, and as I had little else to amuse me I figured out one day, after I had been pacing up and down for several hours, just how much distance I would have covered on my way to Holland if my footsteps had been taking me in that direction instead of just up and down that old room. I was very much surprised that in three hours I crossed the room no less than five thousand times and the distance covered was between nine and ten miles. It was not very gratifying to realize that after walking all that distance I wasn't a step nearer my goal than when I started, but I had to do something while waiting for Huyliger to help me, and pacing up and down was a natural outlet for my restlessness.

While looking out of that top-floor window one day I noticed a cat on a window-ledge of the house across the street. I had a piece of a broken mirror which I had picked up in the house and I used to amuse myself for an hour at a time shining it in the cat's eyes across the street. At first the animal was annoyed by the reflection and would move away, only to come back a few moments later. By and by, however, it seemed to get used to the glare and wouldn't budge, no matter how strong the sunlight was.

Playing with the cat in this way was the means of my getting food a day or two later—at a time when I was so famished that I was ready to do almost anything to appease my hunger.

It was about seven o'clock in the evening. I was expecting Huyliger at eight, but I hadn't the slightest hope that he would bring me food, as he had told me that he wouldn't take the risk of having food in his possession when calling on me. I was standing at the window in such a way that I could see what was going on in the street without being observed by those who passed by, when I noticed my friend the cat coming down the steps of the opposite house with something in his mouth. Without considering the risks I ran, I opened the front door, ran down the steps and across the street, and pounced on the cat before it could get away with its supper, for that, as I had imagined, was what I had seen in its mouth. It turned out to be a piece of stewed rabbit, which I confiscated eagerly and took back with me to the house.

Perhaps I felt a little sorry for the cat, but I certainly had no other qualms about eating the animal's dinner. I was much too hungry to dwell upon niceties, and a piece of stewed rabbit was certainly too good for a cat to eat when a man was starving. I ate it and enjoyed it, and the incident suggested to me a way in which I might possibly obtain food again when all other avenues failed.

From my place of concealment I frequently saw huge carts being pushed through the streets gathering potato peelings, refuse of cabbage, and similar food remnants which, in America, are considered garbage and destroyed. In Belgium they were using this "garbage" to make their bread out of, and while the idea may sound revolting to us, the fact is that the Germans have brought these things down to such a science that the bread they make in this way is really very good to eat. I know it would have been like cake to me when I was in need of food; indeed, I would have eaten the "garbage" direct, let alone the bread.

Although, as I have said, I suffered greatly from hunger while occupying this house, there were one or two things I observed through the keyhole or from the windows which made me laugh, and some of the incidents that occurred during my voluntary imprisonment were really rather funny.

From the keyhole I could see, for instance, a shop window on the other side of the street, several houses down the block. All day long

German soldiers would be passing in front of the house, and I noticed that practically every one of them would stop in front of this store window and look in. Occasionally a soldier on duty bent would hurry past, but I think nine out of ten of them were sufficiently interested to spend at least a minute, and some of them three or four minutes, gazing at whatever was being exhibited in that window, although I noticed that it failed to attract the Belgians.

I have a considerable streak of curiosity in me and I couldn't help wondering what it could be in that window which almost without exception seemed to interest German soldiers, but failed to hold the Belgians, and after conjuring my brains for a while on the problem I came to the conclusion that the shop must have been a book-shop and the window contained German magazines, which, naturally enough, would be of the greatest interest to the Germans, but of none to the Belgians.

At any rate, I resolved that as soon as night came I would go out and investigate the window. When I got the answer I laughed so loud that I was afraid for the moment I must have attracted the attention of the neighbors, but I couldn't help it. The window was filled with huge quantities of sausage. The store was a butcher-shop, and one of the principal things they sold, apparently, was sausage. The display they made, although it consisted merely of quantities of sausage piled in the windows, certainly had plenty of "pulling" power. It "pulled" nine Germans out of ten out of their course and indirectly it "pulled" me right across the street. The idea of those Germans being so interested in that window display as to stand in front of the window for two, three, or four minutes at a time, however, certainly seemed funny to me, and when I got back to the house I sat at the keyhole again and found just as much interest as before in watching the Germans stop in their tracks when they reached the window, even though I was now aware what the attraction was.

One of my chief occupations during those days was catching flies. I would catch a fly, put him in a spider's web—there were plenty of them in the old house—and sit down to wait for the spider to come and get him. But always I pictured myself in the same predicament and rescued the fly just as the spider was about to grab him. Several times when things were dull I was tempted to see the tragedy through, but perhaps the same Providence that guided me safely through all perils was guarding, too, the destiny of those flies, for I always weakened and the flies never did suffer from my lust for amusement.

The house was well supplied with books—in fact, one of the choicest libraries I think I ever saw—but they were all written either in Flemish or in French. I could read no Flemish and very little French. I might have made a little headway with the latter, but the books all seemed too deep for me and I gave it up. There was one thing, though, that I did read and re-read from beginning to end—that was a New York *Herald* which must have arrived just about the time war was declared. Several things in there interested me, and particularly the baseball scores, which I studied with as much care as a real fan possibly would an up-to-date score. I couldn't refrain from laughing when I came to an account of Zimmerman (of the Cubs) being benched for some spat with the umpire, and it afforded me just as much interest three years after it had happened—perhaps more— than some current item of worldwide interest had at the time.

I rummaged the house many times from cellar to garret in my search for something to eat, but the harvest of three years of war had made any success along that line impossible. I was like the man out on the ocean in a boat and thirsty, with water everywhere, but not a drop to drink.

I was tempted while in this city to go to church one Sunday, but my better judgment told me it would be a useless risk. Of course some one would surely say something to me, and I didn't know how many Germans would be there, or what might happen, so I gave up that idea.

During all the time I was concealed in this house I saw but one automobile, and that was a German staff officer's. That same afternoon I had one of the frights of my young life.

I had been gazing out of the keyhole as usual when I heard coming down the street the measured tread of German soldiers. It didn't sound like very many, but there was no doubt in my mind that German soldiers were marching down the street. I went up-stairs and peeked through the window, and sure enough a squad of German infantry was coming down the street, accompanying a military truck. I hadn't the slightest idea that they were coming after me, but still the possibilities of the situation gave me more or less alarm, and I considered how I could make my escape if by any chance I was the man they were after. The idea of hiding in the wine-cellar appealed to me as the most practical; there must have been plenty of places among the wine kegs and cases where a man could conceal himself, but, as a matter of fact, I did not believe that any such contingency would arise.

The marching soldiers came nearer. I could hear them at the next house. In a moment I would see them pass the keyhole through which I was looking.

"Halt!"

At the word of command shouted by a junior officer the squad came to attention right in front of the house.

I waited no longer. Running down the stairs, I flew down into the wine-cellar, and although it was almost pitch dark—the only light coming from a grating which led to the backyard—I soon found a satisfactory hiding-place in the extreme rear of the cellar. I had the presence of mind to leave the door of the wine-cellar ajar, figuring that if the soldiers found a closed door they would be more apt to search for a fugitive behind it than if the door were open.

My decision to get away from the front door had been made and carried out none too soon, for I had only just located myself between two big wine-cases when I heard the tramp of soldiers' feet marching up the front steps, a crash at the front door, a few hasty words of command which I did not understand, and then the noise of scurrying feet from room to room and such a banging and hammering and smashing and crashing that I could not make out what was going on.

If Huyliger had revealed my hiding-place to the Huns, as I was now confident he had, I felt that there was little prospect of their overlooking me. They would search the house from top to bottom and, if necessary, raze it to the ground before they would give up the search. To escape from the house through the backyard through the iron grating, which I had no doubt I could force, seemed to be a logical thing to do, but the chances were that the Huns had thrown a cordon around the entire block before the squad was sent to the house. The Germans do these things in an efficient manner always. They take nothing for granted.

My one chance seemed to be to stand pat in the hope that the officer in charge might possibly come to the conclusion that he had arrived at the house too late—that the bird had flown.

My position in that wine-cellar was anything but a comfortable one. Rats and mice were scurrying across the floor, and the smashing and crashing going on overhead was anything but promising. Evidently those soldiers imagined that I might be hiding in the walls, for it sounded as though they were tearing off the wainscoting, the picture-molding, and, in fact, everything that they could tear or pull apart.

Before very long they would finish their search up-stairs and would come down to the basement. What they would do when they discovered the wine I had no idea. Perhaps they would let themselves loose on it and give me my chance. With a bottle of wine in each hand I figured I could put up a good fight in the dark, especially as I was becoming more and more accustomed to it and could begin to distinguish things here and there, whereas they would be as blind as bats in the sun when they entered the pitchy darkness of the cellar.

Perhaps it was twenty minutes before I heard what sounded like my death-knell to me; the soldiers were coming down the cellar steps. I clutched a wine bottle in each hand and waited with bated breath.

Tramp! Tramp! Tramp! In a moment they would be in the cellar proper. I could almost hear my heart beating. The mice scurried across the floor by the scores, frightened, no doubt, by the vibration and noise made by the descending soldiers. Some of the creatures ran across me where I stood between the two wine-cases, but I was too much interested in bigger game to pay attention to mice.

Tramp! Tramp! "Halt!" Again an order was given in German, and although I did not understand it, I am willing to bless every word of it, because it resulted in the soldiers turning right about face, marching up the stairs again, through the hall, and out of the front door and away!

I could hardly believe my ears. It seemed almost too good to be true that they could have given up the search just as they were about to come on their quarry, but unless my ears deceived me that was what they had done.

The possibility that the whole thing might be a German ruse did not escape me, and I remained in the cellar for nearly an hour after they had apparently departed before I ventured to move, listening intently in the mean while for the slightest sound which would reveal the presence of a sentry up-stairs.

Not hearing a sound, I began to feel that they had indeed given up the hunt, for I did not believe that a German officer would be so considerate of his men as to try to trap me rather than carry the cellar by force if they had the slightest idea that I was there.

I took off my shoes and crept softly and slowly to the cellar steps, and then step by step, placing my weight down gradually so as to prevent the steps from creaking, I climbed to the top. The sight that met my eyes as I glanced into the kitchen told me the whole story. The water faucets had been ripped from the sinks, the water pipes having been torn from the walls. Everything of brass or copper had been torn off, and gas fixtures, cooking utensils, and everything else which contain even only a small proportion of the metals the Germans so badly needed had been taken from the kitchen. I walked up-stairs now with more confidence, feeling tolerably assured that the soldiers hadn't been after me at all, but had been merely collecting metals and other materials which they expected an elaborate dwelling-house like the one in which I was concealed to yield.

Later I heard that the Germans have taken practically every ounce of brass, copper, and wool they could lay their hands on in Belgium. Even the brass out of pianos has been ruthlessly removed, the serious damage done to valuable property by the removal of only an insignificant proportion of metal never being taken into consideration. I learned, too, that all dogs over fourteen inches high had been seized by the Germans. This furnished lots of speculation among the Belgians as to what use the Germans were putting the animals to, the general impression apparently being that they were being used for food.

This, however, seemed much less likely to me than that they were being employed as despatch dogs in the trenches, the same as we use them on our side of the line. They might possibly kill the dogs and use their skins for leather and their carcasses for tallow, but I feel quite sure that the Huns are by no means so short of food that they have to eat dogs yet awhile.

Indeed, I want to repeat here what I have mentioned before: if any one has the idea that this war can be won by *starving* the Huns, he hasn't the slightest idea how well provided the Germans are in that respect. They have considered their food needs in connection with their resources for several years to come, and they have gone at it in such a methodical, systematic way, taking into consideration every possible contingency, that, provided there is not an absolute crop failure, there isn't the slightest doubt in my mind that they can last for years, and the worst of it is they are quite cocksure about it.

It is true that the German soldiers want peace. As I watched them through the keyhole in the door I thought how unfavorably they compared with our men. They marched along the street without laughter, without joking, without singing. It was quite apparent that the war is telling on them. I don't believe I saw a single German soldier who didn't look as if he had lost his best friend—and he probably had.

At the same time, there is a big difference—certainly a difference of several years—between wishing the war was over and giving up, and I don't believe the German rank and file any more than their leaders have the slightest idea at this time of giving up at all.

But to return to my experiences while concealed in the house. After the visit of the soldiers, which left the house in a wretched condition, I decided that I would continue my journey toward the frontier, particularly as I had got all I could out of Huyliger, or rather he had got all he was going to get out of me.

During my concealment in the house I made various sorties into the city at night, and I was beginning to feel more comfortable, even when German soldiers were about. Through the keyhole I had studied very closely the gait of the Belgians, the slovenly droop that characterized most of them, and their general appearance, and I felt that in my own dirty and unshaven condition I must have looked as much like the average poor Belgian as a man could. The only thing that was against me was my height. I was several inches taller than even the tallest Belgians. I had often thought that red hair would have gone well with my name, but now, of course, I was mighty glad that I was not so endowed, for red-haired Belgians are about as rare as German charity.

There are many, no doubt, who will wonder why I did not get more help than I did at this time. It is easily answered. When a man is in hourly fear of his life and the country is full of spies, as Belgium certainly was, he is not going to help just any one that comes along seeking aid.

One of the Germans' most successful ways of trapping the Belgians has been to pose as an English or French prisoner who has escaped; appeal to them for aid; implicate as many as possible, and then turn the whole German police force loose on them.

As I look back now on those days I think it remarkable that I received as much help as I did, but when people are starving under the conditions now forced upon those unfortunate people it is a great temptation to surrender these escaped prisoners to German authorities and receive the handsome rewards offered for them—or for alien spies, as I was classed at that time.

The passport which I had described me as a Spanish sailor, but I was very dubious about its value. If I could have spoken Spanish fluently it might have been worth something to me, but the few words I knew of the language would not have carried me very far if I had been confronted with a Spanish interpreter. I decided to use the passport only as a last resort, preferring to act the part of a deaf and dumb Belgian peasant as far as it would carry me.

Before I finally left the house I had a remarkable experience which I shall remember as long as I live.

CHAPTER XIV

A NIGHT OF DISSIPATION

During the first two days I spent with Huyliger after I had first arrived in the big city he had told me, among other things, of a moving-picture show in town which he said I might have a chance to see while there.

"It is free every night in the week except Saturdays and Sundays," he said, "and once you are inside you would not be apt to be bothered by any one except when they come to take your order for something to drink. While there is no admission, patrons are expected to eat or drink while enjoying the pictures."

A day or two later, while walking the streets at night in search of food, I had passed this place, and was very much tempted to go in and spend a few hours, particularly as it would perhaps give me an opportunity to buy something to eat, although I was at a loss to know how I was going to ask for what I wanted.

While trying to make up my mind whether it was safe for me to go in, I walked half a block past the place, and when I turned back again and reached the entrance with my mind made up that I would take the chance I ran full tilt into a German officer who was just coming out!

That settled all my hankerings for moving pictures that night. "Where you came from, my friend," I figured, "there must be more like you! I guess it is a good night for walking."

The next day, however, in recalling the incident of the evening before, it seemed to me that I had been rather foolish. What I needed more than anything at that time was confidence. Before I could get to the frontier I would have to confront German soldiers many times, because there were more of them between this city and Holland than in any section of the country through which I had so far traveled. Safety in these contingencies would depend largely upon the calmness I displayed. It wouldn't do to get all excited at the mere sight of a spiked helmet. The Belgians, I had noticed, while careful to obey the orders of the Huns, showed no particular fear of them, and it seemed to me the sooner I cultivated the same feeling of indifference the better I would be able to carry off the part I was playing.

For this reason, I made up my mind then and there that, officers or no officers, I would go to that show that night and sit it through, no matter what happened. While people may think that I had decided unwisely because of the unnecessary risk involved in the adventure, it occurred to me that perhaps, after all, that theater was about one of the safest places I could attend, because that was about the last place Germans would expect to find a fugitive English officer in, even if they were searching for one.

As soon as evening came, therefore, I decided to go to the theater. I fixed myself up as well as possible. I had on a fairly decent pair of trousers which Huyliger had given me and I used a clean handkerchief as a collar.

With my hair brushed up and my beard trimmed as neatly as possible with a pair of rusty scissors which I had found in the house, while my appearance was not exactly that of a Beau Brummel, I don't think I looked much worse than the average Belgian. In these days, the average Belgian is very poorly dressed at best.

I can't say I had no misgivings as I made my way to the theater; certainly I was going there more for discipline than pleasure, but I had made up my mind and I was going to see it through.

The entrance to the theater or beer-garden—for it was as much one as the other—was on the side of the building, and was reached by way of an alley which ran along the side. Near the door was a ticket-seller's booth, but as this was one of the free nights there was no one in the booth.

I marched slowly down the alley, imitating as best I could the indifferent gait of the Belgians, and when I entered the theater I endeavored to act as though I had been there many times before. A hasty survey of the layout of the place was sufficient to enable me to select my seat. It was early and there were not more than half a dozen people in the place at that time, so that I had my choice.

There was a raised platform, perhaps two feet high, all round the walls of the place, except at the end where the stage was located. On this platform tables were arranged, and there were tables on the floor proper as well.

I decided promptly that the safest place for me was as far back as possible where I would not be in the line of vision of others in back of me. Accordingly, I slouched over to a table on the platform directly opposite the stage and I took the seat against the wall. The whole place was now in front of me. I could see everything that was going on and every one who came in, but no one, except those who sat at my own table, would notice me unless they deliberately turned around to look.

The place began to fill up rapidly. Every second person who came in the door seemed to me to be a German soldier, but when they were seated at the tables and I got a chance later on to make a rough count, I found that in all there were not more than a hundred soldiers in the place and there must have been several hundred civilians.

The first people to sit at my table were a Belgian and his wife. The Belgian sat next to me and his wife next to him. I was hoping that other civilians would occupy the remaining two seats at my table because I did not relish the idea of having to sit through the show with German soldiers within a few feet of me. That would certainly have spoiled my pleasure for the evening.

Every uniform that came in the door gave me cause to worry until I was sure it was not coming in my direction. I don't suppose there was a single soldier who came in the door whom I didn't follow to his seat—with my eyes.

Just before they lowered the lights two German officers came in the door. They stood there for a moment looking the place over. Then they made a bee-line in my direction, and I must confess my heart started to beat a little faster. I hoped that they would find another seat before they came to my vicinity, but they were getting nearer and nearer, and I realized with a sickening sensation that they were headed directly for the two seats at my table, and that was indeed the case.

These two seats were in front of the table, facing the stage, and except when they would be eating or drinking their backs were toward me, and there was considerable consolation in that. From my seat I could have reached right over and touched one of them on his bald head. It would have been more than a touch, I am afraid, if I could have got away with it safely.

As the officers seated themselves a waiter came to us with a printed bill of fare and a program. Fortunately, he waited on the others first, and I listened intently to their orders. The officers ordered some light wine, but my Belgian neighbor ordered "Bock" for himself and his wife, which was what I had decided to order, anyway, as that was the only thing I could say. Heaven knows I would far rather have ordered something to eat, but the bill of fare meant nothing to me, and I was afraid to take a chance at the pronunciation of the dishes it set forth.

There were a number of drinks listed which I suppose I might safely enough have ordered. For instance, I noticed "Lemon Squash, 1.50," "Ginger Beer, 1-," "Sparkling Dry Ginger Ale, 1-," "Apollinaris, 1-," and "Schweppes Soda, 0.80," but it occurred to me that the mere fact that I selected something that was listed in English might attract attention to me and something in my pronunciation might give further cause for suspicion.

It seemed better to parrot the Belgian and order "Bock," and that was what I decided to do.

One item on the bill of fare tantalized me considerably. Although it was listed among the "Prizzen der dranken," which I took to mean "Prices of drinks," it sounded very much to me like something to eat, and Heaven knows I would rather have had one honest mouthful of food than all the drinks in the world. The item I refer to was "Dubbel Gersten de Flesch (Michaux)." A *double* portion of anything would have been mighty welcome to me, but I would have been quite contented with a *single* "Gersten"— whatever that might happen to be—if I had only had the courage to ask for it.

To keep myself as composed as possible, I devoted a lot of attention to that bill of fare, and I think by the time the waiter came around I almost knew it by heart. One drink that almost made me laugh out loud was listed as "Lemonades Gazeuses," but I might just as well have introduced myself to the German officers by my right name and rank as to have attempted to pronounce it.

When the waiter came to me, therefore, I said "Bock" as casually as I could, and felt somewhat relieved that I got through this part of the ordeal so easily.

While the waiter was away I had a chance to examine the bill of fare, and I observed that a glass of beer cost eighty centimes. The smallest change I had was a two-mark paper bill.

Apparently the German officers were similarly fixed, and when they offered their bill to the waiter he handed it back to them with a remark which I took to mean that he couldn't make change.

Right there I was in a quandary. To offer him my bill after he had just told the officers he didn't have change would have seemed strange, and yet I couldn't explain to him that I was in the same boat and he would have to come to me again later. The only thing to do, therefore, was to offer him the bill as though I hadn't heard or noticed what had happened with the Germans, and I did so. He said the same thing to me as he had said to the officers, perhaps a little more sharply, and gave me back the bill. Later on he returned to the table with a handful of change and we closed the transaction. I gave him twenty-five centimes as a tip—I had never yet been in a place where it was necessary to talk to do that.

During my first half-hour in that theater, to say I was on pins and needles is to express my feelings mildly. The truth of the matter is I was never so uneasy in my life. Every minute seemed like an hour, and I was on the point of getting up and leaving a dozen times. There were altogether too many soldiers in the place to suit me, and when the German officers seated themselves right at my table I thought that was about all I could stand. As it was, however, the lights went out shortly afterward and in the dark I felt considerably easier.

After the first picture, when the lights went up again, I had regained my composure considerably and I took advantage of the opportunity to study the various types of people in the place.

From my seat I had a splendid chance to see them all. At one table there was a German medical corps officer with three Red Cross nurses.

That was the only time I had ever seen a German nurse, for when I was in the hospital I had seen only men orderlies. Nurses don't work so near the first-line trenches.

The German soldiers at the different tables were very quiet and orderly. They drank Bock beer and conversed among themselves, but there was no hilarity or rough-housing of any kind.

As I sat there, within an arm's reach of those German officers and realized what they would have given to know what a chance they had to capture an escaped British officer, I could hardly help smiling to myself, but when I thought of the big risk I was taking, more or less unnecessarily, I began to wonder whether I had not acted foolishly in undertaking it.

Nevertheless, the evening passed off uneventfully, and when the show was over I mixed with the crowd and disappeared, feeling very proud of myself and with a good deal more confidence than I had enjoyed at the start.

I had passed a night which will live in my life as long as I live. The bill of fare, program, and a "throw-away" bill advertising the name of the attraction which was to be presented the following week, which was handed to me as I came out, I still have and they are among the most valued souvenirs of my adventure.

CHAPTER XV

OBSERVATIONS IN A BELGIAN CITY

One night, shortly before I left this city, our airmen raided the place. I didn't venture out of the house at the time, but the next night I thought I would go out and see what damage had been done.

When it became dark I left the house, accordingly, and, mixing with the crowd, which consisted largely of Germans, I went from one place to another to see what our "strafing" had accomplished. Naturally I avoided speaking to any one. If a man or woman appeared about to speak to me, I just turned my head and looked or walked away in some other direction. I must have been taken for an unsociable sort of individual a good many times, and if I had encountered the same person twice I suppose my conduct might have aroused suspicion.

I had a first-class observation of the damage that was really done by our bombs. One bomb had landed very near the main railroad station, and if it had been only thirty yards nearer would have completely demolished it. As the station was undoubtedly our airman's objective, I was very much impressed with the accuracy of his aim. It is by no means an easy thing to hit a building from the air when you are going at anywhere from fifty to one hundred miles an hour and are being shot at from beneath from a dozen different angles—unless, of course, you are taking one of those desperate chances and flying so low that you cannot very well miss your mark, and the Huns can't very well miss you, either!

I walked by the station and mingled with the crowds which stood in the entrances. They paid no more attention to me than they did to real Belgians, and the fact that the lights were all out in this city at night made it impossible, anyway, for any one to get as good a look at me as if it had been light.

During the time that I was in this city I suppose I wandered from one end of it to the other. In one place, where the German staff had its headquarters, a huge German flag hung from the window, and I think I would have given ten years of my life to have stolen it. Even if I could have pulled it down, however, it would have been impossible for me to have concealed it, and to have carried it away with me as a souvenir would have been out of the question.

As I went along the street one night a lady standing on the comer stopped me and spoke to me. My first impulse, of course, was to answer her, explaining that I could not understand, but I stopped myself in time, pointed to my ears and mouth, and shook my head, indicating that I was deaf and dumb, and she nodded understandingly and walked on. Incidents of this kind were not unusual, and I was always in fear that the time would come when some inquisitive and suspicious German would encounter me and not be so easily satisfied.

There are many things that I saw in this city which, for various reasons, it is impossible for me to relate until after the war is over. Some of them, I think, will create more surprise than the incidents I am free to reveal now.

It used to amuse me, as I went along the streets of this town, looking in the shop windows, with German soldiers at my side looking at the same things, to think how close I was to them and they had no way of knowing. I was quite convinced that if I were discovered my fate would have been death, because I not only had the forged passport on me, but I had been so many days behind the German lines after I had escaped that they couldn't safely let me live with the information I possessed.

One night I walked boldly across a park. I heard footsteps behind me and, turning around, saw two German soldiers. I slowed up a trifle to let them get ahead of me. It was rather dark and I got a chance to see what a wonderful uniform the German military authorities have picked out. The soldiers had not gone more than a few feet ahead of me when they disappeared in the darkness like one of those melting pictures on the moving-picture screen.

As I wandered through the streets I frequently glanced in the café windows as I passed. German officers were usually dining there, but they didn't conduct themselves with anything like the light-heartedness which characterizes the Allied officers in London and Paris. I was rather surprised at this, because in this part of Belgium they were much freer than they would have been in Berlin, where, I understand, food is comparatively scarce and the restrictions are very rigid.

As I have said, my own condition in this city was in some respects worse than it had been when I was making my way through the open country. While I had a place to sleep and my clothes were no longer constantly soaking, my opportunities for getting food were considerably less than they had been. Nearly all the time I was half famished, and I decided that I would get out of there at once, since I was entirely through with Huyliger.

My physical condition was greatly improved. While the lack of food showed itself on me, I had regained some of my strength, my wounds were healed, my ankle was stronger, and, although my knees were still considerably enlarged, I felt that I was in better shape than I had been at any time since my leap from the train, and I was ready to go through whatever was in store for me.

CHAPTER XVI

I APPROACH THE FRONTIER

To get out of the city it would be necessary to pass two guards. This I had learned in the course of my walks at night, having frequently traveled to the city limits with the idea of finding out just what conditions I would have to meet when the time came for me to leave.

A German soldier's uniform, however, no longer worried me as it had at first. I had mingled with the Huns so much in the city that I began to feel that I was really a Belgian, and I assumed the indifference that the latter seemed to feel.

I decided, therefore, to walk out of the city in the daytime when the sentries would be less apt to be on the watch. It worked splendidly. I was not held up a moment, the sentries evidently taking me for a Belgian peasant on his way to work.

Traveling faster than I had ever done before since my escape, I was soon out in the open country, and the first Belgian I came to I approached for food. He gave me half his lunch and we sat down on the side of the road to eat it. Of course, he tried to talk to me, but I used the old ruse of pretending I was deaf and dumb and he was quite convinced that it was so. He made various efforts to talk to me in pantomime, but I could not make out what he was getting at, and I think he must have concluded that I was not only half-starved, deaf, and dumb, but "luny" into the bargain.

When night came I looked around for a place to rest. I had decided to travel in the daytime as well as night, because I understood that I was only a few miles from the frontier, and I was naturally anxious to get there at the earliest possible moment, although I realized that there I would encounter the most hazardous part of my whole adventure. To get through that heavily guarded barbed and electrically charged barrier was a problem that I hated to think of, even, although the hours I spent endeavoring to devise some way of outwitting the Huns were many.

It had occurred to me, for instance, that it would not be such a difficult matter to vault over the electric fence, which was only nine feet high. In college, I know, a ten-foot vault is considered a high-school boy's accomplishment, but there were two great difficulties in the way of this solution. In the first place, it would be no easy matter to get a pole of the right length, weight, and strength to serve the purpose. More particularly, however, the pole-vault idea seemed to be out of the question because of the fact that on either side of the electric fence, six feet from it, was a six-foot barbed-wire barrier. To vault safely over a nine-foot electrically charged fence was one thing, but to combine with it a twelve-foot broad vault was a feat which even a college athlete in the pink of condition would be apt to flunk. Indeed, I don't believe it is possible.

Another plan that seemed half-way reasonable was to build a pair of stilts about twelve or fourteen feet high and walk over the barriers one by one. As a youngster I had acquired considerable skill in stilt-walking, and I have no doubt that with the proper equipment it would have been quite feasible to have walked out of Belgium as easily as possible in that way, but whether or not I was going to have a chance to construct the necessary stilts remained to be seen.

There were a good many bicycles in use by the German soldiers in Belgium, and it had often occurred to me that if I could have stolen one, the tires would have made excellent gloves and insulated coverings for my feet in case it was necessary for me to attempt to climb over the electric fence bodily. But as I had never been able to steal a bicycle, this avenue of escape was closed to me.

I decided to wait until I arrived at the barrier and then make up my mind how to proceed.

To find a decent place to sleep that night I crawled under a barbed-wire fence, thinking it led into some field. As I passed under, one of the barbs caught in my coat, and in trying to pull myself free I shook the fence for several yards.

Instantly there came out of the night the nerve-racking command, "Halt!"

Again I feared I was done for. I crouched close down on the ground in the darkness, not knowing whether to take to my legs and trust to the Hun's missing me in the darkness if he fired, or stay right where I was. It was foggy as well as dark, and although I knew the sentry was only a few feet away from me I decided to stand, or rather lie still. I think my heart made almost as much noise as the rattling of the wire in the first place, but it was a tense few moments for me.

I heard the German say a few words to himself, but didn't understand them, of course, and then he made a sound as if to call a dog, and I realized that his theory of the noise he had heard was that a dog had made its way through the fence.

For perhaps five minutes I didn't stir, and then, figuring that the German had probably continued on his beat, I crept quietly under the wire again, this time being mighty careful to hug the ground so close that I wouldn't touch the wire, and made off in a different direction. Evidently the barbed-wire fence had been thrown around an ammunition-depot or something of the kind and it was not a field at all that I had tried to get into.

I figured that other sentries were probably in the neighborhood and I proceeded very gingerly.

After I had got about a mile away from this spot I came to a humble Belgian house, and I knocked at the door and applied for food in my usual way, pointing to my mouth to indicate I was hungry and to my ears and mouth to imply that I was deaf and dumb. The Belgian woman who lived in the house brought me a piece of bread and two cold potatoes, and as I sat there eating them she eyed me very keenly.

I haven't the slightest doubt that she realized I was a fugitive. She lived so near the border that it was more than likely that other fugitives had come to her before, and for that reason I appreciated more fully the extent of the risk she ran, for no doubt the Germans were constantly watching the conduct of these Belgians who lived near the line.

My theory that she realized that I was not a Belgian at all, but probably some English fugitive, was confirmed a moment later when, as I made ready to go, she touched me on the arm and indicated that I was to wait a moment. She went to a bureau and brought out two pieces of fancy Belgian lace, which she insisted upon my taking away, although at that particular moment I had as much use for Belgian lace as an elephant has for a safety-razor, but I was touched with her thoughtfulness and pressed her hand to show my gratitude. She would not accept the money I offered her.

I carried that lace through my subsequent experiences, feeling that it would be a fine souvenir for my mother, although, as a matter of fact, if she had known that it was going to delay my final escape for even a single moment, as it did, I am quite sure she would rather I had never seen it.

On one piece of lace was the Flemish word "*Charité*" and on the other the word "*Espérance.*" At the time, I took these words to mean "Charity" and "Experience," and all I hoped was that I would get as much of the one as I was getting of the other before I finally got through. I learned subsequently that what the words really stood for was "Charity" and "Hope," and then I was sure that my kind Belgian friend had indeed realized my plight and that her thoughtful souvenir was intended to encourage me in the trials she must have known were before me.

I didn't let the old Belgian lady know, because I did not want to alarm her unnecessarily, but that night I slept in her backyard, leaving early in the morning before it became light.

Later in the day I applied at another house for food. It was occupied by a father and mother and ten children. I hesitated to ask them for food without offering to pay for it, as I realized what a task it must have been for them to support themselves without having to feed a hungry man. Accordingly, I gave the man a mark and then indicated that I wanted something to eat. They were just about to eat, themselves, apparently, and they let me partake of their meal, which consisted of a huge bowl of some kind of soup which I was unable to identify and which they served in ordinary wash-basins! I don't know that they ever used the basins to wash in as well, but whether they did or not did not worry me very much. The soup was good and I enjoyed it very much.

All the time I was there I could see the father and the eldest son, a boy about seventeen, were extremely nervous. I had indicated to them that I was deaf and dumb, but if they believed me it didn't seem to make them any more comfortable.

I lingered at the house for about an hour after the meal, and during that time a young man came to call on the eldest daughter, a young woman of perhaps eighteen. The caller eyed me very suspiciously, although I must have resembled anything but a British officer. They spoke in Flemish and I did not understand a word they said, but I think they were discussing my probable identity. During their conversation, I had a chance to look around the rooms. There were three altogether, two fairly large and one somewhat smaller, about fourteen feet long and six deep. In this smaller room there were two double-decked beds, which were apparently intended to house the whole family, although how the whole twelve of them could sleep in that one room will ever remain a mystery to me.

From the kitchen you could walk directly into the cow-barn, where two cows were kept, and this, as I have pointed out before, is the usual construction of the poorer Belgian houses.

I could not make out why the caller seemed to be so antagonistic to me, and yet I am sure he was arguing with the family against me. Perhaps the fact that I wasn't wearing wooden shoes—I doubt whether I could have obtained a pair big enough for me—had convinced him that I was not really a Belgian, because there was nothing about me otherwise which could have given him that idea.

At that time—and I suppose it is true to-day—about ninety per cent. of the people in Belgium were wearing wooden shoes. Among the peasants I don't believe I ever saw any other kind of footwear, and they are more common there than they are in Holland. The Dutch wear them more as a matter of custom. In Belgium they are a dire necessity because of the lack of leather. I was told that during the coming year practically all the peasants and poorer people in Germany, too, will adopt wooden shoes for farm-work, as that is one direction in which wood can be substituted for leather without much loss.

When the young man left I left shortly afterward, as I was not at all comfortable about what his intentions were regarding me. For all I knew, he might have gone to notify the German authorities that there was a strange man in the vicinity—more, perhaps, to protect his friends from suspicion of having aided me than to injure me.

At any rate, I was not going to take any chances and I got out of that neighborhood as rapidly as I could.

That night found me right on the frontier of Holland.

CHAPTER XVII
GETTING THROUGH THE LINES

Waiting until it was quite dark, I made my way carefully through a field and eventually came to the much-dreaded barrier.

It was all that I had heard about it. Every foot of the border-line between Belgium and Holland is protected in precisely the same manner. It is there to serve three purposes: first, to keep the Belgians from escaping into Holland; second, to keep enemies, like myself, from making their way to freedom; and, third, to prevent desertions on the part of Germans themselves. One look at it was enough to convince any one that it probably accomplished all three objects about as well as any contrivance could, and one look was all I got of it that night, for while I lay on my stomach gazing at the forbidding structure I heard the measured stride of a German sentry advancing toward me, and I crawled away as fast as I possibly could, determined to spend the night somewhere in the fields and make another and more careful survey the following night.

The view I had obtained, however, was sufficient to convince me that the pole-vault idea was out of the question even if I had a pole and were a proficient pole-vaulter. The three fences covered a span of at least twelve feet, and to clear the last barbed-wire fence it would be necessary to vault not only at least ten feet high, but at least fourteen feet wide, with certain knowledge that to touch the electrically charged fence meant instant death. There would be no second chance if you came a cropper the first time.

The stilt idea was also impracticable because of the lack of suitable timber and tools with which to construct the stilts.

It seemed to me that the best thing to do was to travel up and down the line a bit in the hope that some spot might be discovered where conditions were more favorable, although I don't know just what I expected along those lines.

It was mighty disheartening to realize that only a few feet away lay certain liberty and that the only thing that prevented me from reaching it were three confounded fences. I thought of my machine and wished that some kind fairy would set it in front of me for just one minute.

I spent the night in a clump of bushes and kept in hiding most of the next day, only going abroad for an hour or two in the middle of the day to intercept some Belgian peasant and beg for food. The Belgians in this section were naturally very much afraid of the Germans, and I fared badly. In nearly every house German soldiers were quartered, and it was out of the question for me to apply for food in that direction. The proximity of the border made every one eye one another with more or less suspicion, and I soon came to the conclusion that the safest thing I could do was to live on raw vegetables, which I could steal from the fields at night as I had previously done.

That night I made another survey of the barrier in that vicinity, but it looked just as hopeless as it had the night before, and I concluded that I only wasted time there.

I spent the night wandering west, guided by the North Star, which had served me so faithfully in all my traveling. Every mile or two I would make my way carefully to the barrier to see if conditions were any better, but it seemed to be the same all along. I felt like a wild animal in a cage, with about as much chance of getting out.

The section of the country in which I was now wandering was very heavily wooded and there was really no very great difficulty in keeping myself concealed, which I did all day long, striving all the time to think of some way in which I could circumvent that cursed barrier.

The idea of a huge step-ladder occurred to me, but I searched hour after hour in vain for lumber or fallen trees out of which I could construct one. If I could only obtain something which would enable me to reach a point about nine feet in the air, it would be a comparatively simple matter to jump from that point over the electric fence.

Then I thought that perhaps I could construct a simple ladder and lean it against one of the posts upon which the electric wires were strung, climb to the top and leap over, getting over the barbed-wire fences in the same way.

This seemed to be the most likely plan, and all night long I sat constructing a ladder for this purpose.

I was fortunate enough to find a number of fallen pine-trees from ten to twenty feet long. I selected two of them which seemed sufficiently strong and broke off all the branches, which I used as rungs, tying them to the poles with grass and strips from my handkerchief and shirt as best I could.

It was not a very workmanlike-looking ladder when I finally got through with it. I leaned it against a tree to test it and it wabbled considerably. It was more like a rope ladder than a wooden one, but I strengthened it here and there and decided that it would probably serve the purpose.

I kept the ladder in the woods all day and could hardly wait until dark to make the supreme test. If it proved successful, my troubles were over; within a few hours I would be in a neutral country out of all danger. If it failed—I dismissed the idea summarily. There was no use worrying about failure; the thing to do was to succeed.

The few hours that were to pass before night came on seemed endless, but I utilized them to reinforce my ladder, tying the rungs more securely with long grass which I plucked in the woods.

At last night came, and with my ladder in hand I made for the barrier. In front of it there was a cleared space of about one hundred yards, which had been prepared to make the work of the guards easier in watching it.

I waited in the neighborhood until I heard the sentry pass the spot where I was in hiding, and then I hurried across the clearing, shoved my ladder under the barbed wire, and endeavored to follow it. My clothing caught in the wire, but I wrenched myself clear and crawled to the electric barrier.

My plan was to place the ladder against one of the posts, climb up to the top, and then jump. There would be a fall of nine or ten feet, and

I might possibly sprain my ankle or break my leg, but if that was all that stood between me and freedom I wasn't going to stop to consider it.

I put my ear to the ground to listen for the coming of the sentry. There was not a sound. Eagerly but carefully I placed the ladder against the post and started up. Only a few feet separated me from liberty, and my heart beat fast.

I had climbed perhaps three rungs of my ladder when I became aware of an unlooked-for difficulty.

The ladder was slipping!

Just as I took the next rung the ladder slipped, came in contact with the live wire, and the current passed through the wet sticks and into my body. There was a blue flash, my hold on the ladder relaxed, and I fell heavily to the ground unconscious!

Of course, I had not received the full force of the current or I would not now be here. I must have remained unconscious for a few moments, but I came to just in time to hear the German guard coming, and the thought came to me that if I didn't get that ladder concealed at once, he would see it even though, fortunately for me, it was an unusually dark night.

I pulled the ladder out of his path and lay down flat on the ground, not seven feet away from his beat. He passed so close that I could have pushed the ladder out and tripped him up.

It occurred to me that I could have climbed back under the barbed-wire fence and waited for the sentry to return and then felled him with a blow on the head, as he had no idea, of course, that there was any one in the vicinity. I wouldn't have hesitated to take life, because my only thought now was to get into Holland, but I thought that as long as he didn't bother me perhaps the safest thing to do was not to bother him, but to continue my efforts during his periodic absences.

His beat at this point was apparently fairly long and allowed me more time to work than I had hoped for.

My mishap with the ladder had convinced me that escape in that way was not feasible. The shock that I had received had unnerved me and I was afraid to risk it again, particularly as I realized that I had fared more fortunately than I could hope to again if I met with a similar mishap. There was no way of making that ladder hold, and I gave up the idea of using it.

I was now right in front of this electric barrier, and as I studied it I saw another way of getting by. If I couldn't get over it, what was the matter with getting under it?

The bottom wire was only two inches from the ground, and, of course, I couldn't touch it, but my plan was to dig underneath it and then crawl through the hole in the ground.

I had only my hands to dig with, but I went at it with a will, and fortunately the ground was not very hard.

When I had dug about six inches, making a distance in all of eight inches from the lowest electric wire, I came to an underground wire. I knew enough about electricity to realize that this wire could not be charged, as it was in contact with the ground, but still there was not room between the live wire and this underground wire for me to crawl through, and I either had to go on digging deep enough under this wire to crawl under it or else pull it up.

This underground wire was about as big around as a lead-pencil and there was no chance of breaking it. The jack-knife I had had at the start of my travels I had long since lost, and even if I had had something to hammer with, the noise would have made that method impracticable.

I went on digging. When the total distance between the live wire and the bottom of the hole I had dug was thirty inches I took hold of the ground wire and pulled on it with all my strength.

It wouldn't budge. It was stretched taut across the narrow ditch I had dug—about fourteen inches wide—and all my tugging didn't serve to loosen it.

I was just about to give it up in despair when a staple gave way in the nearest post. This enabled me to pull the wire through the ground a little, and I renewed my efforts. After a moment or two of pulling as I had never pulled in my life before a staple on the next post gave way, and my work became easier. I had more leeway now and pulled and pulled again until in all eight staples had given way.

Every time a staple gave way it sounded in my ears like the report of a gun, although I suppose it didn't really make very much noise. Nevertheless, each time I would put my ear to the ground to listen for the guard, and, not hearing him, went on with my work.

By pulling on the wire I was now able to drag it through the ground enough to place it back from the fence and go on digging.

The deeper I went the harder became the work, because by this time my finger-nails were broken and I was nervous—afraid every moment that I would touch the charged wire.

I kept at it, however, with my mind constantly on the hole I was digging and the liberty which was almost within my reach.

Finally I figured that I had enough space to crawl through and still leave a couple of inches between my back and the live wire.

Before I went under that wire I noticed that the lace which the Belgian woman had given me as a souvenir made my pocket bulge, and lest it might be the innocent means of electrocuting me by touching the live wire, I took it out, rolled it up, and threw it over the barrier.

Then I lay down on my stomach and crawled or rather writhed under the wire like a snake, with my feet first, and there wasn't any question of my hugging Mother Earth as closely as possible, because I realized that even to touch the wire above me with my back meant instant death.

Anxious as I was to get on the other side, I didn't hurry this operation. I feared that there might be some little detail that I had overlooked, and I exercised the greatest possible care in going under, taking nothing for granted.

When I finally got through and straightened up there were still several feet of Belgium between me and liberty, represented by the six feet which separated the electric barrier from the last barbed-wire fence, but before I went another step I went down on my knees and thanked God for my long series of escapes and especially for this last achievement, which seemed to me to be about all that was necessary to bring me freedom.

Then I crawled under the barbed-wire fence and breathed the free air of Holland! I had no clear idea just where I was, and I didn't much care. I was out of the power of the Germans, and that was enough. I had walked perhaps a hundred yards when I remembered the lace I had thrown over the barrier, and, dangerous as I realized the undertaking to be, I determined to walk back and get it. This necessitated my going back on to Belgian soil again, but it seemed a shame to leave the lace there, and by exercising a little care I figured I could get it easily enough.

When I came to the spot at which I had made my way under the barbed wire I put my ear to the ground and listened for the sentry. I heard him coming and lay prone on the ground till he had passed. The fact that he might observe the hole in the ground or the ladder occurred to me as I lay there, and it seemed like an age before he finally marched out of earshot. Then I went under the barbed wire again, retrieved the lace, and once again made my way to Dutch territory.

It does not take long to describe the events just referred to, but the incidents themselves consumed several hours in all. To dig the hole must have taken me more than two hours, and I had to stop frequently to hide while the sentry passed. Many times, indeed, I thought I heard him coming and stopped my work, and then discovered that it was only my imagination. I certainly suffered enough that night to last me a lifetime. With a German guard on one side, death from electrocution on the other, and starvation staring me in the face, my plight was anything but a comfortable one.

It was the 19th of November, 1917, when I got through the wires. I had made my leap from the train on September 9th. Altogether, therefore, just seventy-two days had elapsed since I escaped from the Huns. If I live to be as old as Methuselah, I never expect to live through another seventy-two days so crammed full of incident and hazard and lucky escapes.

CHAPTER XVIII

EXPERIENCES IN HOLLAND

But I was not yet quite out of the woods.

I now knew that I was in Holland, but just where I had no idea. I walked for about thirty minutes and came to a path leading to the right, and I had proceeded along it but a few hundred yards when I saw in front of me a fence exactly like the one I had crossed.

"This is funny," I said to myself. "I didn't know the Dutch had a fence, too." I advanced to the fence and examined it closely, and judge of my astonishment when I saw beyond it a nine-foot fence apparently holding live wires exactly like the one which had nearly been the death of me!

I had very little time to conjecture what it all meant, for just then I heard a guard coming. He was walking so fast that I was sure it was a Dutch sentry, as the Huns walk much more slowly.

I was so bewildered, however, that I decided to take no chances, and as the road was fairly good I wandered down it and away from that mysterious fence. About half a mile down I could see the light of a sentry station, and I thought I would go there and tell my story to the sentries, realizing that as I was unarmed it was perfectly safe for me to announce myself to the Dutch authorities. I could be interned only if I entered Holland under arms.

As I approached the sentry box I noticed three men in gray uniforms, the regulation Dutch color. I was on the verge of shouting to them when the thought struck me that there was just a chance I might be mistaken, as the German uniforms were the same color, and I had suffered too many privations and too many narrow escapes to lose all at this time.

I had just turned off the road to go back into some bushes when out of the darkness I heard that dread German command:

"Halt! Halt!"

He didn't need to holler twice. I heard and heeded the first time. Then I heard another man come running up, and there was considerable talking, but whether they were Germans or Hollanders I was still uncertain. Evidently, however, he thought the noise must be a dog or the wind.

Finally I heard one of them laugh and heard him walk back to the sentry station where the guard was billeted, and I crawled a little nearer to try to make out just what it all meant. I had begun to think it was all a nightmare.

Between myself and the light in the sentry station I then noticed the stooping figure of a man bending over as if to conceal himself, and on his head was the spiked helmet of a German soldier!

I knew then what another narrow escape I had had, for I am quite sure he would have shot me without ceremony if I had foolishly made myself known. I would have been buried at once and no one would have been any the wiser, even though, technically speaking, I was on neutral territory and immune from capture or attack.

This new shock only served to bewilder me the more. I was completely lost. There seemed to be frontier behind me and frontier in front of me. Evidently, however, what had happened was that I had lost my sense of direction and had wandered in the arc of a circle, returning to the same fence that I had been so long in getting through. This solution of the mystery came to me suddenly, and I at once searched the landscape for something in the way of a landmark to guide me. For once my faithful friend, the North Star, had failed me. The sky was pitch black and there wasn't a star in the heavens.

In the distance, at what appeared to be about three miles away, but which turned out to be six, I could discern the lights of a village, and I knew that it must be a Dutch village, as lights are not allowed in Belgium in that indiscriminate way.

My course was now clear. I would make a bee-line for that village. Before I had gone very far I found myself in a marsh or swamp, and I turned back a little, hoping to find a better path. Finding none, I retraced my steps and kept straight ahead, determined to reach that village at all costs and to swerve neither to the right nor to the left until I got there.

One moment I would be in water up to my knees and the next I would sink in clear up to my waist. I paid no attention to my condition. It was merely a repetition of what I had gone through many times before, but this time I had a definite goal, and, once I reached it, I knew my troubles would be over.

It took me perhaps three hours to reach firm ground. The path I struck led to within half a mile of the village. I shall never forget that path; it was almost as welcome to my feet as the opposite bank of the Meuse had seemed.

The first habitation I came to was a little workshop with a bright light shining outside. It must have been after midnight, but the people inside were apparently just quitting work. There were three men and two boys engaged in making wooden shoes.

It wasn't necessary for me to explain to them that I was a refugee, even if I had been able to speak their language. I was caked with mud up to my shoulders, and I suppose my face must have recorded some of the experiences I had gone through that memorable night.

"I want the British consul," I told them.

Apparently they didn't understand, but one of them volunteered to conduct me to the village. They seemed to be only too anxious to do all they could for me; evidently they realized I was a British soldier.

It was very late when my companion finally escorted me into the village, but he aroused some people he knew from their beds and they dressed and came down to feed me.

The family consisted of an old lady and her husband and a son who was a soldier in the Dutch army. The cold shivers ran down my back while he sat beside me, because every now and again I caught a glimpse of his gray uniform and it resembled very much that of the German soldiers.

Some of the neighbors, aroused by the commotion, got up to see what it was all about, and came in and watched while I ate the meal those good Dutch people prepared for me. Ordinarily, I suppose, I would have been embarrassed with so many people staring at me while I ate, as though I were some strange animal that had just been captured, but just then I was too famished to notice or care very much what other people did.

There will always be a warm place in my heart for the Dutch people. I had heard lots of persons say that they were not inclined to help refugees, but my experience did not bear these reports out. They certainly did much more for me than I ever expected.

I had a little German money left, but as the value of German money is only about half in Holland, I didn't have enough to pay the fare to Rotterdam, which was my next objective. It was due to the generosity of these people that I was able to reach the British consul as quickly as I did. Some day I hope to return to Holland and repay every single soul who played the part of Good Samaritan to me.

With the money that these people gave me I was able to get a third-class ticket to Rotterdam, and I am glad that I didn't have enough to travel first-class, for I would have looked as much out of place in a first-class carriage as a Hun would appear in heaven.

That night I slept in the house of my Dutch friends, where they fixed me up most comfortably. In the morning they gave me breakfast and then escorted me to the station.

While I was waiting in the station a crowd gathered round me, and soon it seemed as if the whole town had turned out to get a look at me. It was very embarrassing, particularly as I could give them no information regarding the cause of my condition, although, of course, they all knew that I was a refugee from Belgium.

As the train pulled out of the station the crowd gave a loud cheer, and the tears almost came to my eyes as I contrasted in my mind the conduct of this crowd and the one that had gathered at the station in Ghent when I had departed a prisoner en route for the reprisal camp. I breathed a sigh of relief as I thought of that reprisal camp and how fortunate I had really been, despite all my suffering, to have escaped it. Now, at any rate, I was a free man and I would soon be sending home the joyful news that I had made good my escape.

At Einhoffen two Dutch officers got into the compartment with me. They looked at me with very much disfavor, not knowing, of course, that I was a British officer. My clothes were still pretty much in the condition they were when I crossed the border, although I had been able to scrape off some of the mud I had collected the night before. I had not shaved nor trimmed my beard for many days, and I must have presented a sorry appearance. I could hardly blame them for edging away from me.

The trip from Einhoffen to Rotterdam passed without special incident. At various stations passengers would get into the compartment and, observing my unusual appearance, would endeavor to start a conversation with me. None of them spoke English, however, and they had to use their own imagination as to my identity.

When I arrived at Rotterdam I asked a policeman who stood in front of the station where I could find the British consul, but I could not make him understand. I next applied to a taxicab driver.

"English consul—British consul—American consul—French consul," I said, hoping that if he didn't understand one he might recognize another.

He eyed me with suspicion and motioned me to get in and drove off. I had no idea where he was taking me, but after a quarter of an hour's ride he brought up in front of the British consulate. Never before was I so glad to see the Union Jack!

I beckoned to the chauffeur to go with me up to the office, as I had no money with which to pay him, and when we got to the consulate I told them that if they would pay the taxi fare I would tell them who I was and how I happened to be there.

They knew at once that I was an escaped prisoner and they readily paid the chauffeur and invited me to give some account of myself.

They treated me most cordially and were intensely interested in the brief account I gave them of my adventures. Word was sent to the consul-general, and he immediately sent for me. When I went in he shook hands with me, greeting me very heartily and offering me a chair.

He then sat down, screwed a monocle on his eye, and viewed me from top to toe. I could see that only good breeding kept him from laughing at the spectacle I presented. I could see he wanted to laugh in the worst way.

"Go ahead and laugh!" I said. "You can't offend me the way I feel this blessed day!" And he needed no second invitation. Incidentally, it gave me a chance to laugh at him, for I was about as much amused as he was.

After he had laughed himself about sick he got up and slapped me on the back and invited me to tell him my story.

"Lieutenant," he said, when I had concluded, "you can have anything you want. I think your experiences entitle you to it."

"Well, Consul," I replied, "I would like a bath, a shave, a hair-cut, and some civilized clothes about as badly as a man ever needed them, I suppose, but before that I would like to get a cable off to America to my mother, telling her that I am safe and on my way to England."

The consul gave the necessary instructions, and I had the satisfaction of knowing before I left the office that the cable, with its good tidings, was on its way to America.

Then he sent for one of the naval men who had been interned there since the beginning of the war and who was able to speak Dutch, and told him to take good care of me.

After I had been bathed and shaved and had a hair-cut, I bought some new clothes and had something to eat, and I felt like a new man.

As I walked through the streets of Rotterdam, breathing the air of freedom again and realizing that there was no longer any danger of being captured and taken back to prison, it was a wonderful sensation.

I don't believe there will ever be a country that will appear in my eyes quite as good as Holland did then. I had to be somewhat careful, however, because Holland was full of German spies, and I knew they would be keen to learn all they possibly could about my escape and my adventures, so that the authorities in Belgium could mete out punishment to every one who was in any respect to blame for it. As I was in Rotterdam only a day, they didn't have very much opportunity to learn anything from me.

The naval officer who accompanied me and acted as interpreter for me introduced me to many other soldiers and sailors who had escaped from Belgium when the Germans took Antwerp, and as they had arrived in Holland in uniform and under arms the laws of neutrality compelled their internment, and they had been there ever since.

The life of a man who is interned in a neutral country, I learned, is anything but satisfactory. He gets one month a year to visit his home. If he lives in England, that is not so bad, but if he happens to live farther away, the time he has to spend with his folks is very short, as the month's leave does not take into consideration the time consumed in traveling to and from Holland.

The possibility of escape from internment is always there, but the British authorities have an agreement with the Dutch government to send refugees back immediately. In this respect, therefore, the position of a man who is interned is worse than that of a prisoner who, if he does succeed in making his escape, is naturally received with open arms in his native land. Apart from this restraint, however, internment, with all its drawbacks, is a thousand times—yes, a million times better than being a prisoner of war in Germany.

It seems to me that when the war is over and the men who have been imprisoned in Germany return home they should be given a bigger and greater reception than the most victorious army that ever marched into a city, for they will have suffered and gone through more than the world will ever be able to understand.

No doubt you will find in the German prison-camps one or two faint-hearted individuals with a pronounced yellow streak who voluntarily gave up the struggle and gave up their liberty rather than risk their lives or limbs. These sad cases, however, are, I am sure, extremely few. Nine hundred and ninety-nine out of a thousand of the men fighting in the Allied lines would rather be in the front-line trenches, fighting every day, with all the horrors and all the risks, than be a prisoner of war in Germany, for the men in France have a very keen realization of what that means.

But to return to my day in Rotterdam.

After I was fixed up I returned to the consulate and arrangements were made for my transportation to England at once. Fortunately there was a boat leaving that very night, and I was allowed to take passage on it.

Just as we were leaving Rotterdam the boat I was on rammed our own convoy, one of the destroyers, and injured it so badly that it had to put back to port. It would have been a strange climax to my adventure if the disaster had resulted in the sinking of my boat and I had lost my life while on my way to England after having successfully outwitted the Huns. But my luck was with me to the last, and while the accident resulted in some delay, our boat was not seriously damaged and made the trip over in schedule time and without further incident, another destroyer having been assigned to escort us through the danger zone in place of the one which we had put out of commission.

When I arrived in London the reaction from the strain I had been under for nearly three months immediately became apparent. My nerves were in such a state that it was absolutely impossible for me to cross the street without being in deadly fear of being run over or trampled on. I stood at the curb, like an old woman from the country on her first visit to the city, and I would not venture across until some knowing policeman, recognizing my condition, came to my assistance and convoyed me across.

Indeed, there are a great number of English officers at home at all times "getting back their nerve" after a long spell of active service at the front, so that my condition was anything but novel to the London bobbies.

It was not many days, however, before I regained control of myself and felt in first-class shape.

Although the British authorities in Holland had wired my mother from Holland that I was safe and on my way to England, the first thing I did when we landed was to send her a cable myself.

The cable read as follows:

Mrs. M. J. O'Brien, Momence, Ill., U. S. A.:
Just escaped from Germany. Letter follows.
Pat.

As I delivered it to the cable-despatcher I could just imagine the exultation with which my mother would receive it and the pride she would feel as she exhibited it among her neighbors and friends.

I could hear the volley of "I told you so's" that greeted her good tidings.

"It would take more than the Kaiser to keep Pat in Germany!" I could hear one of them saying.

"Knew he'd be back for Christmas, anyway," I could hear another remark.

"I had an idea that Pat and his comrades might spend Christmas in Berlin," I could hear another admitting, "but I didn't think any other part of Germany would appeal to him very much."

"Mrs. O'Brien, did Pat write you how many German prisoners he brought back with him?" I could hear still another credulous friend inquiring.

It was all very amusing and gratifying to me, and I must confess I felt quite cocky as I walked into the War Department to report.

For the next five days I was kept very busy answering questions put to me by the military authorities regarding what I had observed as to conditions in Germany and behind the lines.

What I reported was taken down by a stenographer and made part of the official records, but I did not give them my story in narrative form. The information I was able to give was naturally of interest to various branches of the service, and experts in every line of government work took it in turns to question me. One morning would be devoted, for instance, to answering questions of a military nature—German methods behind the front-line trenches, tactics, morale of troops, and similar matters. Then the aviation experts would take a whack at me and discuss with me all I had observed of German flying-corps methods and equipment. Then, again, the food experts would interrogate me as to what I had learned of food conditions in Germany, Luxembourg, and Belgium, and as I had lived pretty close to the ground for the best part of seventy-two days I was able to give them some fairly accurate reports as to actual agricultural conditions, many of the things I told them probably having more significance to them than they had to me.

There were many things I had observed which I have not referred to in these pages because their value to us might be diminished if the Germans knew we were aware of them, but they were all reported to the authorities, and it was very gratifying to me to hear that the experts considered some of them of the greatest value.

One of the most amusing incidents of my return occurred when I called at my banker's in London to get my personal effects.

The practice in the Royal Flying Corps when a pilot is reported missing is to have two of his comrades assigned to go through his belongings, check them over, destroy anything that it might not be to his interest to preserve, and send the whole business to his banker or his home, as the case may be. Every letter is read through, but its contents is never afterward discussed nor revealed in any way. If the pilot is finally reported dead, his effects are forwarded to his next of kin, but while he is officially only "missing" or is known to be a prisoner of war they are kept either at the squadron headquarters or sent to his banker's.

In my case, as soon as it was learned that I had fallen from the sky it was assumed that I had been killed, and my chum, Paid Raney, and another officer were detailed to check over my effects. The list they made and to which they affixed their signatures, as I have previously mentioned, is now in my possession and is one of the most treasured souvenirs of my adventure.

My trunk was sent to Cox & Co. in due course, and now that I was in London I thought I would go and claim it.

When I arrived in the bank I applied at the proper window for my mail and trunk.

"Who are you?" I was asked, rather sharply.

"Well, I guess no one has any greater right to Pat O'Brien's effects than I have," I replied, "and I would be obliged to you if you would look them up for me."

"That may be all right, my friend," replied the clerk, "but according to our records Lieutenant O'Brien is a prisoner of war in Germany, and we can't very well turn over his effects to any one else unless either you present proof that he is dead and that you are his lawful representative, or else deliver to us a properly authenticated order from him to give them to you."

He was very positive about it all, but quite polite, and I thought I would kid him no more.

"Well," I said, "I can't very well present proofs to you that Pat O'Brien is dead, but I will do the best I can to prove to you that he is alive, and if you haven't quite forgotten his signature I guess I can write you out an order that will answer all your requirements and enable you to give me Pat O'Brien's belongings without running any risks." And I scribbled my signature on a scrap of paper and handed it to him.

He looked at me carefully through the latticed window, then jumped down from his chair and came outside to clasp me by the hand.

"Good Heavens, Lieutenant!" he exclaimed as he pumped my hand up and down. "How did you ever get away?" And I had to sit right down and tell him and half a dozen other people in the bank all about my experiences.

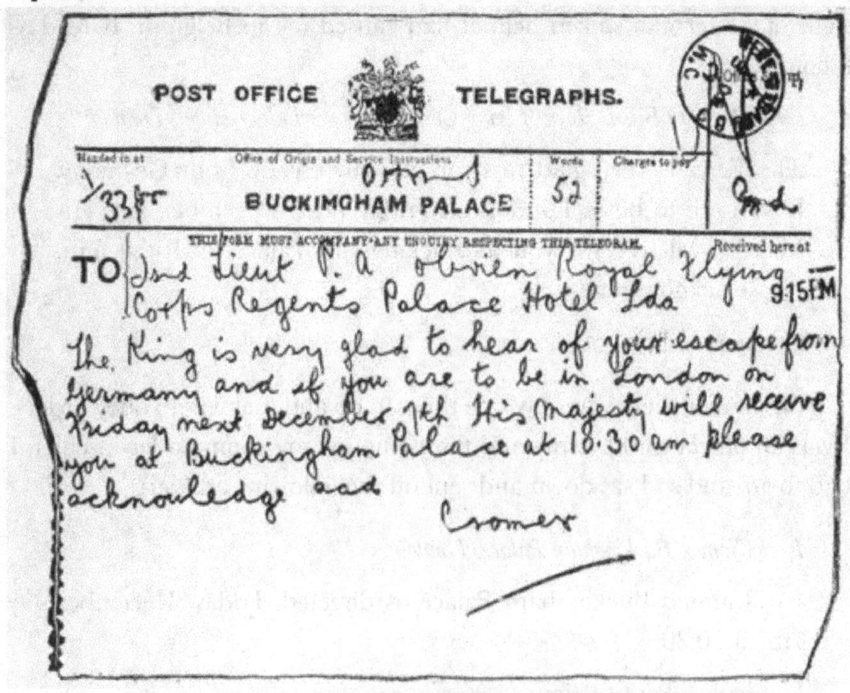

COPY OF TELEGRAM INVITING LIEUTENANT O'BRIEN TO MEET KING GEORGE

COPY OF TELEGRAM SENT BY LIEUTENANT O'BRIEN IN ANSWER TO AN INVITATION TO MEET KING GEORGE

I had been in England about ten days when I received a telegram which, at first, occasioned me almost as much concern as the unexpected sight of a German spiked helmet had caused me in Belgium. It read as follows:

Lieut. P. A. O'Brien, Royal Flying Corps, Regent's Palace Hotel, London:

The King is very glad to hear of your escape from Germany. If you are to be in London on Friday next, December 7th, His Majesty will receive you at Buckingham Palace at 10:30 a.m. Please acknowledge.

Cromer.

Of course, there was only one thing to do and that was to obey orders. I was an officer in the army and the King was my commander-in-chief. I had to go, and so I sat down and sent off the following answer:

Earl Cromer, Buckingham Palace, London:

I will attend Buckingham Palace as directed, Friday, December 7th, at 10:30.

Lieutenant Pat O'Brien.

In the interval that elapsed I must confess, the ordeal of calling on the King of England loomed up more dreadfully every day, and I really believe I would rather have spent another day in that empty house in the big city in Belgium, or, say, two days at Courtrai, than go through what I believed to be in store for me.

Orders were orders, however, and there was no way of getting out of it. As it turned out it wasn't half so bad as I had feared; on the contrary, it was one of the most agreeable experiences of my life.

CHAPTER XIX

I AM PRESENTED TO THE KING

When the dreaded 7th of December arrived I hailed a taxicab and in as matter-of-fact tone of voice as I could command directed the chauffeur to drive me to Buckingham Palace, as though I were paying my regular morning call on the King.

My friends' version of this incident, I have since heard, is that I seated myself in the taxi and, leaning through the window, said, "Buckingham Palace!" whereupon the taxi driver got down, opened the door, and exclaimed, threateningly:

"If you don't get out quietly and chuck your drunken talk, I'll jolly quick call a bobby, bli' me if I won't!"

But I can only give my word that nothing of the kind occurred.

When I arrived at the palace gate the sentry on guard asked me who I was, and then let me pass at once up to the front entrance of the palace.

There I was met by an elaborately uniformed and equally elaborately decorated personage, who, judging by the long row of medals he wore, must have seen long and distinguished service for the King.

I was relieved of my overcoat, hat, and stick and conducted up a long stairway, where I was turned over to another functionary, who led me to the reception-room of Earl Cromer, the King's secretary.

There I was introduced to another earl and a duke whose names I do not remember. I was becoming so bewildered, in fact, that it is a wonder that I remember as much as I do of this eventful day.

I had heard many times that before being presented to the King a man is coached carefully as to just how he is to act and what he is to say and do, and all this time I was wondering when this drilling would commence. I certainly had no idea that I was to be ushered into the august presence of the King without some preliminary instruction.

Earl Cromer and the other noblemen talked to me for a while and got me to relate in brief the story of my experiences, and they appeared to be very much interested. Perhaps they did it only to give me confidence and as a sort of rehearsal for the main performance, which was scheduled to take place much sooner than I expected.

I had barely completed my story when the door opened and an attendant entered and announced:

"The King will receive Leftenant O'Brien!"

If he had announced that the Kaiser was outside with a squad of German guards to take me back to Courtrai my heart could not have sunk deeper.

Earl Cromer beckoned me to follow him, and we went into a large room, where I supposed I was at last to receive my coaching, but I observed the earl bow to a man standing there and realized that I was standing in the presence of the King of England.

"Your Majesty, Leftenant O'Brien!" the earl announced, and then immediately backed from the room. I believed I would have followed right behind him, but by that time the King had me by the hand and was congratulating me, and he spoke so very cordially and democratically that he put me at my ease at once.

He then asked me how I felt and whether I was in a condition to converse, and when I told him I was he said he would be very much pleased to hear my story in detail.

"Were you treated any worse by the Germans, Leftenant," he asked, "on account of being an American? I've heard that the Germans had threatened to shoot Americans serving in the British army if they captured them, classing them as murderers because America was a neutral country and Americans had no right to mix in the war. Did you find that to be the case?"

I told him that I had heard similar reports, but that I did not notice any appreciable difference in my treatment from that accorded Britishers.

The King declared that he believed my escape was due to my pluck and will power, and that it was one of the most remarkable escapes he had ever heard of, which I thought was quite a compliment, coming as it did from the King of England.

"I hope that all the Americans will give as good an account of themselves as you have, Leftenant," he said, "and I feel quite sure they will. I fully appreciate all the service rendered us by Americans before the States entered the war."

At this point I asked him if I was taking too much time.

"Not at all, Leftenant, not at all!" he replied, most cordially. "I was extremely interested in the brief report that came to me of your wonderful escape, and I sent for you because I wanted to hear the whole story first-hand, and I am very glad you were able to come."

I had not expected to remain more than a few minutes, as I understood that four minutes is considered a long audience with the King. Fifty-two minutes elapsed before I finally left there!

During all this time I had done most of the talking, in response to the King's request to tell my story. Occasionally he interrupted to ask a question about a point he wanted me to make clear, but for the most part he was content to play the part of listener.

He seemed to be very keen on everything, and when I described some of the tight holes I got into during my escape he evinced his sympathy. Occasionally I introduced some of the few humorous incidents of my adventure, and in every instance he laughed heartily.

Altogether the impression I got of him was that he is a very genial, gracious, and alert sovereign. I know I have felt more ill at ease when talking to a major than when speaking to the King—but perhaps I had more cause to.

During the whole interview we were left entirely alone, which impressed me as significant of the democratic manner of the present King of England, and I certainly came away with the utmost respect for him.

In all of my conversation, I recalled afterward, I never addressed the King as "Your Majesty," but used the military "sir." As I was a British officer and he was the head of the army, he probably appreciated this manner of address more than if I had used the usual "Your Majesty." Perhaps he attributed it to the fact that I was an American. At any rate, he didn't evince any displeasure at my departure from what I understand is the usual form of address.

Before I left he asked me what my plans for the future were.

"Why, sir, I hope to rejoin my squadron at the earliest possible moment!" I replied.

"No, Leftenant," he rejoined, "that is out of the question. We can't risk losing you for good by sending you back to a part of the front opposed by Germany, because if you were unfortunate enough to be captured again they would undoubtedly shoot you."

"Well, if I can't serve in France, sir," I suggested, "wouldn't it be feasible for me to fly in Italy or Salonica?"

"No," he replied; "that would be almost as bad. The only thing that I can suggest for you to do is either to take up instruction—a very valuable form of service—or perhaps it might be safe enough for you to serve in Egypt; but, just at present, Leftenant, I think you have done enough, anyway."

Then he rose and shook hands with me and wished me the best of luck, and we both said, "Good-by."

In the adjoining room I met Earl Cromer again, and as he accompanied me to the door he seemed to be surprised at the length of my visit.

"His Majesty must have been very much interested in your story," he said.

As I left the palace a policeman and a sentry outside came smartly to attention. Perhaps they figured I had been made a general.

As I was riding back to the hotel in a taxi I reflected on the remarkable course of events which in the short space of nine months had taken me through so much and ended up, like the finish of a book, with my being received by his Majesty the King! When I first joined the Royal Flying Corps I never expected to see the inside of Buckingham Palace, much less to be received by the King.

CHAPTER XX

HOME AGAIN!

That same day, in the evening, I was tendered a banquet at the Hotel Savoy by a fellow-officer who had bet three other friends of mine that I would be home by Christmas. This wager had been made at the time he heard that I was a prisoner of war, and the dinner was the stake.

The first intimation he had of my safe return from Germany and the fact that he had won his bet was a telegram I sent him reading as follows:

Lieutenant Louis Grant:

War-bread bad, so I came home.
Pat.

He said he would not part with that message for a thousand dollars.

Other banquets followed in fast succession. After I had survived nine of them I figured that I was now in as much danger of succumbing to a surfeit of rich food as I had previously been of dying from starvation, and for my own protection I decided to leave London. Moreover, my thoughts and my heart were turning back to the land of my birth, where I knew there was

171

a loving old mother who was longing for more substantial evidence of my safe escape than the cables and letters she had received.

Strangely enough, on the boat which carried me across the Atlantic I saw an R. F. C. man—Lieutenant Lascelles.

I walked over to him, held out my hand, and said, "Hello!"

He looked at me steadily for at least a minute.

"My friend, you certainly look like Pat O'Brien," he declared, "but I can't believe my eyes. Who are you?"

I quickly convinced him that his eyes were still to be relied upon, and then he stared at me for another minute or two, shaking his head dubiously.

His mystification was quite explicable. The last time he had seen me I was going down to earth with a bullet in my face and my machine doing a spinning nose dive. He was one of my comrades in the flying corps and was in the fight which resulted in my capture. He said he had read the report that I was a prisoner of war, but he had never believed it, as he did not think it possible for me to survive that fall.

He was one of the few men living out of eighteen who were originally in my squadron—I do not mean the eighteen with whom I sailed from Canada last May, but the squadron I joined in France. He rehearsed for me the fate of all my old friends in the squadron, and it was a mighty sad story. All of them had been killed except one or two who were in dry-dock for repairs. He himself was on his way to Australia to recuperate and get his nerves back into shape again. He had been in many desperate combats.

As we sat on the deck exchanging experiences I would frequently notice him gazing intently in my face as if he were not quite sure that the whole proposition was not a hoax and that I was not an impostor.

Outside of this unexpected meeting, my trip across was uneventful.

I arrived in St. John, New Brunswick, and eventually the little town of Momence, Illinois, on the Kankakee River.

I have said that I was never so happy to arrive in a country as I was when I first set foot on Dutch soil. Now I'm afraid I shall have to take that statement back. Not until I finally landed in Momence and realized that I was again in the town of my childhood days did I enjoy that feeling of absolute security which one never really appreciates until after a visit to foreign parts.

Now that I am back, the whole adventure constantly recurs to me as a dream, and I'm never quite sure that I won't wake up and find it so.

THE END

Dark Corners
Elmedina Hota

Frozen In Hell

The well known presence was felt in her chambers
as her sight was set at the beauty of the embers,
embracing the sins of her beloved one,
the timing was ideal for her to let go,
the trade was definite and ought to be done,
she was prepared for the events to take the suitable flow

The smell of rotten flesh has filled her nostrils,
her vision remained clear:
she saw herself in Hell,
the time has come to reveal the weight of all the sins,
she was led to the depths of darkness
where she shall dwell

Sacrifices haven't been strange to her,
a chance of joy for the sinner she desired,
abalienating the marks that made his soul slurred
went quicker than waiting for him to be inspired,
bizarre mistakes, obscurity he delivered,
with time, the hope in her heart has been slithered...

Miserable, filled with emptiness inside,
ages ago she's said the last goodbye to her pride,
the coldness of December's Winter flew through her heart,
recklessness of his games turned her mourning into art

State of the melancholy metamorphosed into sorcery,
crawling in the shadows,
yearning for the slice of freedom,
decorating the four walls,
a fantasy of the nursery,
to set her damned soul to Hell
and leave that burning kingdom.

The Letter

A ribbon of words is making the world fade into grey,
the words describing the state of an old heart,
as darkness embraced her and has led her mind astray,
like a disease, mercilessly tearing it apart

A change of reality as it once was;
as she remembered,
of the love in her heart she so dreadfully treasured

"Take this pain and turn it into a beautiful memory,
my heart shall carry it from here to eternity,
I'll remember it everytime I turn on our melody...
Bring the light into my dark, forgotten soul,
that once was eaten by a cruel sorrow,
put the broken pieces together and set them to eternal dreams"

Fragile, seeking for a man of her lost fairytale,
was it, indeed, too late for a fix?
Of midnight skies her skin appeared so pale;
of moon:
black was the blood,
while she faded away,
lost and regretful,
desperate for one last kiss.

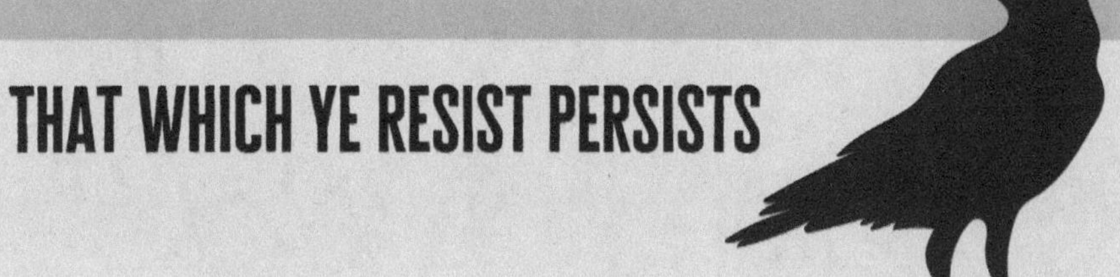

THE TUNNEL UNDER THE WORLD

BY FREDERIK POHL
Illustrations by EMSH

Pinching yourself is no way to see if you are dreaming.
Surgical instruments? Well, yes—but a mechanic's kit is
best of all!

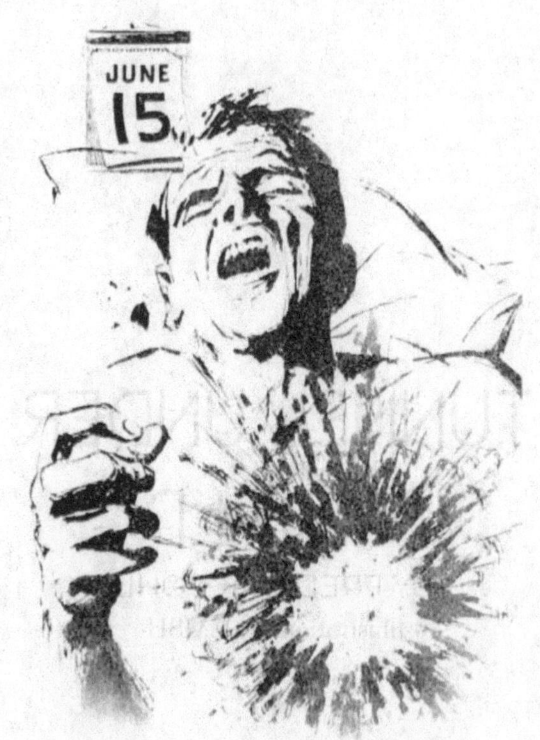

CHAPTER ONE

On the morning of June 15th, Guy Burckhardt woke up screaming out of a dream.

It was more real than any dream he had ever had in his life. He could still hear and feel the sharp, ripping-metal explosion, the violent heave that had tossed him furiously out of bed, the searing wave of heat.

He sat up convulsively and stared, not believing what he saw, at the quiet room and the bright sunlight coming in the window.

He croaked, "Mary?"

His wife was not in the bed next to him. The covers were tumbled and awry, as though she had just left it, and the memory of the dream was so strong that instinctively he found himself searching the floor to see if the dream explosion had thrown her down.

But she wasn't there. Of course she wasn't, he told himself, looking at the familiar vanity and slipper chair, the uncracked window, the unbuckled wall. It had only been a dream.

"Guy?" His wife was calling him querulously from the foot of the stairs. "Guy, dear, are you all right?"

He called weakly, "Sure."

There was a pause. Then Mary said doubtfully, "Breakfast is ready. Are you sure you're all right? I thought I heard you yelling—"

Burckhardt said more confidently, "I had a bad dream, honey. Be right down."

IN THE SHOWER, PUNCHING THE LUKEWARM-AND-COLOGNE HE FAVORED, HE told himself that it had been a beaut of a dream. Still, bad dreams weren't unusual, especially bad dreams about explosions. In the past thirty years of H-bomb jitters, who had not dreamed of explosions?

Even Mary had dreamed of them, it turned out, for he started to tell her about the dream, but she cut him off. "You *did?*" Her voice was astonished. "Why, dear, I dreamed the same thing! Well, almost the same thing. I didn't actually *hear* anything. I dreamed that something woke me up, and then there was a sort of quick bang, and then something hit me on the head. And that was all. Was yours like that?"

Burckhardt coughed. "Well, no," he said. Mary was not one of these strong-as-a-man, brave-as-a-tiger women. It was not necessary, he thought, to tell her all the little details of the dream that made it seem so real. No need to mention the splintered ribs, and the salt bubble in his throat, and the agonized knowledge that this was death. He said, "Maybe there really was some kind of explosion downtown. Maybe we heard it and it started us dreaming."

Mary reached over and patted his hand absently. "Maybe," she agreed. "It's almost half-past eight, dear. Shouldn't you hurry? You don't want to be late to the office."

He gulped his food, kissed her and rushed out—not so much to be on time as to see if his guess had been right.

But downtown Tylerton looked as it always had. Coming in on the bus, Burckhardt watched critically out the window, seeking evidence of an explosion. There wasn't any. If anything, Tylerton looked better than it ever had before: It was a beautiful crisp day, the sky was cloudless, the buildings were clean and inviting. They had, he observed, steam-blasted the Power & Light Building, the town's only skyscraper—that was the penalty of having Contro Chemical's main plant on the outskirts of town; the fumes from the cascade stills left their mark on stone buildings.

None of the usual crowd were on the bus, so there wasn't anyone Burckhardt could ask about the explosion. And by the time he got out at the corner of Fifth and Lehigh and the bus rolled away with a muted diesel moan, he had pretty well convinced himself that it was all imagination.

He stopped at the cigar stand in the lobby of his office building, but Ralph wasn't behind the counter. The man who sold him his pack of cigarettes was a stranger.

"Where's Mr. Stebbins?" Burckhardt asked.

The man said politely, "Sick, sir. He'll be in tomorrow. A pack of Marlins today?"

"Chesterfields," Burckhardt corrected.

"Certainly, sir," the man said. But what he took from the rack and slid across the counter was an unfamiliar green-and-yellow pack.

"Do try these, sir," he suggested. "They contain an anti-cough factor. Ever notice how ordinary cigarettes make you choke every once in a while?"

BURCKHARDT SAID SUSPICIOUSLY, "I NEVER HEARD OF THIS BRAND."

"Of course not. They're something new." Burckhardt hesitated, and the man said persuasively, "Look, try them out at my risk. If you don't like them, bring back the empty pack and I'll refund your money. Fair enough?"

Burckhardt shrugged. "How can I lose? But give me a pack of Chesterfields, too, will you?"

He opened the pack and lit one while he waited for the elevator. They weren't bad, he decided, though he was suspicious of cigarettes that had the tobacco chemically treated in any way. But he didn't think much of Ralph's stand-in; it would raise hell with the trade at the cigar stand if the man tried to give every customer the same high-pressure sales talk.

The elevator door opened with a low-pitched sound of music. Burckhardt and two or three others got in and he nodded to them as the door closed. The thread of music switched off and the speaker in the ceiling of the cab began its usual commercials.

No, not the *usual* commercials, Burckhardt realized. He had been exposed to the captive-audience commercials so long that they hardly registered on the outer ear any more, but what was coming from the recorded program in the basement of the building caught his attention. It wasn't merely that the brands were mostly unfamiliar; it was a difference in pattern.

There were jingles with an insistent, bouncy rhythm, about soft drinks he had never tasted. There was a rapid patter dialogue between what sounded like two ten-year-old boys about a candy bar, followed by an authoritative bass rumble: "Go right out and get a DELICIOUS Choco-Bite and eat your TANGY Choco-Bite *all up*. That's *Choco-Bite!*" There was a sobbing female whine: "I *wish* I had a Feckle Freezer! I'd do *anything* for a Feckle Freezer!" Burckhardt reached his floor and left the elevator in the middle of the last one. It left him a little uneasy. The commercials were not for familiar brands; there was no feeling of use and custom to them.

But the office was happily normal—except that Mr. Barth wasn't in. Miss Mitkin, yawning at the reception desk, didn't know exactly why. "His home phoned, that's all. He'll be in tomorrow."

"Maybe he went to the plant. It's right near his house."

She looked indifferent. "Yeah."

A thought struck Burckhardt. "But today is June 15th! It's quarterly tax return day—he has to sign the return!"

Miss Mitkin shrugged to indicate that that was Burckhardt's problem, not hers. She returned to her nails.

Thoroughly exasperated, Burckhardt went to his desk. It wasn't that he couldn't sign the tax returns as well as Barth, he thought resentfully. It simply wasn't his job, that was all; it was a responsibility that Barth, as office manager for Contro Chemicals' downtown office, should have taken.

HE THOUGHT BRIEFLY OF CALLING BARTH AT HIS HOME OR TRYING TO REACH him at the factory, but he gave up the idea quickly enough. He didn't really care much for the people at the factory and the less contact he had with them, the better. He had been to the factory once, with Barth; it had been a confusing and, in a way, a frightening experience. Barring a handful of executives and engineers, there wasn't a soul in the factory—that is, Burckhardt corrected himself, remembering what Barth had told him, not a *living* soul—just the machines.

According to Barth, each machine was controlled by a sort of computer which reproduced, in its electronic snarl, the actual memory and mind of a human being. It was an unpleasant thought. Barth, laughing, had assured him that there was no Frankenstein business of robbing graveyards and implanting brains in machines. It was only a matter, he said, of transferring a man's habit patterns from brain cells to vacuum-tube cells. It didn't hurt the man and it didn't make the machine into a monster.

But they made Burckhardt uncomfortable all the same.

He put Barth and the factory and all his other little irritations out of his mind and tackled the tax returns. It took him until noon to verify the figures—which Barth could have done out of his memory and his private ledger in ten minutes, Burckhardt resentfully reminded himself.

He sealed them in an envelope and walked out to Miss Mitkin. "Since Mr. Barth isn't here, we'd better go to lunch in shifts," he said. "You can go first."

"Thanks." Miss Mitkin languidly took her bag out of the desk drawer and began to apply makeup.

Burckhardt offered her the envelope. "Drop this in the mail for me, will you? Uh—wait a minute. I wonder if I ought to phone Mr. Barth to make sure. Did his wife say whether he was able to take phone calls?"

"Didn't say." Miss Mitkin blotted her lips carefully with a Kleenex. "Wasn't his wife, anyway. It was his daughter who called and left the message."

"The kid?" Burckhardt frowned. "I thought she was away at school."

"She called, that's all I know."

Burckhardt went back to his own office and stared distastefully at the unopened mail on his desk. He didn't like nightmares; they spoiled his whole day. He should have stayed in bed, like Barth.

A FUNNY THING HAPPENED ON HIS WAY HOME. THERE WAS A DISTURBANCE AT the corner where he usually caught his bus—someone was screaming something about a new kind of deep-freeze—so he walked an extra block. He saw the bus coming and started to trot. But behind him, someone was calling his name. He looked over his shoulder; a small harried-looking man was hurrying toward him.

Burckhardt hesitated, and then recognized him. It was a casual acquaintance named Swanson. Burckhardt sourly observed that he had already missed the bus.

He said, "Hello."

Swanson's face was desperately eager. "Burckhardt?" he asked inquiringly, with an odd intensity. And then he just stood there silently, watching Burckhardt's face, with a burning eagerness that dwindled to a faint hope and died to a regret. He was searching for something, waiting for something, Burckhardt thought. But whatever it was he wanted, Burckhardt didn't know how to supply it.

Burckhardt coughed and said again, "Hello, Swanson."

Swanson didn't even acknowledge the greeting. He merely sighed a very deep sigh.

"Nothing doing," he mumbled, apparently to himself. He nodded abstractedly to Burckhardt and turned away.

Burckhardt watched the slumped shoulders disappear in the crowd. It was an *odd* sort of day, he thought, and one he didn't much like. Things weren't going right.

Riding home on the next bus, he brooded about it. It wasn't anything terrible or disastrous; it was something out of his experience entirely. You live your life, like any man, and you form a network of impressions and reactions. You *expect* things. When you open your medicine chest, your razor is expected to be on the second shelf; when you lock your front door, you expect to have to give it a slight extra tug to make it latch.

It isn't the things that are right and perfect in your life that make it familiar. It is the things that are just a little bit wrong—the sticking latch, the light switch at the head of the stairs that needs an extra push because the spring is old and weak, the rug that unfailingly skids underfoot.

It wasn't just that things were wrong with the pattern of Burckhardt's life; it was that the *wrong* things were wrong. For instance, Barth hadn't come into the office, yet Barth *always* came in.

Burckhardt brooded about it through dinner. He brooded about it, despite his wife's attempt to interest him in a game of bridge with the neighbors, all through the evening. The neighbors were people he liked—Anne and Farley Dennerman. He had known them all their lives. But they were odd and brooding, too, this night and he barely listened to Dennerman's complaints about not being able to get good phone service or his wife's comments on the disgusting variety of television commercials they had these days.

Burckhardt was well on the way to setting an all-time record for continuous abstraction when, around midnight, with a suddenness that surprised him—he was strangely *aware* of it happening—he turned over in his bed and, quickly and completely, fell asleep.

CHAPTER TWO

It was more real than any dream he had ever had in his life. He could still hear the explosion, feel the blast that crushed him against a wall. It did not seem right that he should be sitting bolt upright in bed in an undisturbed room.

His wife came pattering up the stairs. "Darling!" she cried. "What's the matter?"

He mumbled, "Nothing. Bad dream."

She relaxed, hand on heart. In an angry tone, she started to say: "You gave me such a shock—"

But a noise from outside interrupted her. There was a wail of sirens and a clang of bells; it was loud and shocking.

The Burckhardts stared at each other for a heartbeat, then hurried fearfully to the window.

There were no rumbling fire engines in the street, only a small panel truck, cruising slowly along. Flaring loudspeaker horns crowned its top. From them issued the screaming sound of sirens, growing in intensity, mixed with the rumble of heavy-duty engines and the sound of bells. It was a perfect record of fire engines arriving at a four-alarm blaze.

Burckhardt said in amazement, "Mary, that's against the law! Do you know what they're doing? They're playing records of a fire. What are they up to?"

"Maybe it's a practical joke," his wife offered.

"Joke? Waking up the whole neighborhood at six o'clock in the morning?" He shook his head. "The police will be here in ten minutes," he predicted. "Wait and see."

But the police weren't—not in ten minutes, or at all. Whoever the pranksters in the car were, they apparently had a police permit for their games.

The car took a position in the middle of the block and stood silent for a few minutes. Then there was a crackle from the speaker, and a giant voice chanted:

"Feckle Freezers!
Feckle Freezers!
Gotta have aFeckle Freezer!
Feckle, Feckle, Feckle,
Feckle, Feckle, Feckle—"

It went on and on. Every house on the block had faces staring out of windows by then. The voice was not merely loud; it was nearly deafening.

Burckhardt shouted to his wife, over the uproar, "What the hell is a Feckle Freezer?"

"Some kind of a freezer, I guess, dear," she shrieked back unhelpfully.

ABRUPTLY THE NOISE STOPPED AND THE TRUCK STOOD SILENT. IT WAS STILL misty morning; the Sun's rays came horizontally across the rooftops. It was impossible to believe that, a moment ago, the silent block had been bellowing the name of a freezer.

"A crazy advertising trick," Burckhardt said bitterly. He yawned and turned away from the window. "Might as well get dressed. I guess that's the end of—"

The bellow caught him from behind; it was almost like a hard slap on the ears. A harsh, sneering voice, louder than the arch-angel's trumpet, howled:

"Have you got a freezer? *It stinks!* If it isn't a Feckle Freezer, *it stinks!* If it's a last year's Feckle Freezer, *it stinks!* Only this year's Feckle Freezer is any good at all! You know who owns an Ajax Freezer? Fairies own Ajax Freezers! You know who owns a Triplecold Freezer? Commies own Triplecold Freezers! Every freezer but a brand-new Feckle Freezer *stinks!*"

The voice screamed inarticulately with rage. "I'm warning you! Get out and buy a Feckle Freezer right away! Hurry up! Hurry for Feckle! Hurry for Feckle! Hurry, hurry, hurry, Feckle, Feckle, Feckle, Feckle, Feckle, Feckle...."

It stopped eventually. Burckhardt licked his lips. He started to say to his wife, "Maybe we ought to call the police about—" when the speakers erupted again. It caught him off guard; it was intended to catch him off guard. It screamed:

"Feckle, Feckle, Feckle, Feckle, Feckle, Feckle, Feckle, Feckle. Cheap freezers ruin your food. You'll get sick and throw up. You'll get sick and die. Buy a Feckle, Feckle, Feckle, Feckle! Ever take a piece of meat out of the freezer you've got and see how rotten and moldy it is? Buy a Feckle, Feckle, Feckle, Feckle, Feckle. Do you want to eat rotten, stinking food? Or do you want to wise up and buy a Feckle, Feckle, Feckle—"

That did it. With fingers that kept stabbing the wrong holes, Burckhardt finally managed to dial the local police station. He got a busy signal—it was apparent that he was not the only one with the same idea—and while he was shakingly dialing again, the noise outside stopped.

He looked out the window. The truck was gone.

BURCKHARDT LOOSENED HIS TIE AND ORDERED ANOTHER FROSTY-FLIP FROM the waiter. If only they wouldn't keep the Crystal Cafe so *hot*! The new paint job—searing reds and blinding yellows—was bad enough, but some-one seemed to have the delusion that this was January instead of June; the place was a good ten degrees warmer than outside.

He swallowed the Frosty-Flip in two gulps. It had a kind of peculiar flavor, he thought, but not bad. It certainly cooled you off, just as the waiter had promised. He reminded himself to pick up a carton of them on the way home; Mary might like them. She was always interested in something new.

He stood up awkwardly as the girl came across the restaurant toward him. She was the most beautiful thing he had ever seen in Tylerton. Chin-height, honey-blonde hair and a figure that—well, it was all hers. There was no doubt in the world that the dress that clung to her was the only thing she wore. He felt as if he were blushing as she greeted him.

"Mr. Burckhardt." The voice was like distant tomtoms. "It's wonderful of you to let me see you, after this morning."

He cleared his throat. "Not at all. Won't you sit down, Miss—"

"April Horn," she murmured, sitting down—beside him, not where he had pointed on the other side of the table. "Call me April, won't you?"

She was wearing some kind of perfume, Burckhardt noted with what little of his mind was functioning at all. It didn't seem fair that she should be using perfume as well as everything else. He came to with a start and realized that the waiter was leaving with an order for *filets mignon* for two.

"Hey!" he objected.

"Please, Mr. Burckhardt." Her shoulder was against his, her face was turned to him, her breath was warm, her expression was tender and solicitous. "This is all on the Feckle Corporation. Please let them—it's the *least* they can do."

He felt her hand burrowing into his pocket.

"I put the price of the meal into your pocket," she whispered conspiratorially. "Please do that for me, won't you? I mean I'd appreciate it if you'd pay the waiter—I'm old-fashioned about things like that."

She smiled meltingly, then became mock-businesslike. "But you must take the money," she insisted. "Why, you're letting Feckle off lightly if you do! You could sue them for every nickel they've got, disturbing your sleep like that."

WITH A DIZZY FEELING, AS THOUGH HE HAD JUST SEEN SOMEONE MAKE A RAB-
bit disappear into a top hat, he said, "Why, it really wasn't so bad, uh,
April. A little noisy, maybe, but—"

"Oh, Mr. Burckhardt!" The blue eyes were wide and admiring. "I
knew you'd understand. It's just that—well, it's such a *wonderful* freezer
that some of the outside men get carried away, so to speak. As soon as
the main office found out about what happened, they sent representatives
around to every house on the block to apologize. Your wife told us where
we could phone you—and I'm so very pleased that you were willing to let
me have lunch with you, so that I could apologize, too. Because truly, Mr.
Burckhardt, it is a *fine* freezer.

"I shouldn't tell you this, but—" the blue eyes were shyly lowered—
"I'd do almost anything for Feckle Freezers. It's more than a job to me."
She looked up. She was enchanting. "I bet you think I'm silly, don't you?"

Burckhardt coughed. "Well, I—"

"Oh, you don't want to be unkind!" She shook her head. "No, don't
pretend. You think it's silly. But really, Mr. Burckhardt, you wouldn't think
so if you knew more about the Feckle. Let me show you this little booklet—"

Burckhardt got back from lunch a full hour late. It wasn't only the
girl who delayed him. There had been a curious interview with a little
man named Swanson, whom he barely knew, who had stopped him with
desperate urgency on the street—and then left him cold.

But it didn't matter much. Mr. Barth, for the first time since Burckhardt
had worked there, was out for the day—leaving Burckhardt stuck with the
quarterly tax returns.

What did matter, though, was that somehow he had signed a purchase
order for a twelve-cubic-foot Feckle Freezer, upright model, self-defrosting,
list price $625, with a ten per cent "courtesy" discount—"Because of
that *horrid* affair this morning, Mr. Burckhardt," she had said.

And he wasn't sure how he could explain it to his wife.

HE NEEDN'T HAVE WORRIED. AS HE WALKED IN THE FRONT DOOR, HIS WIFE SAID
almost immediately, "I wonder if we can't afford a new freezer, dear.

There was a man here to apologize about that noise and—well, we got to talking and—"

She had signed a purchase order, too.

It had been the damnedest day, Burckhardt thought later, on his way up to bed. But the day wasn't done with him yet. At the head of the stairs, the weakened spring in the electric light switch refused to click at all. He snapped it back and forth angrily and, of course, succeeded in jarring the tumbler out of its pins. The wires shorted and every light in the house went out.

"Damn!" said Guy Burckhardt.

"Fuse?" His wife shrugged sleepily. "Let it go till the morning, dear."

Burckhardt shook his head. "You go back to bed. I'll be right along."

It wasn't so much that he cared about fixing the fuse, but he was too restless for sleep. He disconnected the bad switch with a screwdriver, stumbled down into the black kitchen, found the flashlight and climbed gingerly down the cellar stairs. He located a spare fuse, pushed an empty trunk over to the fuse box to stand on and twisted out the old fuse.

When the new one was in, he heard the starting click and steady drone of the refrigerator in the kitchen overhead.

He headed back to the steps, and stopped.

Where the old trunk had been, the cellar floor gleamed oddly bright. He inspected it in the flashlight beam. It was metal!

"Son of a gun," said Guy Burckhardt. He shook his head unbelievingly. He peered closer, rubbed the edges of the metallic patch with his thumb and acquired an annoying cut—the edges were *sharp*.

The stained cement floor of the cellar was a thin shell. He found a hammer and cracked it off in a dozen spots—everywhere was metal.

The whole cellar was a copper box. Even the cement-brick walls were false fronts over a metal sheath!

BAFFLED, HE ATTACKED ONE OF THE FOUNDATION BEAMS. THAT, AT LEAST, WAS real wood. The glass in the cellar windows was real glass.

He sucked his bleeding thumb and tried the base of the cellar stairs. Real wood. He chipped at the bricks under the oil burner. Real bricks. The retaining walls, the floor—they were faked.

It was as though someone had shored up the house with a frame of metal and then laboriously concealed the evidence.

The biggest surprise was the upside-down boat hull that blocked the rear half of the cellar, relic of a brief home workshop period that Burckhardt had gone through a couple of years before. From above, it looked perfectly normal. Inside, though, where there should have been thwarts and seats and lockers, there was a mere tangle of braces, rough and unfinished.

"But I *built* that!" Burckhardt exclaimed, forgetting his thumb. He leaned against the hull dizzily, trying to think this thing through. For reasons beyond his comprehension, someone had taken his boat and his cellar away, maybe his whole house, and replaced them with a clever mock-up of the real thing.

"That's crazy," he said to the empty cellar. He stared around in the light of the flash. He whispered, "What in the name of Heaven would anybody do that for?"

Reason refused an answer; there wasn't any reasonable answer. For long minutes, Burckhardt contemplated the uncertain picture of his own sanity.

He peered under the boat again, hoping to reassure himself that it was a mistake, just his imagination. But the sloppy, unfinished bracing was unchanged. He crawled under for a better look, feeling the rough wood incredulously. Utterly impossible!

He switched off the flashlight and started to wriggle out. But he didn't make it. In the moment between the command to his legs to move and the crawling out, he felt a sudden draining weariness flooding through him.

Consciousness went—not easily, but as though it were being taken away, and Guy Burckhardt was asleep.

CHAPTER THREE

On the morning of June 16th, Guy Burckhardt woke up in a cramped position huddled under the hull of the boat in his basement—and raced upstairs to find it was June 15th.

The first thing he had done was to make a frantic, hasty inspection of the boat hull, the faked cellar floor, the imitation stone. They were all as he had remembered them—all completely unbelievable.

The kitchen was its placid, unexciting self. The electric clock was purring soberly around the dial. Almost six o'clock, it said. His wife would be waking at any moment.

Burckhardt flung open the front door and stared out into the quiet street. The morning paper was tossed carelessly against the steps—and as he retrieved it, he noticed that this was the 15th day of June.

But that was impossible. *Yesterday* was the 15th of June. It was not a date one would forget—it was quarterly tax-return day.

He went back into the hall and picked up the telephone; he dialed for Weather Information, and got a well-modulated chant: "—and cooler, some showers. Barometric pressure thirty point zero four, rising ... United States Weather Bureau forecast for June 15th. Warm and sunny, with high around—"

He hung the phone up. June 15th.

"Holy heaven!" Burckhardt said prayerfully. Things were very odd indeed. He heard the ring of his wife's alarm and bounded up the stairs.

Mary Burckhardt was sitting upright in bed with the terrified, uncomprehending stare of someone just waking out of a nightmare.

"Oh!" she gasped, as her husband came in the room. "Darling, I just had the most *terrible* dream! It was like an explosion and—"

"Again?" Burckhardt asked, not very sympathetically. "Mary, something's funny! I *knew* there was something wrong all day yesterday and—"

He went on to tell her about the copper box that was the cellar, and the odd mock-up someone had made of his boat. Mary looked astonished, then alarmed, then placatory and uneasy.

She said, "Dear, are you *sure*? Because I was cleaning that old trunk out just last week and I didn't notice anything."

"Positive!" said Guy Burckhardt. "I dragged it over to the wall to step on it to put a new fuse in after we blew the lights out and—"

"After we what?" Mary was looking more than merely alarmed.

"After we blew the lights out. You know, when the switch at the head of the stairs stuck. I went down to the cellar and—"

Mary sat up in bed. "Guy, the switch didn't stick. I turned out the lights myself last night."

Burckhardt glared at his wife. "Now I *know* you didn't! Come here and take a look!"

He stalked out to the landing and dramatically pointed to the bad switch, the one that he had unscrewed and left hanging the night before....

Only it wasn't. It was as it had always been. Unbelieving, Burckhardt pressed it and the lights sprang up in both halls.

Mary, looking pale and worried, left him to go down to the kitchen and start breakfast. Burckhardt stood staring at the switch for a long time. His mental processes were gone beyond the point of disbelief and shock; they simply were not functioning.

He shaved and dressed and ate his breakfast in a state of numb introspection. Mary didn't disturb him; she was apprehensive and soothing. She kissed him good-by as he hurried out to the bus without another word.

Miss Mitkin, at the reception desk, greeted him with a yawn. "Morning," she said drowsily. "Mr. Barth won't be in today."

Burckhardt started to say something, but checked himself. She would not know that Barth hadn't been in yesterday, either, because she was tearing a June 14th pad off her calendar to make way for the "new" June 15th sheet.

He staggered to his own desk and stared unseeingly at the morning's mail. It had not even been opened yet, but he knew that the Factory Distributors envelope contained an order for twenty thousand feet of the new acoustic tile, and the one from Finebeck & Sons was a complaint.

After a long while, he forced himself to open them. They were.

By lunchtime, driven by a desperate sense of urgency, Burckhardt made Miss Mitkin take her lunch hour first—the June-fifteenth-that-was-yesterday, *he* had gone first. She went, looking vaguely worried about his strained insistence, but it made no difference to Burckhardt's mood.

The phone rang and Burckhardt picked it up abstractedly. "Contro Chemicals Downtown, Burckhardt speaking."

The voice said, "This is Swanson," and stopped.

Burckhardt waited expectantly, but that was all. He said, "Hello?"

Again the pause. Then Swanson asked in sad resignation, "Still nothing, eh?"

"Nothing what? Swanson, is there something you want? You came up to me yesterday and went through this routine. You—"

The voice crackled: "Burckhardt! Oh, my good heavens, *you remember*! Stay right there—I'll be down in half an hour!"

"What's this all about?"

"Never mind," the little man said exultantly. "Tell you about it when I see you. Don't say any more over the phone—somebody may be listening. Just wait there. Say, hold on a minute. Will you be alone in the office?"

"Well, no. Miss Mitkin will probably—"

"Hell. Look, Burckhardt, where do you eat lunch? Is it good and noisy?"

"Why, I suppose so. The Crystal Cafe. It's just about a block—"

"I know where it is. Meet you in half an hour!" And the receiver clicked.

THE CRYSTAL CAFE WAS NO LONGER PAINTED RED, BUT THE TEMPERATURE WAS still up. And they had added piped-in music interspersed with commercials. The advertisements were for Frosty-Flip, Marlin Cigarettes—"They're sanitized," the announcer purred—and something called Choco-Bite candy bars that Burckhardt couldn't remember ever having heard of before. But he heard more about them quickly enough.

While he was waiting for Swanson to show up, a girl in the cellophane skirt of a nightclub cigarette vendor came through the restaurant with a tray of tiny scarlet-wrapped candies.

"Choco-Bites are *tangy*," she was murmuring as she came close to his table. "Choco-Bites are *tangier* than tangy!"

Burckhardt, intent on watching for the strange little man who had phoned him, paid little attention. But as she scattered a handful of the confections over the table next to his, smiling at the occupants, he caught a glimpse of her and turned to stare.

"Why, Miss Horn!" he said.

The girl dropped her tray of candies.

Burckhardt rose, concerned over the girl. "Is something wrong?"

But she fled.

The manager of the restaurant was staring suspiciously at Burckhardt, who sank back in his seat and tried to look inconspicuous. He hadn't insulted the girl! Maybe she was just a very strictly reared young lady, he thought—in spite of the long bare legs under the cellophane skirt—and when he addressed her, she thought he was a masher.

Ridiculous idea. Burckhardt scowled uneasily and picked up his menu.

"Burckhardt!" It was a shrill whisper.

Burckhardt looked up over the top of his menu, startled. In the seat across from him, the little man named Swanson was sitting, tensely poised.

"Burckhardt!" the little man whispered again. "Let's get out of here! They're on to you now. If you want to stay alive, come on!"

There was no arguing with the man. Burckhardt gave the hovering manager a sick, apologetic smile and followed Swanson out. The little man seemed to know where he was going. In the street, he clutched Burckhardt by the elbow and hurried him off down the block.

"Did you see her?" he demanded. "That Horn woman, in the phone booth? She'll have them here in five minutes, believe me, so hurry it up!"

ALTHOUGH THE STREET WAS FULL OF PEOPLE AND CARS, NOBODY WAS PAYING any attention to Burckhardt and Swanson. The air had a nip in it—more like October than June, Burckhardt thought, in spite of the weather bureau. And he felt like a fool, following this mad little man down the street, running away from some "them" toward—toward what? The little man might be crazy, but he was afraid. And the fear was infectious.

"In here!" panted the little man.

It was another restaurant—more of a bar, really, and a sort of second-rate place that Burckhardt had never patronized.

"Right straight through," Swanson whispered; and Burckhardt, like a biddable boy, side-stepped through the mass of tables to the far end of the restaurant.

It was "L"-shaped, with a front on two streets at right angles to each other. They came out on the side street, Swanson staring coldly back at the question-looking cashier, and crossed to the opposite sidewalk.

They were under the marquee of a movie theater. Swanson's expression began to relax.

"Lost them!" he crowed softly. "We're almost there."

He stepped up to the window and bought two tickets. Burckhardt trailed him in to the theater. It was a weekday matinee and the place was almost empty. From the screen came sounds of gunfire and horse's hoofs. A solitary usher, leaning against a bright brass rail, looked briefly at them and went back to staring boredly at the picture as Swanson led Burckhardt down a flight of carpeted marble steps.

They were in the lounge and it was empty. There was a door for men and one for ladies; and there was a third door, marked "MANAGER" in gold letters. Swanson listened at the door, and gently opened it and peered inside.

"Okay," he said, gesturing.

Burckhardt followed him through an empty office, to another door—a closet, probably, because it was unmarked.

But it was no closet. Swanson opened it warily, looked inside, then motioned Burckhardt to follow.

It was a tunnel, metal-walled, brightly lit. Empty, it stretched vacantly away in both directions from them.

Burckhardt looked wondering around. One thing he knew and knew full well:

No such tunnel belonged under Tylerton.

THERE WAS A ROOM OFF THE TUNNEL WITH CHAIRS AND A DESK AND WHAT looked like television screens. Swanson slumped in a chair, panting.

"We're all right for a while here," he wheezed. "They don't come here much any more. If they do, we'll hear them and we can hide."

"Who?" demanded Burckhardt.

The little man said, "Martians!" His voice cracked on the word and the life seemed to go out of him. In morose tones, he went on: "Well, I think they're Martians. Although you could be right, you know; I've had plenty of time to think it over these last few weeks, after they got you, and it's possible they're Russians after all. Still—"

"Start from the beginning. Who got me when?"

Swanson sighed. "So we have to go through the whole thing again. All right. It was about two months ago that you banged on my door, late at night. You were all beat up—scared silly. You begged me to help you—"

"*I* did?"

"Naturally you don't remember any of this. Listen and you'll understand. You were talking a blue streak about being captured and threatened, and your wife being dead and coming back to life, and all kinds of mixed-up nonsense. I thought you were crazy. But—well, I've always had a lot of respect for you. And you begged me to hide you and I have this darkroom, you know. It locks from the inside only. I put the lock on myself. So we went in there—just to humor you—and along about midnight, which was only fifteen or twenty minutes after, we passed out."

"Passed out?"

Swanson nodded. "Both of us. It was like being hit with a sandbag. Look, didn't that happen to you again last night?"

"I guess it did," Burckhardt shook his head uncertainly.

"Sure. And then all of a sudden we were awake again, and you said you were going to show me something funny, and we went out and bought a paper. And the date on it was June 15th."

"June 15th? But that's today! I mean—"

"You got it, friend. It's *always* today!"

It took time to penetrate.

Burckhardt said wonderingly, "You've hidden out in that darkroom for how many weeks?"

"How can I tell? Four or five, maybe. I lost count. And every day the same—always the 15th of June, always my landlady, Mrs. Keefer, is sweeping the front steps, always the same headline in the papers at the corner. It gets monotonous, friend."

CHAPTER FOUR

It was Burckhardt's idea and Swanson despised it, but he went along. He was the type who always went along.

"It's dangerous," he grumbled worriedly. "Suppose somebody comes by? They'll spot us and—"

"What have we got to lose?"

Swanson shrugged. "It's dangerous," he said again. But he went along.

Burckhardt's idea was very simple. He was sure of only one thing—the tunnel went somewhere. Martians or Russians, fantastic plot or crazy hallucination, whatever was wrong with Tylerton had an explanation, and the place to look for it was at the end of the tunnel.

They jogged along. It was more than a mile before they began to see an end. They were in luck—at least no one came through the tunnel to spot them. But Swanson had said that it was only at certain hours that the tunnel seemed to be in use.

Always the fifteenth of June. Why? Burckhardt asked himself. Never mind the how. *Why?*

And falling asleep, completely involuntarily—everyone at the same time, it seemed. And not remembering, never remembering anything— Swanson had said how eagerly he saw Burckhardt again, the morning after Burckhardt had incautiously waited five minutes too many before retreating into the darkroom. When Swanson had come to, Burckhardt was gone. Swanson had seen him in the street that afternoon, but Burckhardt had remembered nothing.

And Swanson had lived his mouse's existence for weeks, hiding in the woodwork at night, stealing out by day to search for Burckhardt in pitiful hope, scurrying around the fringe of life, trying to keep from the deadly eyes of *them*.

Them. One of "them" was the girl named April Horn. It was by seeing her walk carelessly into a telephone booth and never come out that Swanson had found the tunnel. Another was the man at the cigar stand in Burckhardt's office building. There were more, at least a dozen that Swanson knew of or suspected.

They were easy enough to spot, once you knew where to look—for they, alone in Tylerton, changed their roles from day to day. Burckhardt was on that 8:51 bus, every morning of every day-that-was-June-15th, never different by a hair or a moment. But April Horn was sometimes gaudy in the cellophane skirt, giving away candy or cigarettes; sometimes plainly dressed; sometimes not seen by Swanson at all.

Russians? Martians? Whatever they were, what could they be hoping to gain from this mad masquerade?

Burckhardt didn't know the answer—but perhaps it lay beyond the door at the end of the tunnel. They listened carefully and heard distant sounds that could not quite be made out, but nothing that seemed dangerous. They slipped through.

And, through a wide chamber and up a flight of steps, they found they were in what Burckhardt recognized as the Contro Chemicals plant.

NOBODY WAS IN SIGHT. BY ITSELF, THAT WAS NOT SO VERY ODD—THE AUTOMatized factory had never had very many persons in it. But Burckhardt remembered, from his single visit, the endless, ceaseless busyness of the plant, the valves that opened and closed, the vats that emptied themselves and filled themselves and stirred and cooked and chemically tasted the bubbling liquids they held inside themselves. The plant was never populated, but it was never still.

Only—now it *was* still. Except for the distant sounds, there was no breath of life in it. The captive electronic minds were sending out no commands; the coils and relays were at rest.

Burckhardt said, "Come on." Swanson reluctantly followed him through the tangled aisles of stainless steel columns and tanks.

They walked as though they were in the presence of the dead. In a way, they were, for what were the automatons that once had run the factory, if not corpses? The machines were controlled by computers that were really not computers at all, but the electronic analogues of living brains. And if they were turned off, were they not dead? For each had once been a human mind.

Take a master petroleum chemist, infinitely skilled in the separation of crude oil into its fractions. Strap him down, probe into his brain with searching electronic needles. The machine scans the patterns of the mind, translates what it sees into charts and sine waves. Impress these same waves on a robot computer and you have your chemist. Or a thousand copies of your chemist, if you wish, with all of his knowledge and skill, and no human limitations at all.

Put a dozen copies of him into a plant and they will run it all, twenty-four hours a day, seven days of every week, never tiring, never overlooking anything, never forgetting....

Swanson stepped up closer to Burckhardt. "I'm scared," he said.

They were across the room now and the sounds were louder. They were not machine sounds, but voices; Burckhardt moved cautiously up to a door and dared to peer around it.

It was a smaller room, lined with television screens, each one—a dozen or more, at least—with a man or woman sitting before it, staring into the screen and dictating notes into a recorder. The viewers dialed from scene to scene; no two screens ever showed the same picture.

The pictures seemed to have little in common. One was a store, where a girl dressed like April Horn was demonstrating home freezers. One was a series of shots of kitchens. Burckhardt caught a glimpse of what looked like the cigar stand in his office building.

It was baffling and Burckhardt would have loved to stand there and puzzle it out, but it was too busy a place. There was the chance that someone would look their way or walk out and find them.

THEY FOUND ANOTHER ROOM. THIS ONE WAS EMPTY. IT WAS AN OFFICE, LARGE and sumptuous. It had a desk, littered with papers. Burckhardt stared at them, briefly at first—then, as the words on one of them caught his attention, with incredulous fascination.

He snatched up the topmost sheet, scanned it, and another, while Swanson was frenziedly searching through the drawers.

Burckhardt swore unbelievingly and dropped the papers to the desk.

Swanson, hardly noticing, yelped with delight: "Look!" He dragged a gun from the desk. "And it's loaded, too!"

Burckhardt stared at him blankly, trying to assimilate what he had read. Then, as he realized what Swanson had said, Burckhardt's eyes sparked. "Good man!" he cried. "We'll take it. We're getting out of here with that gun, Swanson. And we're going to the police! Not the cops in Tylerton, but the F.B.I., maybe. Take a look at this!"

The sheaf he handed Swanson was headed: "Test Area Progress Report. Subject: Marlin Cigarettes Campaign." It was mostly tabulated figures that made little sense to Burckhardt and Swanson, but at the end was a summary that said:

> Although Test 47-K3 pulled nearly double the number of new users of any of the other tests conducted, it probably cannot be used in the field because of local sound-truck control ordinances.

> The tests in the 47-K12 group were second best and our recommendation is that retests be conducted in this appeal, testing each of the three best campaigns with and without the addition of sampling techniques.

> An alternative suggestion might be to proceed directly with the top appeal in the K12 series, if the client is unwilling to go to the expense of additional tests.

> All of these forecast expectations have an 80% probability of being within one-half of one per cent of results forecast, and more than 99% probability of coming within 5%.

Swanson looked up from the paper into Burckhardt's eyes. "I don't get it," he complained.

Burckhardt said, "I don't blame you. It's crazy, but it fits the facts, Swanson, *it fits the facts*. They aren't Russians and they aren't Martians. These people are advertising men! Somehow—heaven knows how they did it—they've taken Tylerton over. They've got us, all of us, you and me and twenty or thirty thousand other people, right under their thumbs.

"Maybe they hypnotize us and maybe it's something else; but however they do it, what happens is that they let us live a day at a time. They pour advertising into us the whole damned day long. And at the end of the day, they see what happened—and then they wash the day out of our minds and start again the next day with different advertising."

SWANSON'S JAW WAS HANGING. HE MANAGED TO CLOSE IT AND SWALLOW. "Nuts!" he said flatly.

Burckhardt shook his head. "Sure, it sounds crazy—but this whole thing is crazy. How else would you explain it? You can't deny that most of Tylerton lives the same day over and over again. You've *seen* it! And that's the crazy part and we have to admit that that's true—unless we are the crazy ones. And once you admit that somebody, somehow, knows how to accomplish that, the rest of it makes all kinds of sense.

"Think of it, Swanson! They test every last detail before they spend a nickel on advertising! Do you have any idea what that means? Lord knows how much money is involved, but I know for a fact that some companies spend twenty or thirty million dollars a year on advertising. Multiply it, say, by a hundred companies. Say that every one of them learns how to cut its advertising cost by only ten per cent. And that's peanuts, believe me!

"If they know in advance what's going to work, they can cut their costs in half—maybe to less than half, I don't know. But that's saving two or three hundred million dollars a year—and if they pay only ten or twenty per cent of that for the use of Tylerton, it's still dirt cheap for them and a fortune for whoever took over Tylerton."

Swanson licked his lips. "You mean," he offered hesitantly, "that we're a—well, a kind of captive audience?"

Burckhardt frowned. "Not exactly." He thought for a minute. "You know how a doctor tests something like penicillin? He sets up a series of little colonies of germs on gelatine disks and he tries the stuff on one after another, changing it a little each time. Well, that's us—we're the germs, Swanson. Only it's even more efficient than that. They don't have to test more than one colony, because they can use it over and over again."

It was too hard for Swanson to take in. He only said: "What do we do about it?"

"We go to the police. They can't use human beings for guinea pigs!"

"How do we get to the police?"

Burckhardt hesitated. "I think—" he began slowly. "Sure. This place is the office of somebody important. We've got a gun. We'll stay right here until he comes along. And he'll get us out of here."

Simple and direct. Swanson subsided and found a place to sit, against the wall, out of sight of the door. Burckhardt took up a position behind the door itself—

And waited.

THE WAIT WAS NOT AS LONG AS IT MIGHT HAVE BEEN. HALF AN HOUR, PERHAPS. Then Burckhardt heard approaching voices and had time for a swift whisper to Swanson before he flattened himself against the wall.

It was a man's voice, and a girl's. The man was saying, "—reason why you couldn't report on the phone? You're ruining your whole day's test! What the devil's the matter with you, Janet?"

"I'm sorry, Mr. Dorchin," she said in a sweet, clear tone. "I thought it was important."

The man grumbled, "Important! One lousy unit out of twenty-one thousand."

"But it's the Burckhardt one, Mr. Dorchin. Again. And the way he got out of sight, he must have had some help."

"All right, all right. It doesn't matter, Janet; the Choco-Bite program is ahead of schedule anyhow. As long as you're this far, come on in the office and make out your worksheet. And don't worry about the Burckhardt business. He's probably just wandering around. We'll pick him up tonight and—"

They were inside the door. Burckhardt kicked it shut and pointed the gun.

"That's what you think," he said triumphantly.

It was worth the terrified hours, the bewildered sense of insanity, the confusion and fear. It was the most satisfying sensation Burckhardt had ever had in his life. The expression on the man's face was one he had read about but never actually seen: Dorchin's mouth fell open and his eyes went wide, and though he managed to make a sound that might have been a question, it was not in words.

The girl was almost as surprised. And Burckhardt, looking at her, knew why her voice had been so familiar. The girl was the one who had introduced herself to him as April Horn.

Dorchin recovered himself quickly. "Is this the one?" he asked sharply.

The girl said, "Yes."

Dorchin nodded. "I take it back. You were right. Uh, you—Burckhardt. What do you want?"

SWANSON PIPED UP, "WATCH HIM! HE MIGHT HAVE ANOTHER GUN."

"Search him then," Burckhardt said. "I'll tell you what we want, Dorchin. We want you to come along with us to the FBI and explain to them how you can get away with kidnapping twenty thousand people."

"Kidnapping?" Dorchin snorted. "That's ridiculous, man! Put that gun away—you can't get away with this!"

Burckhardt hefted the gun grimly. "I think I can."

Dorchin looked furious and sick—but, oddly, not afraid. "Damn it—" he started to bellow, then closed his mouth and swallowed. "Listen," he said persuasively, "you're making a big mistake. I haven't kidnapped anybody, believe me!"

"I don't believe you," said Burckhardt bluntly. "Why should I?"

"But it's true! Take my word for it!"

Burckhardt shook his head. "The FBI can take your word if they like. We'll find out. Now how do we get out of here?"

Dorchin opened his mouth to argue.

Burckhardt blazed: "Don't get in my way! I'm willing to kill you if I have to. Don't you understand that? I've gone through two days of hell and every second of it I blame on you. Kill you? It would be a pleasure and I don't have a thing in the world to lose! Get us out of here!"

Dorchin's face went suddenly opaque. He seemed about to move; but the blonde girl he had called Janet slipped between him and the gun.

"Please!" she begged Burckhardt. "You don't understand. You mustn't shoot!"

"*Get out of my way!*"

"But, Mr. Burckhardt—"

She never finished. Dorchin, his face unreadable, headed for the door. Burckhardt had been pushed one degree too far. He swung the gun, bellowing. The girl called out sharply. He pulled the trigger. Closing on him with pity and pleading in her eyes, she came again between the gun and the man.

Burckhardt aimed low instinctively, to cripple, not to kill. But his aim was not good.

The pistol bullet caught her in the pit of the stomach.

DORCHIN WAS OUT AND AWAY, THE DOOR SLAMMING BEHIND HIM, HIS FOOT-steps racing into the distance.

Burckhardt hurled the gun across the room and jumped to the girl.

Swanson was moaning. "That finishes us, Burckhardt. Oh, why did you do it? We could have got away. We could have gone to the police. We were practically out of here! We—"

Burckhardt wasn't listening. He was kneeling beside the girl. She lay flat on her back, arms helter-skelter. There was no blood, hardly any sign of the wound; but the position in which she lay was one that no living human being could have held.

Yet she wasn't dead.

She wasn't dead—and Burckhardt, frozen beside her, thought: *She isn't alive, either.*

There was no pulse, but there was a rhythmic ticking of the outstretched fingers of one hand.

There was no sound of breathing, but there was a hissing, sizzling noise.

The eyes were open and they were looking at Burckhardt. There was neither fear nor pain in them, only a pity deeper than the Pit.

She said, through lips that writhed erratically, "Don't—worry, Mr. Burckhardt. I'm—all right."

Burckhardt rocked back on his haunches, staring. Where there should have been blood, there was a clean break of a substance that was not flesh; and a curl of thin golden-copper wire.

Burckhardt moistened his lips.

"You're a robot," he said.

The girl tried to nod. The twitching lips said, "I am. And so are you."

CHAPTER FIVE

Swanson, after a single inarticulate sound, walked over to the desk and sat staring at the wall. Burckhardt rocked back and forth beside the shattered puppet on the floor. He had no words.

The girl managed to say, "I'm—sorry all this happened." The lovely lips twisted into a rictus sneer, frightening on that smooth young face, until she got them under control. "Sorry," she said again. "The—nerve center was right about where the bullet hit. Makes it difficult to—control this body."

Burckhardt nodded automatically, accepting the apology. Robots. It was obvious, now that he knew it. In hindsight, it was inevitable. He thought of his mystic notions of hypnosis or Martians or something stranger still—idiotic, for the simple fact of created robots fitted the facts better and more economically.

All the evidence had been before him. The automatized factory, with its transplanted minds—why not transplant a mind into a humanoid robot, give it its original owner's features and form?

Could it know that it was a robot?

"All of us," Burckhardt said, hardly aware that he spoke out loud. "My wife and my secretary and you and the neighbors. All of us the same."

"No." The voice was stronger. "Not exactly the same, all of us. I chose it, you see. I—" this time the convulsed lips were not a random contortion of the nerves—"I was an ugly woman, Mr. Burckhardt, and nearly sixty years old. Life had passed me. And when Mr. Dorchin offered me the chance to live again as a beautiful girl, I jumped at the opportunity. Believe me, I *jumped*, in spite of its disadvantages. My flesh body is still alive—it is sleeping, while I am here. I could go back to it. But I never do."

"And the rest of us?"

"Different, Mr. Burckhardt. I work here. I'm carrying out Mr. Dorchin's orders, mapping the results of the advertising tests, watching you and the others live as he makes you live. I do it by choice, but you have no choice. Because, you see, you are dead."

"Dead?" cried Burckhardt; it was almost a scream.

The blue eyes looked at him unwinkingly and he knew that it was no lie. He swallowed, marveling at the intricate mechanisms that let him swallow, and sweat, and eat.

He said: "Oh. The explosion in my dream."

"It was no dream. You are right—the explosion. That was real and this plant was the cause of it. The storage tanks let go and what the blast didn't get, the fumes killed a little later. But almost everyone died in the blast, twenty-one thousand persons. You died with them and that was Dorchin's chance."

"The damned ghoul!" said Burckhardt.

THE TWISTED SHOULDERS SHRUGGED WITH AN ODD GRACE. "WHY? YOU WERE gone. And you and all the others were what Dorchin wanted—a whole town, a perfect slice of America. It's as easy to transfer a pattern from a dead brain as a living one. Easier—the dead can't say no. Oh, it took work and money—the town was a wreck—but it was possible to rebuild it entirely, especially because it wasn't necessary to have all the details exact.

"There were the homes where even the brains had been utterly destroyed, and those are empty inside, and the cellars that needn't be too perfect, and the streets that hardly matter. And anyway, it only has to last for one day. The same day—June 15th—over and over again; and if someone finds something a little wrong, somehow, the discovery won't have time to snowball, wreck the validity of the tests, because all errors are canceled out at midnight."

The face tried to smile. "That's the dream, Mr. Burckhardt, that day of June 15th, because you never really lived it. It's a present from Mr. Dorchin, a dream that he gives you and then takes back at the end of the day, when he has all his figures on how many of you responded to what variation of which appeal, and the maintenance crews go down the tunnel to go through the whole city, washing out the new dream with their little electronic drains, and then the dream starts all over again. On June 15th.

"Always June 15th, because June 14th is the last day any of you can remember alive. Sometimes the crews miss someone—as they missed you, because you were under your boat. But it doesn't matter. The ones who are missed give themselves away if they show it—and if they don't, it doesn't affect the test. But they don't drain us, the ones of us who work for Dorchin. We sleep when the power is turned off, just as you do. When we wake up, though, we remember." The face contorted wildly. "If I could only forget!"

Burckhardt said unbelievingly, "All this to sell merchandise! It must have cost millions!"

The robot called April Horn said, "It did. But it has made millions for Dorchin, too. And that's not the end of it. Once he finds the master words that make people act, do you suppose he will stop with that? Do you suppose—"

The door opened, interrupting her. Burckhardt whirled. Belatedly remembering Dorchin's flight, he raised the gun.

"Don't shoot," ordered the voice calmly. It was not Dorchin; it was another robot, this one not disguised with the clever plastics and cosmetics, but shining plain. It said metallically: "Forget it, Burckhardt. You're not accomplishing anything. Give me that gun before you do any more damage. Give it to me *now*."

BURCKHARDT BELLOWED ANGRILY. THE GLEAM ON THIS ROBOT TORSO WAS steel; Burckhardt was not at all sure that his bullets would pierce it, or do much harm if they did. He would have put it to the test—

But from behind him came a whimpering, scurrying whirlwind; its name was Swanson, hysterical with fear. He catapulted into Burckhardt and sent him sprawling, the gun flying free.

"Please!" begged Swanson incoherently, prostrate before the steel robot. "He would have shot you—please don't hurt me! Let me work for you, like that girl. I'll do anything, anything you tell me—"

The robot voice said. "We don't need your help." It took two precise steps and stood over the gun—and spurned it, left it lying on the floor.

The wrecked blonde robot said, without emotion, "I doubt that I can hold out much longer, Mr. Dorchin."

"Disconnect if you have to," replied the steel robot.

Burckhardt blinked. "But you're not Dorchin!"

The steel robot turned deep eyes on him. "I am," it said. "Not in the flesh—but this is the body I am using at the moment. I doubt that you can damage this one with the gun. The other robot body was more vulnerable. Now will you stop this nonsense? I don't want to have to damage you; you're too expensive for that. Will you just sit down and let the maintenance crews adjust you?"

Swanson groveled. "You—you won't punish us?"

The steel robot had no expression, but its voice was almost surprised. "Punish you?" it repeated on a rising note. "How?"

Swanson quivered as though the word had been a whip; but Burckhardt flared: "Adjust *him*, if he'll let you—but not me! You're going to have to do me a lot of damage, Dorchin. I don't care what I cost or how much trouble it's going to be to put me back together again. But I'm going out of that door! If you want to stop me, you'll have to kill me. You won't stop me any other way!"

The steel robot took a half-step toward him, and Burckhardt involuntarily checked his stride. He stood poised and shaking, ready for death, ready for attack, ready for anything that might happen.

Ready for anything except what did happen. For Dorchin's steel body merely stepped aside, between Burckhardt and the gun, but leaving the door free.

"Go ahead," invited the steel robot. "Nobody's stopping you."

Outside the door, Burckhardt brought up sharp. It was insane of Dorchin to let him go! Robot or flesh, victim or beneficiary, there was nothing to stop him from going to the FBI or whatever law he could find away from Dorchin's synthetic empire, and telling his story. Surely the corporations who paid Dorchin for test results had no notion of the ghoul's technique he used; Dorchin would have to keep it from them, for the breath of publicity would put a stop to it. Walking out meant death, perhaps—but at that moment in his pseudo-life, death was no terror for Burckhardt.

There was no one in the corridor. He found a window and stared out of it. There was Tylerton—an ersatz city, but looking so real and familiar that Burckhardt almost imagined the whole episode a dream. It was no dream, though. He was certain of that in his heart and equally certain that nothing in Tylerton could help him now.

It had to be the other direction.

It took him a quarter of an hour to find a way, but he found it—skulking through the corridors, dodging the suspicion of footsteps, knowing for certain that his hiding was in vain, for Dorchin was undoubtedly aware of every move he made. But no one stopped him, and he found another door.

It was a simple enough door from the inside. But when he opened it and stepped out, it was like nothing he had ever seen.

First there was light—brilliant, incredible, blinding light. Burckhardt blinked upward, unbelieving and afraid.

He was standing on a ledge of smooth, finished metal. Not a dozen yards from his feet, the ledge dropped sharply away; he hardly dared approach the brink, but even from where he stood he could see no bottom to the chasm before him. And the gulf extended out of sight into the glare on either side of him.

No wonder Dorchin could so easily give him his freedom! From the factory, there was nowhere to go—but how incredible this fantastic gulf, how impossible the hundred white and blinding suns that hung above!

A voice by his side said inquiringly, "Burckhardt?" And thunder rolled the name, mutteringly soft, back and forth in the abyss before him.

Burckhardt wet his lips. "Y-yes?" he croaked.

"This is Dorchin. Not a robot this time, but Dorchin in the flesh, talking to you on a hand mike. Now you have seen, Burckhardt. Now will you be reasonable and let the maintenance crews take over?"

Burckhardt stood paralyzed. One of the moving mountains in the blinding glare came toward him.

It towered hundreds of feet over his head; he stared up at its top, squinting helplessly into the light.

It looked like—

Impossible!

The voice in the loudspeaker at the door said, "Burckhardt?" But he was unable to answer.

A heavy rumbling sigh. "I see," said the voice. "You finally understand. There's no place to go. You know it now. I could have told you, but you might not have believed me, so it was better for you to see it yourself. And after all, Burckhardt, why would I reconstruct a city just the way it was before? I'm a businessman; I count costs. If a thing has to be full-scale, I build it that way. But there wasn't any need to in this case."

From the mountain before him, Burckhardt helplessly saw a lesser cliff descend carefully toward him. It was long and dark, and at the end of it was whiteness, five-fingered whiteness....

"Poor little Burckhardt," crooned the loudspeaker, while the echoes rumbled through the enormous chasm that was only a workshop. "It must have been quite a shock for you to find out you were living in a town built on a table top."

CHAPTER SIX

It was the morning of June 15th, and Guy Burckhardt woke up screaming out of a dream.

It had been a monstrous and incomprehensible dream, of explosions and shadowy figures that were not men and terror beyond words.

He shuddered and opened his eyes.

Outside his bedroom window, a hugely amplified voice was howling.

Burckhardt stumbled over to the window and stared outside. There was an out-of-season chill to the air, more like October than June; but the scent was normal enough—except for the sound-truck that squatted at curbside halfway down the block. Its speaker horns blared:

"Are you a coward? Are you a fool? Are you going to let crooked politicians steal the country from you? NO! Are you going to put up with four more years of graft and crime? NO! Are you going to vote straight Federal Party all up and down the ballot? YES! *You just bet you are!*"

Sometimes he screams, sometimes he wheedles, threatens, begs, cajoles ... but his voice goes on and on through one June 15th after another.

THE MAN OF FLESH AND BLOOD

BY SUSAN GLASPELL

he elements without were not in harmony with the spirit which it was desired should be engendered within. By music, by gay decorations, by speeches from prominent men, the board in charge of the boys' reformatory was striving to throw about this dedication of the new building an atmosphere of cheerfulness and good-will--an atmosphere vibrant with the kindness and generosity which emanated from the State, and the thankfulness and loyalty which it was felt should emanate from the boys.

Outside the world was sobbing. Some young trees which had been planted along the driveway of the reformatory grounds, and which were expected to grow up in the way they should go, were rocking back and forth in passionate insurrection. Fallen leaves were being spit viciously through the air. It was a sullen-looking landscape which Philip Grayson, he who was to be the last speaker of the afternoon, saw stretching itself down the hill, across the little valley, and up another little hill of that rolling prairie state. In his ears was the death wail of the summer. It seemed the spirit of out-of-doors was sending itself up in mournful, hopeless cries.

The speaker who had been delivering himself of pedantic encouragement about the open arms with which the world stood ready to receive the most degraded one, would that degraded one but come to the world in proper spirit, sat down amid perfunctory applause led by the officers and attendants of the institution, and the boys rose to sing. The brightening of their faces told that their work as performers was more to their liking than their position as auditors. They threw back their heads and waited with well-disciplined eagerness for the signal to begin. Then, with the strength and native music there are in some three hundred boys' throats, there rolled out the words of the song of the State.

There were lips which opened only because they must, but as a whole they sang with the same heartiness, the same joy in singing, that he had heard a crowd of public-school boys put into the song only the week before. When the last word had died away it seemed to Philip Grayson that the sigh of the world without was giving voice to the sigh of the world within as the well-behaved crowd of boys sat down to resume their duties as auditors.

And then one of the most important of the professors from the State University was telling them about the kindness of the State: the State had provided for them this beautiful home; it gave them comfortable clothing and nutritious food; it furnished that fine gymnasium in which to train their bodies, books and teachers to train their minds; it provided those fitted to train their souls, to work against the unfortunate tendencies--the professor stumbled a little there--which had led to their coming. The State gave liberally, gladly, and in return it asked but one thing: that they come out into the world and make useful, upright citizens, citizens of which any State might be proud. Was that asking too much? the professor from the State University was saying.

The sobbing of the world without was growing more intense. Many pairs of eyes from among the auditors were straying out to where the summer lay dying. Did they know--those boys whom the State classed as unfortunates--that out of this death there would come again life? Or did they see but the darkness--the decay--of to-day?

The professor from the State University was putting the case very fairly. There were no flaws--seemingly--to be picked in his logic. The State had been kind; the boys were obligated to good citizenship. But the coldness!--comfortlessness!--of it all. The open arms of the world!--how mocking in its abstractness. What did it mean? Did it mean that they--the men who uttered the phrase so easily--would be willing to give these boys aid, friendship when they came out into the world? What would they say, those boys whose ears were filled with high-sounding, non-committal phrases, if some man were to stand before them and say, "And so, fellows, when you get away from this place, and are ready to get your start in the world, just come around to my office and I'll help you get a job?" At thought of it there came from Philip Grayson a queer, partly audible laugh, which caused those nearest him to look his way in surprise.

But he was all unconscious of their looks of inquiry, absorbed in the thoughts that crowded upon him. How far away the world--his kind of people--must seem to these boys of the State Reform School. The speeches they had heard, the training that had been given them, had taught them--unconsciously perhaps, but surely--to divide the world into two great classes: the lucky and the unlucky, those who made speeches and those who must listen, the so-called good and the so-called bad; perhaps--he smiled a little at his own cynicism--those who were caught and those who were not.

There came to him these words of a poet of whom he used to be fond:

In men whom men pronounce as ill,
I find so much of goodness still;
In men whom men pronounce divine,
I find so much of sin and blot;
I hesitate to draw the line
Between the two, when God has not.

When God has not! He turned and looked out at the sullen sky, returning--as most men do at times--to that conception of his childhood that somewhere beyond the clouds was God. God! Did God care for the boys of the State Reformatory? Was that poet of the western mountains right when he said that God was not a drawer of lines, but a seer of the good that was in the so-called bad, and of the bad in the so-called good, and a lover of them both?

If that was God, it was not the God the boys of the reformatory had been taught to know. They had been told that God would forgive the wicked, but it had been made clear to them--if not in words, in implications--that it was they who were the wicked. And the so-called godly men, men of such exemplary character as had been chosen to address them that afternoon, had so much of the spirit of God that they, too, were willing to forgive, be tolerant, and--he looked out at the bending trees with a smile--disburse generalities about the open arms of the world.

What would they think--those three hundred speech-tired boys--if some man who had been held before them as exemplary were to rise and lay bare his own life--its weaknesses, its faults, perhaps its crimes--and tell them there was weakness and there was strength in every human being, and that the world-old struggle of life was to overcome one's weakness with one's strength.

The idea took strange hold on him. It seemed the method of the world--at any rate it had been the method of that afternoon--for the men who stood before their fellows with clean hands to plant themselves on the far side of a chasm of conventions, or narrow self-esteem, or easily won virtue, and cry to those beings who struggled on the other side of that chasm--to those human beings whose souls had never gone to school: "Look at us! Our hands are clean, our hearts are pure. See how beautiful it is to be good! Come ye, poor sinners, and be good also." And the poor sinners, the untaught, birthmarked human souls, would look over at the self-acclaimed goodness they could see far across the chasm, and even though attracted to it (which, he grimly reflected, would not seem likely) the thing that was left with them was a sense of the width of the chasm.

He had a sense of needless waste, of unnecessary blight. He looked down at those three hundred faces and it was as if looking at human waste; and it was human stupidity, human complacency and cowardice kept those human beings human drift.

With what a smug self-satisfaction--under the mask of benevolence--the speakers of that afternoon had flaunted their virtue--their position! How condescendingly they had spoken of the home which we, the good, prepare for you, the bad, and what namby-pambyness there was, after all, in that sentiment which all of them had voiced--and now you must pay us back by being good!

Oh for a man of flesh and blood to stand up and tell how he himself had failed and suffered! For a man who could bridge that chasm with strong, broad, human understanding and human sympathies--a man who would stand among them pulse-beat to pulse-beat and cry out, "I know! I understand! I fought it and I'll help you fight it too!"

The sound of his own name broke the spell that was upon him. He looked to the centre of the stage and saw that the professor from the State University had seated himself and that the superintendent of the institution was occupying the place of the speaker. And the superintendent was saying:

"We may esteem ourselves especially fortunate in having him with us this afternoon. He is one of the great men of the State, one of the men who by high living, by integrity and industry, has raised himself to a position of great honour among his fellow men. A great party--may I say the greatest of all parties?--has shown its unbounded confidence in him by giving him the nomination for the governorship of the State. No man in the State is held in higher esteem to-day than he. And so it is with special pleasure that I introduce to you that man of the future--Philip Grayson."

The superintendent sat down then, and he himself--Philip Grayson--was standing in the place where the other speakers had stood. It was with a rush which almost swept away his outward show of calm that it came to him that he--candidate for the governorship--was well fitted to be that man of flesh and blood for whom he had sighed. That he himself was within grasp of an opportunity to get beneath the jackets and into the very hearts and souls of those boys, and make them feel that a man of sins and virtues, of weaknesses and strength, a man who had had much to conquer, and for whom the fight would never be finally won, was standing before them stripped of his coat of conventions and platitudes, and in nakedness of soul and sincerity of heart was talking to them as a man who understood.

Almost with the inception of the idea was born the consciousness of what it might cost. And as in answer to the silent, blunt question, Is it worth it? there looked up at him three hundred pairs of eyes--eyes behind which there was good as well as bad, eyes which had burned with the fatal rush of passion, and had burned, too, with the hot tears of remorse--eyes which had opened on a hostile world.

And then the eyes of Philip Grayson could not see the eyes which were before him, and he put up his hand to break the mist--little caring what the men upon the platform would think of him, little thinking what effect the words which were crowding into his heart would have upon his candidacy. But one thing was vital to him now: to bring upon that ugly chasm the levelling forces of a common humanity, and to make those boys who were of his clay feel that a being who had fallen and risen again, a fellow being for whom life would always mean a falling and a rising again, was standing before them, and--not as the embodiment of a distant goodness, not as a pattern, but as one among them, verily as man to man--was telling them a few things which his own life had taught him were true.

It was his very consecration which made it hard to begin. He was fearful of estranging them in the beginning, of putting between them and him that very thing he was determined there should not be.

"I have a strange feeling," he said, with a winning little smile, "that if I were to open my heart to-day, just open it clear up the way I'd like to if I could, that you boys would look into it, and then jump back in a scared kind of way and cry, 'Why--that's me!' You would be a little surprised--wouldn't you?--if you could look back and see the kind of boy I was, and find I was much the kind of boy you are?

"Do you know what I think? I think hypocrisy is the worst thing in the world. I think it's worse than stealing, or lying, or any of the other bad things you can name. And do you know where I think lots of the hypocrisy comes from? I think it comes from the so-called self-made men--from the real good men, the men who say 'I haven't got one bad thing charged up to my account.'

"Now the men out campaigning for me call me a self-made man. Your superintendent just now spoke of my integrity, of the confidence reposed in me, and all that. But do you know what is the honest truth? If I am any kind of a man worth mentioning, if I am deserving of any honour, any confidence, it is not because I was born with my heart filled with good and beautiful things, for I was not. It is because I was born with much in my heart that we call the bad, and because, after that bad had grown stronger and stronger through the years it was unchecked, and after it had brought me the great shock, the great sorrow of my life, I began then, when older than you boys are now, to see a little of that great truth which you can put briefly in these words: 'There is good and there is bad in every human heart, and it is the struggle of life to conquer the bad with the good.' What I am trying to say is, that if I am worthy any one's confidence to-day, it is because, having seen that truth, I have been able, through never ceasing trying, through slow conquering, to crowd out some of the bad and make room for a little of the good.

"You see," he went on, three hundred pairs of eyes hard upon him now, "some of us are born to a harder struggle than others. There are people who would object to my saying that to you, even if I believed it. They would say you would make the fact of being born with much against which to struggle an excuse for being bad. But look here a minute; if you were born with a body not as strong as other boys' bodies, if you couldn't run as far, or jump as high, you wouldn't be eternally saying, 'I can't be expected to do much; I wasn't born right.' Not a bit of it! You'd make it your business to get as strong as you could, and you wouldn't make any parade of the fact that you weren't as strong as you should be. We don't like people who whine, whether it's about weak bodies or weak souls.

"I've been sitting here this afternoon wondering what to say to you boys. I had intended telling some funny stories about things which happened to me when I was a boy. But for some reason a serious mood has come over me, and I don't feel just like those stories now. I haven't been thinking of the funny side of life in the last half-hour. I've been thinking of how much suffering I've endured since the days when I, too, was a boy."

He paused then; and when he went on his voice tested to the utmost the silence of the room: "There is lots of sorrow in this old world. Maybe I'm on the wrong track, but as I see it to-day human beings are making a much harder thing of their existence than there is any need of. There are millions and millions of them, and year after year, generation after generation, they fight over the same old battles, live through the same old sorrows. Doesn't it seem all wrong that after the battle has been fought a million times it can't be made a little easier for those who still have it before them?

"If a farmer had gone over a bad road, and the next day saw another farmer about to start over the same road, wouldn't he send him back? Doesn't it seem too bad that in things which concern one's whole life people can't be as decent as they are about things which involve only an inconvenience? Doesn't it seem that when we human beings have so much in common we might stand together a little better? I'll tell you what's the matter. Most of the people of this world are coated round and round with self-esteem, and they're afraid to admit any understanding of the things which aren't good. Suppose the farmer had thought it a disgrace to admit he had been over that road, and so had said: 'From what I have read in books, and from what I have learned in a general way, I fancy that road isn't good.' Would the other farmer have gone back? I rather think he would have said he'd take his chances. But you see the farmer said he *knew*; and how did he know? Why, because he'd been over the road himself."

As he paused again, looking at them, he saw it all with a clarifying simplicity. He himself knew life for a fine and beautiful thing. He had won for himself some of the satisfactions of understanding, certain rare delights of the open spirit. He wanted to free the spirits of these boys to whom he talked; wanted to show them that spirits could free themselves, indicate to them that self-control and self-development carried one to pleasures which sordid self-indulgences had no power to bestow. It was a question of getting the most from life. It was a matter of happiness.

It was thus he began, slowly, the telling of his life's story:

"I was born with strange, wild passions in my heart. I don't know where they came from; I only know they were there. I resented authority. If someone who had a right to dictate to me said, 'Philip, do this,' then Philip would immediately begin to think how much he would rather do the other thing. And," he smiled a little, and some of the boys smiled with him in anticipation, "it was the other thing which Philip usually did.

"I didn't go to a reform school, for the very good reason that there wasn't any in the State where I lived." Some of he boys smiled again, and he could hear the nervous coughing of one of the party managers sitting close to him. "I was what you would call a very bad boy. I didn't mind any one. I was defiant--insolent. I did bad things just because I knew they were bad, and--and I took a great deal of satisfaction out of it."

The sighing of the world without was the only sound which vibrated through the room. "I say," he went on, "that I got a form of satisfaction from it. I did not say I got happiness; there is a vast difference between a kind of momentary satisfaction and that thing--that most precious of all things--which we call happiness. Indeed, I was very far from happy. I had hours when I was so morose and miserable that I hated the whole world. And do you know what I thought? I thought there was no one in all the world who had the same kind of things surging up in his heart that I did. I thought there was no one else with whom it was as easy to be bad, or as hard to be good. I thought that no one understood. I thought that I was all alone.

"Did you ever feel like that? Did you ever feel that no one else knew anything about such feelings as you had? Did you ever feel that here was you, and there was the rest of the world, and that the rest of the world didn't know anything about you, and was just generally down on you? Now that's the very thing I want to talk away from you to-day. You're not the only one. We're all made of the same kind of stuff, and there's none of us made of stuff that's flawless. We all have a fight; some an easy one, and some a big one, and if you have formed the idea that there is a kind of dividing-line in the world, and that on the one side is the good, and on the other side the bad, why, all I can say is that you have a wrong notion of things.

"Well, I grew up to be a man, and because I hadn't fought against any of the stormy things in my heart they kept growing stronger and stronger. I did lots of wild, ugly things, things of which I am bitterly ashamed. I went to another place, and I fell in with the kind of fellows you can imagine I felt at home with. I had been told when I was a boy that it was wrong to drink and gamble. I think that was the chief reason I took to drink and gambling."

There was another cough, more pronounced this time, from the party manager, and the superintendent was twisting uneasily in his seat. It was the strangest speech that had ever been delivered at the boys' reformatory. The boys were leaning forward--self-forgetful, intent. "One night I was playing cards with a crowd of my friends, and one of the men, the best friend I had, said something that made me mad. There was a revolver right there which one of the men had been showing us. Some kind of a demon got hold of me, and without so much as a thought I picked up that revolver and fired at my friend."

The party manager gave way to an exclamation of horror, and the superintendent half rose from his seat. But before any one could say a word Philip Grayson continued, looking at the half-frightened faces before him: "I suppose you wonder why I am not in the penitentiary. I had been drinking, and I missed my aim; and I was with friends, and it was hushed up."

He rested his hand upon the table, and looked out at the sullen landscape. His voice was not steady as he went on: "It's not an easy thing to talk about, boys. I never talked about it to any one before in all my life. I'm not telling it now just to entertain you or to create a sensation. I'm telling it," his voice grew tense in its earnestness, "because I believe that this world could be made a better and a sweeter place if those who have lived and suffered would not be afraid to reach out their hands and cry: 'I know that road--it's bad! I steered off to a better place, and I'll help you steer off, too.'"

There was not one of the three hundred pairs of eyes but was riveted upon the speaker's colourless face. The masks of sullenness and defiance had fallen from them. They were listening now--not because they must, but because into their hungry and thirsty souls was being poured the very sustenance for which--unknowingly--they had yearned.

"We sometimes hear people say," resumed the candidate for Governor, "that they have lived through hell. If by that they mean they've lived through the deepest torments the human heart can know, then I can say that I, too, have lived through hell. What I suffered after I went home that night no one in this world will ever know. Words couldn't tell it; it's not the kind of thing words can come anywhere near. My whole life spread itself out before me; it was not a pleasant thing to look at. But at last, boys, out of the depths of my darkness, I began to get a little light. I began to get some understanding of the battle which it falls to the lot of some of us human beings to wage. There was good in me, you see, or I wouldn't have cared like that, and it came to me then, all alone that terrible night, that it is the good which lies buried away somewhere in our hearts must fight out the bad. And so--all alone, boys--I began the battle of trying to get command of my own life. And do you know--this is the truth--it was with the beginning of that battle I got my first taste of happiness. There is no finer feeling in this world than the sense of coming into mastery of one's self. It is like opening a door that has shut you in. Oh, you don't do it all in a minute. This is no miracle I'm talking about. It's a fight. But it's a fight that can be won. It's a fight that's gloriously worth the winning. I'm not saying to you, 'Be good and you'll succeed.' Maybe you won't succeed. Life as we've arranged it for ourselves makes success a pretty tough proposition. But that doesn't alter the fact that it pays to be a decent sort. You and I know about how much happiness there is in the other kind of thing. And there is happiness in feeling you're doing what you can to develop what's in you. Success or failure, it brings a sense of having done your part,--that bully sense of having put up the best fight you could."

He leaned upon the table then, as though very weary. "I don't know, I am sure, what the people of my State will think of all this. Perhaps they won't want a man for their Governor who once tried to kill another man. But," he looked around at them with that smile of his which got straight to men's hearts, "there's only one of me, and there are three hundred of you, and how do I know but that in telling you of that stretch of bad road ahead I've made a dozen Governors this very afternoon!"

He looked from row to row of them, trying to think of some last word which would leave them with a sense of his sincerity. What he did say was: "And so, boys, when you get away from here, and go out into the world to get your start, if you find the arms of that world aren't quite as wide open as you were told they would be, if there seems no place where you can get a hold, and you are saying to yourself, 'It's no use--I'll not try,' before you give up just remember there was one man who said he knew all about it, and give that one man a chance to show he meant what he said. So look me up, if luck goes all against you, and maybe I can give you a little lift." He took a backward step, as though to resume his seat, and then he said, with a dry little smile which took any suggestion of heroics from what had gone before, "If I'm not at the State-house, you'll find my name in the directory of the city where your programme tells you I live."

He sat down, and for a moment there was silence. Then, full-souled, heart-given, came the applause. It was not led by the attendants this time; it was the attendants who rose at last to stop it. And when the clapping of the hands had ceased, many of those hands were raised to eyes which had long been dry.

The exercises were drawn to a speedy close, and he found the party manager standing by his side. "It was very grand," he sneered, "very high-sounding and heroic, but I suppose you know," jerking his hand angrily toward a table where a reporter for the leading paper of the opposition was writing, "that you've given them the winning card."

As he replied, in far-off tone, "I hope so," the candidate for Governor was looking, not at the reporter who was sending out a new cry for the opposition, but into those faces aglow with the light of new understanding and new-born hopes. He stood there watching them filing out into the corridor, craning their necks to throw him a last look, and as he turned then and looked from the window it was to see that the storm had sobbed itself away, and that along the driveway of the reformatory grounds the young trees--unbroken and unhurt--were rearing their heads in the way they should go.

SODUKO ANSWERS

9	1	6	2	4	7	3	5	8
2	3	8	9	5	6	1	7	4
4	5	7	1	3	8	9	6	2
5	2	1	8	6	3	4	9	7
3	8	9	4	7	2	5	1	6
7	6	4	5	9	1	2	8	3
6	4	5	3	8	9	7	2	1
8	9	2	7	1	4	6	3	5
1	7	3	6	2	5	8	4	9

Thanks for Reading!
Issue 7 Coming in spring 2023
Visit OffBeatReads.com
for more adventures.

9 781950 464272